"I'm sorry," Elise whispered. "What must you think of me?"

"That you're the most intriguing woman I've ever known," Drake said as he reached for her hand. "I don't think you're silly. Tell me why you're afraid."

Elise pulled away, a lonely ache forming in her chest at that moment. "What is it, sweet?" Drake reached for her hand again. "Come back to me. Don't go."

Elise fought the temptation to lean on a person other than herself or her sister. She wanted to open up to Drake, share a deeper bond, but what could she say that wouldn't spur more questions and the revelation of her darkest secrets? She wanted to trust him, but in reality he was little more than a stranger....

Books by Carla Capshaw

Love Inspired Historical

The Gladiator
The Duke's Redemption

CARLA CAPSHAW

Florida native Carla Capshaw is a preacher's kid who grew up grateful for her Christian home and loving family. Always dreaming of being a writer and world traveler, she followed her wanderlust around the globe, including a year spent in the People's Republic of China, before beginning work on her first novel.

A two-time RWA Golden Heart Award winner, Carla loves passionate stories with compelling, nearly impossible conflicts. She's found inspirational historical romance is the perfect vehicle to combine lush settings, vivid characters and a Christian worldview. Currently at work on her next manuscript for Steeple Hill Love Inspired Historical, she still lives in Florida, but is always planning her next trip…and plotting her next story.

Carla loves to hear from readers. To contact her, visit www.carlacapshaw.com or write to Carla@carlacapshaw.com.

The Duke's Redemption
CARLA CAPSHAW

Steeple
Hill®

Published by Steeple Hill Books™

STEEPLE HILL BOOKS

Steeple Hill®

ISBN-13: 978-0-373-82828-9

THE DUKE'S REDEMPTION

www.SteepleHill.com

Printed in U.S.A.

God is our refuge and strength;
always ready to help in times of trouble.
—*Psalms* 46:1

Dedicated to:

My wonderful family.
I love each one of you!

My first critique partners—Carole McPhee,
Lydia Hawke and Mary Veelle—who read and
*re*read this book without ever complaining.
Also, Sheila Raye, Paisley Kirkpatrick,
Stacey Kayne and Jean Mason.
I appreciate you more than I can say.

As always, thank You, Lord!

Prologue

Charles Towne, South Carolina
December 1780

The cold muzzle of a pistol scraped her temple. The hammer cocked a warning beside her ear. A familiar voice rasped, "Don't move, Fox, or I'll be forced to relieve you of your thinking power."

Elise Cooper froze in the middle of her escape through the tavern's second-story window. Her hands gripped either side of the narrow frame, one booted foot on the floor, one planted on the sill. A chilly, smoke-tinged breeze swept through the open space, ruffling her long cloak and loose black breeches.

Hawk had startled her, but she wasn't concerned about the weapon. The real danger lurked outside. Her gaze never left the moonlit alley that cut behind the tavern. More redcoats crept from the darkness.

"Hawk," she said, thankful her mask helped disguise

not only her face, but her voice, "we have no time for your nonsense tonight. Blow out the candle and hurry your pace. Redcoats are infesting the room downstairs and may suspect we're here."

"Of a certainty, they do," he replied. "You've finally been bagged. Your days as a spy have come to an end."

Elise released an exasperated sigh. Hawk, the alias by which she knew him, possessed a fiendish sense of humor. To protect her identity as a woman, she always wore a mask when disguised as the Fox. Though he'd refused to tell her why, Hawk wore one, too. Neither had ever seen the face of the other, but she'd been privy to his games on more than one occasion. She fully expected him to lower the pistol and howl with laughter. He thought himself astoundingly clever, but under the circumstances, she found him most trying. "Cease this, Hawk. We have no time to linger. The English—"

"Are coming," he interrupted gleefully. "Yes, I know. I arranged this meeting. The soldiers are awaiting my signal to make your arrest. I'll be rewarded quite handsomely once I deliver you to my superiors."

Surprised to hear the pride in his voice, she tried to turn and look him in the eye. He jammed the muzzle harder against her temple. "I said don't move."

The menace in his tone convinced her he was serious. Her stomach lurched with fear. Anger blazed through her. "Why hand me over now when you've had the opportunity to do so for well over a year?"

He chuckled. "And give up my play? I think not. Posing as the Hawk has been quite amusing. Sadly, my superiors have ordered your arrest. Since we work so often together, they chose me to do the deed."

Elise bristled at how easily he betrayed her. "And the ransom being offered didn't hurt, I suppose. If I may ask, when did you become a turncoat?"

He stiffened in response. "Turncoat? Not I. My loyalty has always been to my king and England."

Her eyes searched the back alley in hope of seeing a loyal fellow who might aid in her escape. No one appeared save another pair of redcoats. There were eight of them now. Their freshly polished Hessian boots gleamed in the moonlight.

As the gravity of her situation compounded, her thoughts raced in time to her quickening heart. The enemy soldiers moved closer, their indistinct voices carried on the breeze.

"If you're no traitor, explain the many secrets that have passed from your hand to mine?"

"I've shared only what my superiors wanted you rebel scum to know. Remember last month, when I sent you the message about supply wagons leaving Charles Towne for Savannah?"

"Of course." She tried to ease away from the pistol. The Colonial army never ceased being desperate for supplies. At the time, the information she'd carried from Hawk to her spymaster had been considered a boon. "Then the attack *was* a trap. It seemed too coincidental. Did you assist in the murder of those men yourself?"

He laughed. "What do you think?"

She broke into a clammy sweat. If Hawk succeeded in turning her in, she doubted even her gender would save her from hanging.

Dear Lord, please help me.

Four of the redcoats made for the tavern's back door. Her pulse throbbed in her ears as her thoughts shifted frantically. So much began to make sense. How many times had she rendezvoused with Hawk, only to find his information had become mysteriously inaccessible? Yet, many of his leads had been first-rate. Hawk had earned a glowing reputation within the Patriot ranks. Now she understood why. He'd kept her and her contacts hooked with promises of important information, providing just enough to earn their trust.

"This is ridiculous." She stalled in an effort to reason with him. "There must be a bargain we can strike."

She had to flee, but how? Hawk held a pistol to her head. Soldiers waited below, both inside and out. She could no longer make use of the ladder Josiah had propped outside the window. She'd be shot, either by Hawk or his lobsterback friends before she ever touched the ground.

"Ridiculous?" Hawk's hot, menacing breath fanned the back of her neck. "I disagree. If anything, I find the situation most unfortunate. More than once I wished we weren't on opposing sides in this war. Under different circumstances, you're a man I could respect."

"Then kill me if you plan to. I've no wish to meet my captors, and you know I'll tell them nothing."

"Most likely not. All the same, keep your hands against the panes. 'Tis safer when I can make out where they are."

While she considered her options, she allowed him the liberty of searching her, careful not to give him an impatient trigger finger. His hand dipped beneath her cloak and inside her loose wool coat, feeling for weapons. Waiting for the right moment to strike, she held her breath. She'd bound her breasts with strips of cloth under her billowy black shirt and vest, but failed to flatten them completely. When his hand passed over her chest, she heard his sharp intake of breath. "No! You can't be a woman!"

In one quick movement, she swung her arm and knocked the pistol away from her temple. The foot she had poised on the windowsill slammed downward. Her heel found its mark, crushing his toes. Hawk bellowed in pain. His hold slackened enough for her to face him.

The candle's small flame sputtered in the draft, providing meager light to see the masked man she stood with eye to eye. She rammed her fist into his stomach, winding him. He recovered quickly, raising the pistol an inch from her face. She swiped the barrel away, then tried to wrench it from his grasp.

Hawk released her waist and lashed out with the back of his hand. The blow to her jaw stunned her. She stumbled back in pain, loosening her grip on the weapon as she hit the wall behind her.

"Hold your ground!" Hawk snarled. "I'd hate to shoot a woman, but I will if you force me to."

Staring down the barrel of the pistol, Elise stilled. She could turn and run, making her back a perfect target, or she could stand and fight. Hawk was bigger, stronger, but she was fighting for her life. The redcoats considered a captured spy fair game for hanging. She had no wish to die in so shameful a manner.

Better to take a bullet than dangle in the breeze.

She ducked and threw herself forward, scrambling to reach him before he fired. Leading with her shoulder, Elise plowed into him with the full force of her weight, driving him back several paces until he slammed against a table. Hawk fumbled the weapon and dropped it to the floor, where it landed with a solid thump on the wood planks.

Their eyes locked for an instant. They both lunged for the pistol. Hawk reached it first.

Elise rallied before he took aim and fought with all her might. Her ribs ached. Her jaw throbbed. Fear coursed through her blood. Her arms and legs burned from the exertion of fighting her stronger opponent. Finally, she succeeded in twisting his wrist until the pistol's barrel pointed at his belly.

"Stop this wretched business," she demanded, panting for breath. "Let me go!"

"Ha! Think again, you rebel wench."

He grabbed for her once more, but she sidestepped his advance. With one last effort to disarm him, she aimed her knee and made contact with his groin. He groaned in agony and doubled over. She dug her nails deep into his hand, praying he'd drop the weapon.

A blinding flash of light and a loud explosion jolted Elise. Hawk jerked and groaned in pain. Acrid smoke stung her eyes and nostrils.

"Hawk?" Frozen with shock, Elise stared into his horrified and slowly dimming eyes. The scrap of black silk he wore concealed the rest of his expression.

The firearm slipped from his fingers and thumped on the floor. A bone-chilling gurgle escaped his throat and gaping mouth. He reached for her, his fingers clawing weakly at her upper arms. Another frigid breeze whipped through the small room. The candle flickered out the same moment his body went slack.

In the darkness, he fell toward her. She braced against the wall, her body absorbing his heavy weight as he slid down the front of her and fell to his knees.

"Please Lord, no…." She covered his nose and mouth, searching for breath, but found none. Hawk…dead? The prospect was unimaginable.

As gently as she could, she lowered him to the floor. Shouting drew her to the window. More redcoats ran toward the tavern. The shot had warned them to investigate without waiting for his signal. Her cloak swirled around her as she raced to the dead spy and knelt beside him.

Frantic, Elise reached for his jacket. Moonlight exposed the growing stain of blood on the floor. She'd never killed anyone. Bile and remorse clogged her throat. Her hand trembled as it slipped inside the garment, searching for anything to aid her. Hawk had planned to deliver her to the English. He must have some kind of identification to offer them.

His warm blood oozed through her fingers. A sheen of tears blinded her before she blinked them away. The bullet had blown a hole in his belly. For him to die so quickly, it must have also found a vital organ to rupture. She shuddered, fighting nausea when lack of time denied her the luxury of turning squeamish.

Heavy footsteps pounded on the stairs leading from the tavern below. Outside her door, she heard multiple voices, a rattle of keys, the shuffle of boots on wood.

A key scraped in the lock just as her fingers made contact with a sheet of folded parchment. She pulled it free of Hawk's inner pocket a moment before the redcoats stormed through the door.

Chapter One

Hawk Haven Manor, England
February 1781

The moment the coach rolled to a stop, Drake Amberly, Fifth Duke of Hawk Haven, shoved open the door and leapt to the cobblestone drive. Icy rain struck his face, ran off the brim of his hat and slid down his neck, under the collar of his greatcoat. He marched up the wide front steps of his family's palatial home, his mood fouler than the weather.

Chaney, his wizened butler, opened the ornately carved front door in perfect time, allowing him to enter the manor's grandiose hall without slowing his pace.

"Good day, Your Grace."

"I've yet to find the good in it." Drake shed his hat and coat before passing them to the efficient servant. He raked his fingers through his black hair and turned in the direction of the sweeping staircase. Changing his mind, he headed for his study. His mud-splashed boots clapped on the marble floor, echoing in the domed space as he passed gilded mirrors and a display of fine porcelain. "I'm not available for the rest of this miserable day."

"Yes, Your Grace."

Drake crossed the threshold of his mahogany-paneled study, the sound of his steps muffled by the room's thick red carpet. The welcoming crackle of a roaring fire in the hearth and the familiar smell of leather-bound books did little to soothe his irritation.

He took his place behind the massive antique desk and without pause snatched up a quill. Dabbing the tip in ink, he flipped open one of his journals and began ciphering the figures from his latest shipping venture. Trade was an unpopular activity for the nobility, but Drake gave little credence to convention. Convention had caused him nothing but grief. Besides, he enjoyed dabbling in business to relieve his boredom, or annoyance, as was the case today.

Drake slammed the quill down on the desk, sneering as flecks of ink splashed across his accounts. Shoving the book away in disgust, he leaned back in his chair, his thoughts turning toward his former fiancée.

Were all women deceivers? He'd heard the rumors about Penelope, but finding her in the arms of another man was not something he could tolerate. He'd broken their engagement this morning and would speak with her father tomorrow. No strip of land was worth having a wife who couldn't be trusted.

A knock sounded at the door. Chaney peered into the room. "Pardon, Your Grace, but a Lieutenant Kirby is here.

I explained you're unavailable, but he claims to have news of Lord Anthony. I thought you might wish to see him straightaway."

Drake frowned. "Show him in. If they've sent someone, it must be urgent."

The butler departed. Drake closed his journal. An image of his brash younger brother came to mind. From childhood, Anthony had longed for adventure. When the revolt began in the Colonies six years ago, he'd booked passage on the first ship bound for New York. Determined to join their distant cousin's regiment, Anthony had been blinded by his ambition and lust for glory.

"Your Grace?" Chaney spoke from the doorway. "Please allow me to present Lieutenant John Kirby."

Drake studied the new arrival as he walked into the room and stopped several feet away. The man was short, wiry thin. Dirt marred his craggy face and sodden wig. His bulging eyes held respect and a hint of fear.

Kirby bowed low. His uneasy gaze flicked down at his less-than-spotless uniform. "Please forgive my appearance, Your Grace. The ghastly weather—"

"No matter, Lieutenant." Drake remembered his own battle with the soggy roads earlier in the day. Impatient, he motioned toward one of the chairs in front of his desk. "It would appear none of us is at his best this afternoon. Have a seat and tell me what news have you of my brother? I've received no word from him since before the new year."

Kirby sat on the edge of one of the leather chairs. Fidgeting, the soldier cleared his throat. His nervous gaze fell to the floor. "The news I have is ill indeed, Your Grace. I regret to say I've been sent here on the worst sort of errand.

There's no delicate way to put this. Your brother, Lord Anthony, is…dead."

"Dead?" Drake choked, inwardly absorbing the news like a blow to his gut. He'd anticipated something dire, an injury perhaps, but dead…? Not Anthony.

"Yes, Your Grace. I'm sorry to be the bearer of such tragic tidings."

Drake stood and faced the windows that framed the gray winter sky and constant drizzle. Though it was just after one o'clock, the dreary weather made it dark as early evening.

He took a deep breath, desperate to relieve the sudden painful tightening of his chest.

Anthony will never come home.

The thought went round and round in his head. If only he'd insisted Anthony remain in England. He should have found a way to curb his brother's tempestuous nature. Now he'd lost the opportunity forever. "Are you certain? There's been no mistake?"

"I'm positive, Your Grace."

"How? Which battle?"

Kirby cleared his throat as though he had more news he was reluctant to convey. "No battle, Your Grace. A notorious spy known as the Fox murdered him."

Drake clamped his jaw. Fury mingled with his initial shock and raged through him. His brother wasn't the casualty of an honorable fight on the field of battle. A traitor had killed him in cold blood. "When?"

"The last week of December. In Charles Towne, South Carolina colony."

"Was this 'Fox' apprehended?" Drake swung around to

face the messenger. "If so, I want his neck in a noose posthaste."

Kirby squirmed in his chair. "That's the rub, Your Grace. The Fox escaped. The soldiers who caught him—"

"I thought you said the spy eluded capture. Make up your mind, man. Did he or did he not?"

After an uncomfortable pause, Lieutenant Kirby explained. "He…he *was* caught, but the soldiers let him go without realizing who they'd bagged."

Drake seethed. "What ineptitude! 'Tis a wonder the rebels haven't won the war with lackwits such as those to fight."

"Yes, Your Grace, but you see, Lord Anthony arranged the Fox's capture with Captain Beaufort, my superior officer. As a cousin to your family, Captain Beaufort knew your brother on sight, but the men he sent to meet him did not.

"When our men arrived, Lord Anthony was dead. The Fox remained, or so I heard, refusing to remove his mask. Apparently, the spy had rummaged Lord Anthony's clothing and found his identification after he shot him. The Fox then used the papers to switch his true identity with that of your brother. Our men believed the Fox was dead until they took the body to camp. Once there, Captain Beaufort immediately realized the deception. By then, the Fox had flown, reward and all."

"Reward?"

"Aye, there's a price on the brigand's head. Your brother, also known as Hawk, was to collect it from the soldiers sent by Captain Beaufort."

Drake's brow furrowed in disbelief. "You're suggesting my brother was involved in espionage?"

Kirby gulped. "Yes, Your Grace. Lord Anthony spied for His Majesty. The traitors believed he worked for them, but I assure you, his loyalty to England never wavered."

Drake considered the information. Truthfully, he couldn't imagine Anthony being self-disciplined enough to make a successful spy. That his brother had chosen such a reviled occupation surprised him. Its need for secrecy conflicted with his brother's demand for attention. "How long did he work in that capacity?"

"I don't know, Your Grace, but I suspect for some time. From what I understand, the rebels thought highly of him, too."

"The rebels," Drake said scornfully.

"They're tenacious and unpredictable," the soldier added. "None is so bold as the Fox."

Drake's jaw worked as he struggled to conquer his temper. "So, the scum got away with murder and the reward. Very clever."

"Aye, Your Grace. Your cousin, Captain Beaufort, thought you might prefer to keep this matter secret until the Fox is found and punished. Because of that, he dispatched me to deliver the news, rather than someone from Whitehall. I secured passage from Charles Towne the day after your brother's shooting and arrived in London yesterday morn."

Drake returned to his place behind the desk. "Who is leading the hunt for this Fox?"

"As far as I know, Captain Beaufort remains in charge. However, he did say he would post further information to

Hawk Haven by way of special courier if any became available."

The muted sound of rain outside filtered through the lead glass windows. Grim resolve filled Drake's mind. No one could be allowed to kill an Amberly and escape unpunished. "Tell me everything you know about this rebel spy."

Kirby tugged at his ear, and his brow pleated with concentration. "I don't know much. No one does. The Fox is the most elusive spy in the Colonies, Your Grace. So little is known about the sly dog, stories boast he's a phantom."

Drake snorted in contempt. "Phantoms do not murder people."

"No, of course not, Your Grace. In truth, the only certain information is the Fox resides in Charles Towne or the nearby environs. Most likely he's a man of wealth, perhaps a planter."

Frustrated, Drake rubbed his angular chin. His pain and fury grew with each tick of the clock. "There must be a suspect or two. Anthony must have known something of the person with whom he dealt. Why didn't he tell Beaufort the traitor's whereabouts, and simply have the man arrested?"

Kirby shook his head. "He couldn't, not without compromising his position in the enemy spy ring."

Drake had heard enough for one sitting. He stood, barely controlling the need to smash something. He snapped his fingers, and Chaney entered from where he'd been waiting in the hall. "That will be all, Lieutenant. My butler will show you to a room. Prepare for a possible journey. Should I hear no word from Beaufort by week's end, you and I shall return to the Colonies to root out this slippery vermin ourselves."

"Yes, Your Grace. With God's help we'll find him soon." Kirby stood, clicked his heels and bowed as he backed out the door.

With God's help, indeed.

Drake stared through the window at the mournful weather. In his youth, he'd trusted in God, but no longer. Years of grief and disappointment had hardened his heart until he'd been able to forget God as effectively as God had forgotten him. Now, there was no room in his life for forgiveness or faith. It was vengeance he needed to set things right.

His fingers drumming steadily on the desktop, his mind quickly formed a plan. He'd wait two days to hear from Beaufort. Then he'd hunt down the unsuspecting Fox. When he located him, and he had no doubt of his success, he'd make certain the fellow danced at the end of a noose posthaste.

Chapter Two

Charles Towne, South Carolina
July 1781

Elise patted her powdered wig into place, smoothed the green silk gown over her hips and took a deep, relaxing breath as she prepared to leave the safety of her bedchamber.

Dear Lord, You've promised You'll never leave me. Please help me through tonight.

Taking a deep breath, she stepped into the dimly lit hall and closed the heavy door behind her. A moment later, Christian Sayer departed his own chamber two doors down. A handsome young man, Christian looked the picture of a wealthy planter's son in a finely woven white shirt, honey-toned breeches and matching embroidered waistcoat. A well-cropped wig disguised his dark brown hair. His blue eyes sparkled with their usual mischief. Like her, he possessed unquestioning loyalty to the American cause, and worked under the directive of his father, spy-master Zechariah Sayer.

Christian greeted her with an appreciative glance and bowed gallantly. "You look sublime, dearest. That bright shade of green you're wearing matches your eyes precisely." He sighed as though put upon. "I can see tonight's ball will offer me little enjoyment. I'll be far too busy fending off the sea of gents bent on wooing you."

Elise rolled her eyes and restrained her laughter. She wasn't the plainest of women, but there was nothing spectacular about her brown hair, and her lips were too full for her oval face. Christian loved to tease. More oft than not, she was his favorite target. Other than her half sister, Princess, he was the only person she held dear. She loved him like a brother.

"I can take care of myself, thank you. If one of us must defend the other this night, it will be I protecting you. Alice Harris has marriage on her mind, or so I hear."

"Alice Harris, you say? She's fetching enough. Since you won't have me, I suppose she'll do. Tell me of her plans, will you? With a woman like Alice, I'll need to be prepared."

"What makes you think I know her full intentions? Alice and I are hardly confidants."

Christian flashed a wicked grin. "I'm aware that you know everything, my dear Fox."

Elise swatted him with her folded fan. "Shh, you silly dolt. Don't bandy that name about. Do you wish to see me dangling from the nearest hangman's tree?"

"Rest easy. There's no one here. Do you think I'd be that foolhardy?"

"I suppose not, *Wolf*," she agreed, using his own alias. "But we can't be too careful. Charles Towne is crawling with redcoats. So many will be in attendance tonight, one would think King George himself planned to call."

"Aye, you know father has little choice but to include them if he hopes to maintain control of Brixton Hall. Thank God they believe he's a Loyalist or we'd all be out on our ear."

Elise said nothing as they meandered toward the top of the stairs. What she wouldn't do to be released and away from the Hall. But then where would Prin go? Surely the war would end soon, and she and her sister would be free. "There's no doubt Zechariah is convincing in all that he does."

"Do I detect a note of bitterness, Elise?"

"What would I have to be bitter about?"

"I can think of a good many things," Christian said with sympathy.

"It's just that I'm so tired of this life, of always playing the role of someone other than myself," she said, sorry the conversation had taken a personal turn.

"We all wear masks of one kind or another to protect ourselves, m'dear. You play the scatterbrain, Zechariah the Tory and I—"

"The soulless rake," she interjected sweetly.

He grinned, unrepentant. "I do my part. Innocent girl that you are, it might surprise you to know that the wives and mistresses of British officers are more forthcoming with their secrets once they've been exposed to my charm. It's delicate and dangerous work."

"Dangerous? Ha!"

"Of course it's dangerous. Have you not heard? There is no fury like a woman scorned. Once I've gleaned my information I'm required to move on to the next fair dove—"

"Sitting duck, you mean."

"Ah, but it is the least I can do for our cause."

They stopped at the top of the stairs. Once again Elise suffered a twinge of unease. Christian squeezed her hand in commiseration. "We all do what we must. Seven months have passed since Hawk's betrayal. Father is growing impatient with you. If you don't join the ranks again soon, he'll send you back to Roger."

At the mention of her stepfather, she grimaced. Roger was akin to a viper in her mind. He lived for profit no matter the pain he caused others. Her voice dipped to a whisper. "No one is more aware of my precarious position than I. I'll act my part, and no one will ever guess I'm a murderess."

Christian frowned. "Shush, don't speak nonsense. You did what you had to do and defended yourself against the traitor. Should you have died or allowed your capture in order to line our enemy's pockets with silver?"

She sighed. T'was a familiar argument. "I know I had no choice. Still, the nightmare plagues me. I've prayed and I know the Lord has forgiven me, but I can still feel Hawk's blood on my hands."

In the flickering candlelight of the stairwell, her friend's expression changed to one of concern as he displayed a rare moment of seriousness. "I know, but you should put your mind at ease. You didn't pull the trigger or intend to see him dead. In my estimation, the world is a far better place without a turncoat among us."

"Perhaps, but I wish I'd not been the one involved."

"Trust me, the memory will fade in time." Christian pulled her close for a brief hug. "Now, tell me of your new orders."

They continued down the stairs, and she grew more reluctant with each step. "His name is Drake Amberly. He claims to be a ship owner interested in reestablishing trade with colonies under British control. Zechariah wants to know if he can be persuaded to join our cause."

Christian frowned. "I met Amberly yesterday in Charles Towne. He's a disturbing gent, not one to tangle with, I'd wager. He conveys an easy temper, but there's a menace about him, a danger he fails to conceal completely. Be careful of the man."

Elise took his advice to heart. "It's time we changed our conversation. This close to our destination even the walls are listening."

They finished their descent in silence. Elise used the time to compose herself like an actress preparing for opening night. The chatter of their guests' conversation wafted through the house, growing louder until it became a roar as she and Christian reached the mansion's first floor. House slaves hustled past carrying silver trays laden with food. The scents of roast pork, fowl and spiced fruit blended to create an appealing combination.

"So, the pair of you has finally decided to join us." They turned in unison to see Zechariah walking toward them, a scowl pinching his shiny brow.

A short, rotund man, the elder Sayer possessed a massive belly that separated his crimson waistcoat from the top of his fuchsia trousers. His stock appeared as though he'd tied it without benefit of a looking glass and his skin shone more ruddy than usual thanks to the chalked wig that sat askew atop his head.

In the eighteen months since she'd arrived at Brixton Hall, it never ceased to amaze Elise that a man unable to harmonize his own clothing could effectively coordinate one of the Patriots' most successful assemblies of espionage.

"Of course, Father," Christian said. "I'd never miss so grand a gathering, especially one given in my honor. A man turns five and twenty but once in his life. Nothing could keep me away."

Known for his sour disposition, Zechariah grunted, obviously not amused by his son's facetious manner. "I don't appreciate being left to greet our guests alone."

Before Christian could reply, the strains of a harpsichord and stringed quartet shifted tempo, announcing the commencement of dancing. Merry laughter drifted into the foyer from several nearby rooms.

"Our guests seem happy enough," Elise commented in an effort to change the subject. Now was not the time for the two men to quarrel, as they were wont to do far too often.

The spymaster took her hand, but continued to eye his son. "Yes, and we should join them. As usual, the ladies are eager for this young buck's attentions. The gentlemen have already begun to ask after you, Elise. In fact, there's one in particular I want you to meet."

Drake leaned against the mantel, watching the festivities with sharp eyes. The merriment of the party might have cheered him under different circumstances, but frustration flayed his nerves and wore his patience thin. Kirby hadn't exaggerated the Fox's elusiveness. Drake had spent a fortune in bribes, yet learned little concerning the rebel spy. Only a nearly nonexistent trail had led him here to Brixton Hall, one of the largest plantations in the Carolinas.

His contacts had assured him the Fox would be in attendance tonight. A ball such as this provided the perfect opportunity for spies and their web of associates to carry out their business unnoticed and unhindered.

Drake raised his glass and sampled the sweet punch. He suffered no illusions the Fox would give himself away. He planned to keep a watchful eye, search for clues that might reveal the man's identity at a later date.

He perused the room, absorbing each detail. Compared to the drawing rooms he frequented in England, this one was small and plain, though artfully decorated in bright shades of yellow and blue. An abundance of Chippendale furniture lined three walls. The rugs had been rolled back to reveal a polished, wood-planked floor where a group of laughing dancers performed a reel.

Since his arrival in the Colonies three months prior, Drake had done his best to change his manner, dress and speech to match that of a man of trade. Lieutenant Kirby assured him he'd succeeded in his deception though they hadn't stayed anywhere long enough to put his disguise to a serious test.

Drake located Lieutenant Kirby near the refreshment table. The soldier had been contributing to the hunt by eavesdropping as he moved from place to place about the room.

The music faded. All eyes turned toward the doorway as Zechariah, his son, Christian, and a stunning young woman entered the room. The guests clapped for long moments, quieting for Zechariah when he raised his hands to plead for silence. The planter welcomed his friends and neighbors before offering a joyous toast in honor of his son.

It was the woman, however, who arrested Drake's attention. He watched her, his interest keen. Like the other women in attendance, she wore an elaborately arranged wig. Quite inexplicably he felt a prick of irritation at being denied a view of her hair's true color. Her face was pure beauty, with large wide eyes, a slender nose and full luscious lips that begged to be savored.

His eyes roamed over her tall, gently curved frame. The green gown she wore shimmered against her luminous skin. Diamonds around her neck and dangling from her delicate ears sparkled in the luster light, but it was her bright smile that lit up her face, and for him, the room.

He straightened into a more attentive posture, unable to divert his eyes from the girl as she allowed Christian Sayer to lead her to the dance floor, where the other guests followed them in a minuet.

Drake's fingers clenched the glass in his hand. He didn't care for the scene before him. The girl gazed into her escort's eyes too often for Drake's liking, flashing Christian a beautiful smile that Drake began to covet for himself.

Kirby joined him. "She's fair to look upon, is she not, sir?"

With his eyes riveted on the couple, Drake nodded. "Indeed. Who is she?"

"Her name is Elise Cooper. I heard the wallflowers discussing her while I enjoyed the refreshments. According to them she's an orphan and Zechariah's ward. They also mentioned she's as dimwitted as she is pretty."

"Jealous harpies, I'd wager. What of her relationship with the son? 'Tis clear the puppy's besotted with her. Are they affianced?"

"I don't believe so, sir. I've heard no word. Perhaps they will be."

Not if I win her first. Startled by the thought, Drake rejected it immediately. He had no time nor inclination to court her, no matter how beautiful she was. Still, he breathed a sigh of relief when the girl relinquished Christian to another partner and went to stand with Zechariah at the edge of the dance floor.

Across the room, the fine hairs on Elise's arms and the back of her neck stood to attention, alerting her to the odd sensation of being watched.

She looked around, trying to appear nonchalant. Her breath caught in her throat when she noticed the man observing her. He was dark, handsome in a fierce sort of way. His sculpted lips turned in a seductive half smile, but it was the long scar along his jaw that intrigued her.

Tall and broad-shouldered, he cut a fine figure in a black waistcoat and breeches. His stark white shirt and elegant but simple stock stood in sharp contrast with his golden skin. He wore his black hair tied at the nape, one of only a few men in the room bold enough to refuse a wig.

His gaze captured hers, and his magnetic eyes seemed to discern her darkest secrets. His stare rattled her nerves and made her instantly more aware of herself in a manner that was most disconcerting.

To a woman used to being in the midst of trouble, he seemed the essence of it. She decided then to steer clear of him, for in one glance she knew his ilk: pure danger in masculine form.

Zechariah patted her hand. "Elise? Are you ill?"

She blinked and looked down into his round face. "I'm fine. Why do you ask?"

"You've nearly drawn blood."

Her gaze fell to where her fingernails dug into his linen-clad arm. She released him immediately.

Her spymaster fiddled with the froth of lace at his wrist. "Get hold of yourself, girl. You'll never accomplish what you must if you're more skittish than a colt."

Elise narrowed her eyes and bit back a sharp retort. She kept her expression cheerful so as not to give away the game to onlookers, but she resented his tone.

She despised Zechariah's hold on her life. But he'd offered the escape she'd prayed for as part of the bargain she'd made to free her sister. For now, she could do little but accept his sharp ways. Others believed she was his ward, when in actuality he was her warden.

"I'm neither skittish nor incapable of performing my task. The man by the mantel, the dark one, he startled me is all. I turned to see him staring a hole in my back."

Zechariah observed the man covertly. "That, my dear, is Drake Amberly, the man you're to investigate. You'd do well to encourage his interest. If he were to become besotted with you, it would make your task that much easier."

Elise bit back a sharp retort. Her instincts warned that Amberly was the one man in the Colonies she should avoid at all costs. "I have a troublesome feeling about him."

"Perhaps meeting him will alleviate the sensation." His amiable tone cloaked a rod of iron. "Allow me to introduce you."

She took a deep breath and released it slowly. The unease she'd labored under for much of the day increased. Her palms grew moist. The closer she walked toward Amberly, the faster her heart raced.

When they came abreast of the man, Zechariah extended his beefy paw in greeting. He spoke loudly, competing with the party's din of music, dancers and conversation. "Amberly, I'm pleased to see you've joined us. I hope the journey from Charles Towne was not too taxing."

"Not in the least. The river was smooth, the boat swift. I arrived in no time at all."

"Excellent, I'm glad to hear it." Zechariah rocked on his heels, his hands clamped behind his back. "I trust the maid saw you settled?"

"Most comfortably, thank you. Your hospitality is much appreciated."

Even as he spoke with Zechariah, Amberly's eyes returned to her face again and again. Heat rose to her cheeks. She hoped the powder and rouge she'd applied before the party disguised her reaction.

"We're pleased to have you here." Zechariah turned to her. "Amberly, I'd like you to meet my ward, Miss Elise Cooper. Elise, this is Mr. Drake Amberly, direct from London. He'll be staying with us for the next few weeks while he convinces me to contract his shipping line."

No one told her he'd be a long-term guest. She offered her hand politely, schooling her features to prevent her dismay from reflecting on her face.

His large, tanned hand engulfed her much smaller one. He bowed and kissed the back of her knuckles. His scent of spice and soap teased her senses. She shivered, aware her response to him was profoundly peculiar. Every nerve in her body warned her to make an excuse and run away. Only the force of her will kept her planted before him.

Intense, lushly lashed eyes caught and held hers. "The pleasure is all mine, Miss Cooper. I am most fortunate to make your acquaintance."

His voice was deep and smooth except for a few clipped words that reminded her of the English upper class. The observation brought her halfway back to her senses. She had to remember her orders and not allow herself to be waylaid by a handsome face.

She giggled, resorting to her role as a featherbrain. Experience had taught her a man let his guard down around a woman he considered a simpleton. "I'm charmed, Mr. Amberly. A girl could lose her head with a man as handsome as you in the room."

"Why thank you, Miss Cooper. I'm flattered."

He seemed more amused than complimented. She tapped him playfully with her fan and gifted him with a flirtatious grin. "Surely not. I've seen the other ladies swarming you tonight. Most likely you've grown weary of praise." She motioned toward the dancers behind her. "Forgive my boldness, but would you be so kind, sir? I truly love to dance. Since my escort is the guest of honor, he's obliged to take a turn with the other ladies tonight. I fear I'll be left to sit with the matrons if one of you fine gentlemen doesn't take pity on me."

"It would be my honor, Miss Cooper. However, I never acquired the skill of dancing. May I interest you in some refreshment instead?"

"You never learned to dance? How unusual," she remarked, her eyes as wide and innocent as a babe's.

"Dancing isn't a sport in large demand on a ship."

She smiled coyly. His refusal to dance might work to her advantage. Perhaps she could get him alone, away from the crowd and music that would disrupt conversation and her ability to uncover more about him. "I so wanted to dance, but I suppose a glass of refreshment will do. Why don't you fetch us a drink? I'll gather my shawl and meet you in the garden. It's such a pretty night. I see no reason to waste it indoors."

Amberly grinned. "A superb idea, Miss Cooper. To the garden it is."

Drake enjoyed the view of Elise's slim back as she departed. What an intriguing female. He wondered how many men swallowed her act. She played the part of an empty-headed chit, but intelligence shone from her startling green eyes. He wondered what game she played at. In his experience, all women had something to hide. Despite his earlier decision not to pursue her, he found uncovering her secrets might provide an interesting diversion during his stay in South Carolina.

Zechariah cleared his throat, reclaiming Drake's attention. "I apologize, Amberly. Our Elise possesses a double portion of boldness. I hope you weren't offended."

"No, indeed I find her delightful."

"Excellent. She's a wonderful girl, if not the smartest one. Now, if you'll excuse me, I must see to my other guests."

With a nod, Zechariah left and entered conversation with a nearby couple. Drake made his way to the refreshment table and accepted two glasses of punch from a servant before heading to the garden.

Not far from the open French doors, Christian Sayer intercepted him. "Evening, Amberly. I trust you're enjoying our hospitality."

"Very much. I just spoke with your father and his ward—"

"That's why I'm here. Is one of those glasses for Miss Cooper?"

Drake nodded.

"Then I'll tell you this as a friend," Christian's smile held an edge of warning. "Miss Cooper requires the greatest respect. Should you harm her, I'd be gravely disappointed. Treat her well. I'd hate to have to shoot you."

Drake cocked an eyebrow in mild disbelief. The puppy was actually warning him off—an unusual event to be sure for a man used to being hounded by every flesh-peddling mama in England. His sister would howl with laughter if she were here to witness Sayer's threat.

Drake suppressed his amusement and considered Christian with new eyes. The younger man possessed the demeanor of an open, friendly individual, yet it was clear he had darker, hidden depths. Could *he* be the Fox?

Making a mental note to watch Christian more closely, Drake tipped his head. "Save your threats for someone who will be impressed by them, puppy. Now, if you'll excuse me, Miss Cooper is waiting for her drink."

Chapter Three

Drake shouldered his way past the unyielding younger man and followed the sparsely furnished hall to the front of the red-brick mansion.

A servant in a white-and-scarlet uniform opened the door for him to cross into the balmy night. A full moon shone from the velvety black sky. Strategically placed lanterns lit the English garden spread out before him. Beyond its hedges and curved walkways, a wide, well-tended lawn sloped into the inky ribbon of the Ashley River.

He searched for Elise among the strolling guests partaking of the floral-scented air, but it seemed she'd disappeared. His fingers clenched round the glasses he held as disappointment assailed him. He found himself quite put out at the idea of not being able to speak with her. She was by far the most captivating woman he'd met in the whole of his twenty-eight years.

His eyes lit with pleasure when he finally located her across the expansive lawn, near the water's edge. She stood half turned toward him, a lace shawl draped around her slender shoulders. She appeared to be speaking with someone, but he saw no one in the shadows cast by a towering oak. He hoped it wasn't another man because he pitied the chap who tried to snatch her from him.

Drake shook his head to clear it. The fervor of his response to Elise surprised him. He brushed away the sensation, refusing to ponder the speed, the intensity of his reaction to the woman, for he'd never experienced a like emotion to compare with it.

Surely he'd learned his lesson, he thought in self-disgust. Women weren't to be trusted. His wife had ended their union with betrayal, and the recent episode with his faithless fiancée had surely soured him on marriage for good.

So why did sighting Elise bring him such relief? Was it simply her beauty? Or perhaps it was the light of mystery in her eyes? Whatever it was, she was the first thing to please him since he'd learned of Anthony's death. The long winter voyage across the Atlantic had put him in a fouler mood than when he'd left England, and the added frustration of finding so little information about the Fox proved infuriating. For the first time in months he looked forward to concentrating on a subject other than his brother's murderer.

Elise lifted her head and caught him watching her. She tossed him a jaunty smile and beckoned him with a wave of her hand. He descended the steps at a leisurely pace, not wanting to seem overeager in his haste to reach her. His boots crunched the gravel as he followed the garden path to her side.

From her place beside the tree, Elise watched, transfixed by the predatory confidence Drake exuded and the warm manner in which he studied her. She was relieved to see he wasn't offended by her bold request to meet her in the garden. He was by far the most intriguing man she'd ever met. Pity she had no wish to fall in love. If she did, he would be a mighty temptation indeed.

Princess whistled low and quiet from the shadows. "The man carrying the glasses is him, isn't it? I can't tell rightly in the moonlight, but he seems awful dark to be an Englishman."

Without taking her eyes from Drake, Elise nodded. "From what I understand, he spends most of his time on a ship."

"What's his name again?"

"Drake Amberly."

"He reminds me of a loaded pistol that's primed and cocked. Maybe even more dangerous."

"My thought precisely, Prin."

Elise focused on her sister, hoping Amberly thought a view of the river interested her. Her sister's large eyes, straight nose and high cheekbones were similar to her own and their shared father's, but the night hid the mocha-brown skin and simple muslin gown that proclaimed her position as a house slave.

Prin's mother, Abigail, had been their father's property for a handful of years before Samuel decided he needed to marry and produce the legitimate son he longed for. Another girl, Elise had been a bitter disappointment for him.

Prin had been raised among the other slaves, but she'd

done her best to protect Elise from their father's drunken rages. An airtight bond of love had been forged between the two girls. Now their situations were reversed. Elise protected Prin. As long as she did what Zechariah dictated, she'd be given ownership of Prin once the war ended. From there, Elise planned to use the funds she collected from spying to create a new life for them both somewhere free from the hated chains of slavery.

"You can't be too careful round a man like that," Prin warned. "He walks like he owns the whole earth."

"True," Elise whispered. "He's arrogant, but not meanly so, I think. I suppose it comes naturally to him. Men like him seem to acquire that particular trait at birth."

Elise glanced back over her shoulder. Amberly had traversed half the lawn, but remained too far away to hear their conversation. She watched him, disliking the way her heart fluttered in anticipation of his arrival. He carried himself like a nobleman, as though he were well aware of and comfortable with his position in life. With purpose and a complete disregard for others' opinions of him.

"Jus' be careful," Prin warned.

"You know I will be." Her sister never ceased to play the part of mother hen. "You should go before he gets here. Tell Zechariah you delivered his message and I've learned no news as yet. I'll meet with him after I've had a chance to speak with Amberly."

"That old dragon wants a miracle," Prin reminded her, speaking of Zechariah. "Your past work has spoiled him. You're usually so quick to give him the information he wants, he thinks you can read minds and don't need to talk or listen none."

"Well, then, he's deceived. I—"

"My, that man looks dangerous," her sister interrupted.

Elise frowned and continued to focus on the river. "Prin, please go back to the house and deliver my message. Then wait in our room, all right? I want you safe. You know how the soldiers like to make free with their hands."

"Maybe I'll just hide over there in the bushes. When you get ready to head back to the house, I'll go up with you."

"No. What if Amberly sees you? There's enough lantern light to expose you, and how would I explain your presence in the shrubs?"

"I'm your chaperone?"

Elise shook her head at her sister's persistence. "I don't need one with all the other guests strolling about."

"Fine," Prin grouched. "I'm going. Just remember the trick I taught you. A knee to—"

"'If he tries to touch what he shouldn't.' Yes, I know. Now *go*," she whispered.

A snapping twig announced Amberly's arrival. Elise spun to face him just as he joined her. He offered her one of the crystal glasses he held. "Miss Cooper, the drink you requested."

Smiling brightly, she accepted the glass. Her fingertips brushed his, and a pleasant sensation danced up her arm. Surprised by the contact, she forgot the clever quip she'd devised to begin the conversation and gain the upper hand.

She took a sip of fruity punch while gathering her wits. Amberly's intense gaze flustered her, making it difficult to concentrate when questioning him should have been foremost in her mind. Forcing her thoughts to regroup, she flashed him a flirtatious grin, and slipped back into her least favorite role. "Why, thank you, Mr. Amberly. I do believe you've saved me from disgracing myself in a faint. I'm as parched as a hot summer day."

"My pleasure, Miss Cooper. I'm pleased to be of service." He peered into the darkness behind her. "You seem to be alone, but I thought I saw you speaking with someone. I trust I didn't interrupt?"

"No. My maid brought a message from Mr. Sayer. I sent her back to the house."

Drake's brow furrowed. "I spoke with him moments ago. He warned me off you."

Perplexed that Zechariah would do such a thing, she lowered her lashes to hide her confusion. "He did?"

Drake stepped closer, dried leaves crunching beneath his boots. His dark presence engulfed her, made her feel tiny. Nervous excitement shimmied in her belly. She had to crane her neck to look into his eyes.

"It's obvious he's smitten with you, but I hope you don't feel the same way about him."

Realization dawned. Christian must have been the one to warn him off. The tension tightening her muscles suddenly released. Laughter bubbled to her lips. "Christian isn't smitten—"

"He is. I've no doubt." He paused. "But, I fear I'm more so."

Elise's heart beat out of control. She flipped open her fan and fluttered it rapidly, hoping to cool the blush that warmed her cheeks. "You must be jesting. We've just met. Perhaps you were out to sea too long, and the sun has addled your brain?"

He grinned. "No, I simply know beauty when I see it."

His comment sent a gush of relief through her. Her nervousness receded, though her disappointment increased. He was just another shallow man interested in a woman's outward appearance. She'd dealt with such nonsense before.

She dropped her fan, letting it dangle from the silk cord about her wrist, and batted her lashes. "Thank you, Mr. Amberly. I feared with all the other lovely ladies here tonight, I'd be the least noticed among them."

"You needn't have worried, sweet. You outshine all the other ladies of my acquaintance—here and in England."

Determined not to be taken in by his flattery, she took another sip of punch. "You're a prince to say so, sir."

"I'm not a prince, Miss Cooper." His white teeth flashed in a grin. "Perhaps something slightly less grand. Perhaps a duke?"

She knew he jested, but something in his words suggested a double meaning, one she had yet to grasp. Another couple walked close by, admiring the river. She nodded to them as they passed but didn't speak until they were out of earshot. "Hardly, sir. It's just an expression. You needn't worry I'd mistake you for a genuine member of royalty. You've not the bearing for it."

His smile faltered imperceptibly. One dark brow rose in question. "Is that so? How many royals have you known?"

"Few to none," she admitted, glancing out over the river where moon and lantern light shimmered on the calm surface. "Although, I did have the pleasure of meeting Lord Cornwallis and his entourage at a ball I attended last summer."

Amberly gave no reaction when she expected him to be impressed by the announcement. Whenever she mentioned the general's name, most English men and women expressed a keen interest in the details of the man leading Britain's southern campaign.

· She changed the subject, searching for a topic that would encourage him to speak of himself. "Still, I suppose no ball competes with plying the open sea. I envy you, Mr. Amberly. Shipping must be a fascinating occupation."

His thick eyelashes dipped to shield his eyes. If she hadn't been watching him so closely, she wouldn't have noticed. "To be sure, Miss Cooper. 'Tis quite fascinating if one enjoys endless days of bobbing along like a cork, going mad from boredom and smelling of fish. One can only scan the horizon so often. Two weeks into an Atlantic crossing, a ship, no matter how large, becomes excessively small indeed."

"You surprise me, sir. The few sailors I've met love their lot in life more than they love their own mothers. You speak as though you can't bear it."

"On the contrary. I enjoy the sea and all its wonders, but I'm a practical and truthful man. Sailors who have naught but good to say about it are lying or victims of brain rot."

She laughed. "I doubt I'd make a good sailor. I hate the feeling of being penned in. Yet, I must admit the sense of freedom one must feel holds great appeal for me."

Drake moved closer and leaned against the tree. He crossed his arms over his broad chest and gave her a lazy smile.

This close to him she could smell his spicy cologne.

Prin was right, he was dark for an Englishman, almost as dark as the Indians who lived near her father's Virginia farm, and so mysterious she found it impossible to drag her eyes away from him.

Somewhere behind Elise a woman laughed, drawing her back to the task at hand. She had to focus. Prin's future freedom, as well as her own, depended upon her being in control and sober of mind. She took her thoughts in hand and continued her quest with renewed purpose. "I'm curious about you, Mr. Amberly. I'd wager you have more than a few secrets."

He shrugged in casual affirmation. "A few perhaps. No more than most men, a lot less than most women."

She glanced away. Her entire existence was a blend of shadow and light. She possessed so many secrets even she had trouble remembering them all.

He reached out and ran his fingertip down her cheek. Startled by the caress, she caught her breath. She wasn't used to being touched with such gentleness, and the feather-soft brush of his finger was a pleasurable sensation she loathed to end.

Straining her willpower to the seams, she pulled away. Her hand trembled as she tugged the edges of her shawl tighter around her shoulders. "I…I must go."

"Don't," he said.

"I must."

"Why?"

Matters had gotten out of hand. She'd lost her concentration. She needed to regroup her thoughts and felt sure she'd swim in confusion as long as she stayed in his company. "We have other guests. Mr. Amberly and I must see to them."

She turned in the direction of the well-lit brick mansion. "Fare thee well. Goodnight."

He reached for her wrist, but she pretended not to notice as she moved beyond his grasp. He followed her. She heard his pursuit and stepped up her pace.

"I shall see you again soon, Miss Cooper."

His tone was sincere enough, but to her flustered senses the statement sounded like a threat. "Not if I see you first, sir."

His rich laughter stretched across the velvety night. "My heart is broken, dear girl, but thank you for the warning. I'll be sure to sneak up on you the next time we meet."

"Well," Zechariah demanded a few hours later in the study. "What news have you, girl? You and Amberly seemed cozy enough."

Elise shifted on her feet. She stood before the study's waning fire, summoned to the old man like a disobedient servant. "*Cozy* isn't the word I'd use."

Her spymaster kept his back to her as he poured a drink and replaced the bottle's crystal stop. Christian sat in the corner, hidden in shadow. The ball had ended several hours prior, and their guests had gone or sought out a bed for the night.

The old man faced her, took off his flowing powdered wig and tossed it to a nearby chair, where it landed in a cloud of chalk. Candlelight reflected on his bald head. He scratched his scaly crown and sighed before eyeing her with what she thought was suspicion. "I care not about the word, girl. I only wish to know if you discovered something useful."

"No—"

"Then what am I to do with you? If you've forever lost your ability to aid our cause, I'll ship you back to Williamsburg in the blink of an eye."

Her jaw tightened. He'd used the same threat on many occasions. Before Hawk's death she would have paid it no mind, but since that fateful night her guilt made her nearly useless as a spy. His irate expression signaled a real cause for concern. If he sent her back to Williamsburg, she'd be under Roger's thumb once more. All hope of freeing Prin would be lost. "You didn't allow me to fin—"

"We're all risking our lives in this business. Some of us more than that," Zechariah continued with an angry slash of his hand. "We have to stay sharp and spare no opportunity to locate the information we must acquire."

Elise listened to the lecture, biding her time with a prayer for patience. Zechariah would run out of steam soon. Then she'd have her say.

Sayer's tirade came to an abrupt stop. His countenance softened imperceptibly. "You're not the first of our number to have a part in killing a man, you know. Hawk was our enemy. You did right to lay him low. I'll have no more of this pouting. You must move on."

He forestalled her when she began to protest. "Elise, I'd hate to lose you. In the past, you've proven your worth, but the war situation is grim. I cannot coddle you a moment longer."

"You've no need to coddle me," she said between clenched teeth. "I learned no information to support Amberly's claims, but I observed something you may wish to consider."

Sayer's eyes gleamed. "Ah, I knew you'd not disappoint."

Elise bit her tongue and refrained from reminding him of the diatribe he'd cast her way a moment ago. "I believe he's more than he says he is. A minor aristocrat, perhaps."

Christian stood and entered the candlelight. "What makes you think so?"

"His manner and his story conflict. He told Zechariah he operates in trade, that he's come to America to reestablish shipping lines between Carolina planters and England. But Amberly proclaims his finer breeding with each word he speaks."

"I didn't notice anything out of the ordinary," Zechariah said.

"I'd wager he's changed his accent as best he can, but if you listen closely, you can hear his cultured tones."

"It's possible he's putting on airs," Christian offered.

Elise nodded in agreement. "Yes, but I've spoken with sea captains and sailors before. I know many men of trade. None have his confidence or air of command. It's as though he owns the world and accepts it as his due. I've only seen that sort of bearing in the lords and ladies I met in Williamsburg, or more recently, in the entourage of General Cornwallis."

The spymaster rubbed his whiskered chin. "The maid who unpacked for him saw nothing out of the ordinary. His clothing and trinkets are of good quality, but nothing is especially grand—"

"Of course it isn't," Elise said with a touch of impatience. "If a man wishes to hide his identity, what does he do? He pretends to be the opposite of who he really is."

Zechariah gave her a sharp look. "Don't sass me, girl.

I know what a man does to hide his identity. I've been doing it for a good many years."

Chastised, she nodded, but didn't apologize.

"Still," he said, "you've said nothing to convince me he's a spy."

"No, but if I'm right, there's trouble afoot. Everything he's told us regarding himself would be a lie. He'd have to be here for some other purpose...."

The room fell into silence as each of its occupants considered the situation.

"The man *is* hiding something," Zechariah conceded. "I can smell it. If he's a spy, then you must find him out."

Elise nodded. Christian frowned.

"Spend every possible moment with him until the truth is discovered." The spymaster's gaze pinned to her face. "He's taken with you, girl. And you need to reestablish your worth. This is the perfect opportunity to do so."

Elise thought of her strange reaction to Amberly. The oddly delicious, frightening way he'd made her feel. "Zechariah, I...I'm not the best choice for this errand."

"Nonsense, there's no one better. Prove yourself once more or I'll be forced to replace you with someone willing to face the noose if necessary. I'm sure your mother and your weasel of a stepfather will accept you back in Williamsburg, but I might have to sell your sister."

Like a foul stench, his words hung in the air.

"You've no need for concern. I'll do your bidding, as you well know."

"Excellent. Within a week, I want more information on Amberly than even his parents possess of him. Do we understand one another?"

Christian interrupted from beside her. "I'll help, Elise. The two of us might enjoy more success if we work together. However, there is one small problem."

"What?" Zechariah asked irritably.

"I warned him off before he followed Elise into the garden."

"Aye, he told me." she said.

"And why, pray tell, did you do that?" Zechariah slapped the top of the tidy desk. To Elise, "Did Amberly listen? Did the man keep his distance?"

Elise hesitated, recalling Drake's vibrant presence, the way he'd affected her. Yet, to tell Zechariah of her reaction would make her weak in his eyes. He might think she'd grown unable to separate her feelings from her work. "He must have, for none of his actions were untoward."

Zechariah frowned in Christian's direction, but spoke to her. "Pity. Now you'll have to convince him his attentions are welcome."

She doubted that would pose a serious challenge. "I understand."

Zechariah passed her a small packet tied with string. "Good. Now that's settled, here are the letters I want you to deliver to Tabby tomorrow. She'll need to pass them near a flame's heat for the message to appear."

Elise accepted the envelopes. The recent invention of invisible ink amazed her. "If I'm to take these to Tabby, how am I to spend time with Amberly?"

"He has business in Charles Towne. You'll have time on the ferry to charm him."

Never more unsure of herself, she nodded and made for the door.

Chapter Four

Sleep refused to visit Elise. Despite the cool breeze ruffling the white lace curtains of her bedchamber, she was hot and sticky with perspiration. Moonlight illuminated the far side of the room, but barely reached the mosquito-netted bed where she tossed and turned.

More and more of late, her prayers seemed to go unanswered. Without the Lord's guidance she felt adrift and abandoned. With her future and the future of her sister in ever-increasing peril, she clung to the scripture that promised the Lord would never leave her.

But, she had to admit, her faith had begun to bow under the weight of His silence in the midst of her endless concerns.

Prin released a long-suffering breath. "Who you wrestlin' over there?"

"I can't sleep," Elise mumbled. The ropes holding the feather mattress creaked as she flipped to her back. "I believe I'd find more comfort on a stone slab."

"It's a mite better than the mats and cold musty ground of the slave cabins."

"I know," she whispered. "I have no right to complain."

"What's ailing you, then? The truth, if you please."

"Nothing." She couldn't talk about Zechariah's threats with her sister. Prin would protest by way of silent mutiny and hot cups of tea in the spymaster's lap at breakfast. In all likelihood, Zechariah would use the excuse to relegate Prin to the slave cabins instead of turning a blind eye to her presence in his home as he did now.

"So you've taken to lying? I thought my mother taught you better."

Prin was like a hound with a strong scent in her nose. If she ran true to form, Prin wouldn't leave her sister alone until she was fed a satisfactory tale.

"Nothing in particular, I should have said." Elise sighed. "In truth I have much on my mind, none of which I wish to trouble you with."

"I'll wager you do have much on your mind. My name may be Princess but you're the *queen* of frettin'." Her sister turned smug. "Good thing I'm here. I knew you'd come to me for the truth."

"You know I'm always glad you're here with me, but in this case, I wouldn't know what truth you speak of."

Prin rolled her eyes. "Of course you do, Lisie, you're not the brainless girl you play so well. You're not blind either. Your problem's a simple one—man trouble. Did you find out whether Amberly's married or not?"

Truth to tell, she'd forgotten to inquire about such basic information. In retrospect, she felt quite inept. If her reaction to the man hadn't distracted her so, she would have had him volunteering those simple facts without him realizing. "No, but then you're the one determined to see me wed."

"I want to see you settled and protected."

"But I have no wish to marry."

"You're nineteen," Prin pointed out. "Fast becomin' an old maid."

Elise groaned. "And any man within five colonies is an acceptable candidate?"

"I just want you safe and happy."

Elise crossed her arms behind her head and closed her eyes. Her sister's concern tugged at her heart. Still. "I can't see how being shackled to a man can provide any woman with happiness."

"Why are you being such a mulehead?" Prin huffed. "Marriage and misfortune don't have to mean the same thing."

Elise turned her head and strained to see her sister's face. The fat candle she'd lit while preparing for bed no longer burned. In the faint moonlight, she could make out little except the outline of Prin's cheek and the brightness of her eyes. "Just because you've found happiness with Kane doesn't mean we're all destined for an equally joyful end."

"But findin' a husband would solve all your problems."

Aghast, Elise sat up in the bed and twisted toward her sister. "I believe it's finally happened."

"What?"

"You've gone daft."

"Have not."

Elise scrunched the bedsheets in her fists. It was illegal for slaves to wed, but ever since she'd found a minister willing to officiate a secret marriage between Prin and Kane, her sister had become convinced Elise needed to marry as well. "In all seriousness, how can you be foolish enough to believe marriage would solve my difficulties? It's more likely a husband would multiply them. Recall, if you will, how our father treated both our mothers."

"Aye, Pa was a bad seed, but not all men are such fiends."

"Then let's consider Roger."

"Why? The man's a goat's bottom, nothing more. Just 'cause your ma believed his sweet talk and found misery in matrimony, don't mean all church aisles lead in the same direction."

Elise wasn't so certain. Without care for her reputation, her own mother had abandoned her in favor of a handsome man's honey-coated promises. Once she and her new lover were free to wed, Roger showed his true colors, and in the end, her mother found herself tied to a second wicked husband.

Her voice husky with remembered pain, she whispered, "Zechariah is another fine example of male selfishness gone awry."

Prin clucked her tongue and shook her head on the pillow. "You're just bein' a goose. Zechariah has principals even if he's *far* from perfect. And before you mention some other poor fool, what about Kane? Or how 'bout Christian? They're as good and fine men as there ever was born."

"True enough."

"Then why not your friend? You both have this spy business in common. He won't keep you from carryin' out your stubborn convictions. You could chase around the countryside together, bring down all the redcoats.... 'Sides, he fancies you."

Elise rolled her eyes. "Christian is a gentleman and a dear, but he fancies *many* women. Besides, how could I think to marry a man who stirs nothing in me but feelings of the brotherly sort?"

Prin took a deep breath and let it out slowly. "You're just too hard to please."

"Can we cease this?" Elise lay down, her back to her sister. "I'm tired and must get some rest. I'm off to Charles Towne in the morning, and the ferry leaves at half past seven. Amberly will be on it, so I must sparkle."

Prin laughed at her sarcasm. "I'm right for sure. That Englishman must have got under your skin like a hungry tick. You only desert subjects and get all huffy when you know I'm right and you're feelin' hooked."

Elise pulled up the sheet and punched her pillow. "Enough, Prin, truly. You couldn't be more wrong about my interest in that man. Beyond finding out his background for Zechariah, he doesn't concern me in the least. Now go to sleep."

"I wasn't the one tossin' and turnin'. That was you in a tumble."

"Do be quiet, will you?"

"It *is* that man." Prin leaned over her. A giggle in her voice, she whispered, "That tall, mysterious and darkly handsome *English* man."

Elise gritted her teeth. An unsolicited image of Amberly invaded her mind. She saw again his golden eyes and knowing smile. Heard his smooth, rich voice in her head.

She squeezed her eyes closed tight, desperate to ward off the warmth that suffused her heart when she thought of him. "Believe what you will. You always do, no matter what I say."

"It's your own fault, you know. You prove me right so often I'd be silly to doubt myself."

A rooster's crowing startled Drake from a deep sleep. The creature sounded as though it were right outside his window. He pushed back the mosquito net and swung his legs over the side of the bed. His bare feet hit the smooth wood, and he took a moment to clear the grogginess from his mind.

Last night he'd declined Zechariah's offer to have a servant wake him. Normally an early riser, he hadn't anticipated the image of Elise occupying his thoughts or disturbing his rest enough to make him oversleep.

Wearing the same clothes from the previous night, he stood and stretched his knotted muscles. He crossed to the open window, hoping for a breeze that was, unfortunately, not to be. The sun had barely risen, but the heat was high and the air steamy with humidity.

He looked out across the lush green lawn to the dock. The ferry to Charles Towne had yet to arrive, though a few people waited along the bank of the smooth-flowing river.

Abandoning the window, he made use of the pitcher of cool water and ornate basin on top of the bureau. He changed into fresh clothes, pausing to tie his hair back with a leather string before heading to the first floor.

Downstairs, the clatter of cutlery lead him to the dining room. Zechariah Sayer sat at the head of a long, polished pine table, a plate of bacon, eggs and fresh rolls arranged before him. An array of foods filled the silver trays along the sideboard, scenting the room with the aroma of cinnamon and fried bacon. A handful of servants stood along the bright green walls, obviously waiting for Sayer's other guests to arrive and break their fast.

Zechariah picked up his steaming cup of coffee and gestured toward one of the chairs. "I'm afraid most everyone else is still abed. I'm an early riser myself. Can't abide the idea of frittering away half the day in idleness."

Drake pulled out the chair and made himself comfortable. He snapped his napkin from its neat fold and spread it across his lap. One of the female servants placed a plate of breakfast in front of him. He noted how attractive the girl looked with her lovely brown eyes and full lips. She reminded him of Elise, which was nonsense. He must be going round the bend. The chit was invading his dreams and now he was starting to see her in every pretty face he came across.

He took a drink of his coffee and added a teaspoon of sugar to mute its bitterness. "I, too, prefer an early start. At home I enjoy exercising my horses in the cool of the day."

"We have a full stable here. Make use of it if you wish." The older man took a bite of egg and chewed with greedy enjoyment. He poked his fork in Drake's direction. "Just stay clear of Elise's gelding, Freedom. She's in love with the mount. I'd hate to have to rescue you from her ire if you borrow him."

A half smile curved Drake's lips. He accepted a roll from the pretty, light-skinned slave. "Thank you for the offer—and the warning. I shall look forward to riding tomorrow. I believe you said the ferry leaves for Charles Towne this morn at half past seven?"

"Aye," Sayer said, motioning toward the mantel clock with his knife. "It should be here by now. You'd best hurry if you hope to be aboard."

Ten minutes later, Drake joined the other passengers waiting on the riverbank near the garden house. Birds chirped, hidden in the towering oaks. The musty smell of moss hung in the steamy air. Kirby had stayed behind to continue the hunt for clues to the Fox's identity. Drake had yet to see Elise, and his disappointment was acute. With the ferry leaving soon, he'd have no chance to see her for the rest of the day.

Waving, the ginger-haired ferry captain jumped onto the dock, his freckled face split in a huge, snaggle-toothed grin. "Miss Cooper!"

Drake pivoted on his heel to find Elise rushing up the path. His chest tightened in appreciation. She was exceptional. The daylight allowed him to see details of her face previously concealed. Her smooth skin and startling green eyes were no mistake of the candlelight. She'd forgone a wig and a cap, allowing him to indulge his curiosity about her hair. Dark brown with thick strands of red and gold that glinted in the morning sun. Tied at the nape, the long tresses hung over her shoulder and swayed below her waist as she walked.

With a smile and a wave to the captain, Elise joined Drake at the back of the queue. All bright smiles and vivacious energy, she reminded him of a perfect spring morning.

"Hello, Mr. Amberly. Fine day for a sail."

"Fine day, indeed, Miss Cooper. Most fine, now that I'm aware you're following me."

"Following you, sir? You're mad if you think so." She lifted the leather satchel she held. "If not for a friend in need, I'd still be asleep."

He smiled. "Then thank heaven you're a friend willing to help."

Elise ignored the sudden racing of her heart. With the letters for Tabby hidden in her satchel, an emergency stop at Riverwood Plantation to rescue muskets and Drake Amberly to dissect for information, she had too much to do to be taken in by his charm.

The bell rang, announcing their imminent departure. The other dozen or so passengers, some carrying chickens or leading goats on leashes, moved en masse onto the ferry's deck.

Drake helped her onboard, but the captain was there to meet her. He doffed his tricorn. "Good mornin', Miss Cooper."

"Good morning, Captain Travis. How's your mother since her illness last week? Did the honey and lemons I sent make a difference?"

The young man beamed. "She's back up to snuff, ma'am, and told me to thank you. The toddy she made did the trick. Her lung rattle's gone."

"I'm glad to hear it. Let me know if she needs anything else."

The captain nodded his appreciation and reluctantly went back to his work. Elise moved starboard. She placed the satchel between her feet and beneath the hem of her yellow skirt before taking hold of the ferry's rail. Drake joined her, his height and broad shoulders casting a long shadow over the deck.

"I dare say our young captain is another of your smitten conquests."

"Don't be silly, Mr. Amberly. Travis isn't smitten, he's my friend." In truth, he was her partner in espionage. Over the past year she'd taken this particular journey more times than she could count. Beyond her regularly scheduled trips, Travis aided her often when an unexpected need to travel presented itself. Zechariah paid him well for his inconvenience, but his loyalty was free.

"Like Christian?"

The ferry wobbled as it launched. She gave him a saucy grin. "Careful, Mr. Amberly. We haven't known each other long enough for you to be jealous."

He frowned. "Perhaps not, but I do believe I am."

He sounded as surprised by his confession as she was to hear it. Facing him, she was struck by how dangerous he was to her peace of mind. Something rare and beyond her experience had snuck up and bloomed between them. Other men had been as blunt, but they'd left her cold. With Drake, she felt as if she were being bathed with the sun.

He brushed her cheek with his fingertips and slipped a tendril of her hair behind her ear. "It's my fondest hope we'll grow our acquaintance."

Breathless, she stared into his golden eyes, wishing she was the carefree young miss she pretended to be. She forced her gaze out across the river. *Focus, focus,* she warned herself. *Prin is depending on you. The patriots need you. Dear Lord, please help me!* Determined to carry out her task, she straightened her shoulders and lifted her chin. "I agree, Mr. Amberly, we *should* grow our acquaintance. By all means, let's chat."

Chapter Five

"Shall I begin, Mr. Amberly?" Elise prayed their discussion would go well. What a blessing it would be if she were able to uncover all the information Zechariah required before they reached Charles Towne. With her orders fulfilled, she would be free to avoid the man and no longer have to worry about the disturbing emotions he stirred in her.

"If you like. But first, please call me Drake?"

"It wouldn't be proper."

His golden eyes danced with mirth. "Last night I was given to understand you care little for propriety."

"What of your family and background?" she asked, determined to keep the conversation focused on him. "Are your parents living? Have you any siblings?"

His expression sobered. "My mother was of Roman extraction. My parents and older brother perished on a return voyage from Rome ten years past. I was left with the care of my two younger siblings. A sister, Eva, and brother, Anthony. Anthony passed away a few months ago."

Her heart twisted with pity. "I'm so sorry. There's nothing worse than losing a loved one."

"I agree. Especially when he died by means of foul play."

"My goodness! That's doubly distressing."

"I've come to terms with his death, but I won't rest until his murderer is punished."

She leaned forward and touched his hand in commiseration. "I'd want to do the same if it were my brother, but I hope you won't allow your vengeance to rule you."

"Anthony has no one else to avenge his honor."

The fire in Amberly's eyes frightened her. "I believe vengeance is best left to God."

"Are you a religious woman, Miss Cooper?"

"Religious? Not terribly," she admitted. "However, I am a Christian and do my best to follow God's word."

Drake glanced across the river to the passing shore. "I gave up on God ages ago. A man can only endure so many disappointments before he realizes his faith has been misplaced."

Elise noticed his white-knuckled grip on the ferry's rail. Her heart went out to him. "I don't believe the Lord abandoned you. Not when His word promises He'll never leave or forsake us."

His mouth tightened into a hard line. "I hope you're right."

She recognized the bitterness and grief churning beneath his matter-of-fact tone. She understood loss. In the past two years, her home, freedom and many of her loved ones had all been taken from her, yet she couldn't imagine how empty her life would be without her faith to sustain her.

A flock of birds landed on the river's calm surface.

Elise used the distraction to gather her thoughts. "What of your sister? I'm certain you must miss her."

His expression softened and she could tell he and the girl were close.

"Eva is fifteen. She's a hoyden despite my best efforts. She's still in the schoolroom and loathes every moment of it. I've no doubt the servants have their hands full while I'm away."

"I'm sure she'd prefer sailing the seven seas with you."

"Most doubtful. She prefers horses to anything or anyone else. I understand you also have a horse you're quite fond of. Zechariah warned me of your ire should I borrow him."

"Zechariah exaggerates."

"He said you'd take a horsewhip to me. That he'd have to scrape me from the stable walls if I dared to touch the beast."

An indignant retort bubbled to her lips until she noticed the teasing gleam in his eyes. She laughed at her own quick temper. "I see that you jest at my expense, but Freedom is dear to me."

"No doubt."

"Zechariah loaned him to me when I first arrived to stay at Brixton Hall."

"And when was that?"

"Eighteen months ago."

"I'm sorry."

"Why? The Sayers are amicable people."

He nodded in agreement. "I, too, have found them as such. But the circumstances that brought you to Zechariah's wardship must have been tragic for you."

She bowed her head and her fingers fiddled with the end of the silk tie joining her bodice. She knew he must think her an orphan. Most people assumed she needed a protector because they believed the history Zechariah had created for her when she came to work for him at Brixton Hall. "Aye, most tragic."

She looked beyond him to the calm river and marshy green banks that stretched as far as the eye could see. In truth, her situation was grim for entirely different reasons. She'd come to work for Zechariah because of her stepfather's greed. After Roger wed her mother, Anne, he'd claimed the Virginia land and slaves as Anne's property, then sold everything off for a tidy sum.

When Roger sold Prin to Zechariah, Elise did all she could to see her set free. Sayer refused to sell her, but had offered Prin's freedom as the prize in exchange for Elise's loyalty and work as a spy until the war's end.

At the time, she'd been praying for a way to escape Roger and thought the Lord had made a way. For half her spy's pay, she and Prin received room and board. In exchange for his silence, Roger gleaned another quarter of her profits though he never let her forget he could make just as much or more by turning her over to the British if she refused to compensate him for his silence.

Up until the night of Hawk's death, she'd been convinced the Lord would see her through. That her success as a spy had been God's reward for serving a just cause. Now, racked by guilt for her part in a man's death, she wasn't so certain.

"Have you been in shipping long?" she asked in an effort to draw the conversation back to Drake.

"Twelve years, counting my stint in the Royal Navy."

"The navy?" Elise asked with interest.

"Aye, I left home at sixteen and went to sea. Over the next two years, I learned to love all things nautical and decided to make my fortune in shipping. When my father and older brother passed away unexpectedly, I took on the responsibilities of family matters, though I never forgot my own aspirations. I bought my first ship at twenty. Since then, I'm happy to say, I've steadily added to the line and hope to see its continued growth and prosperity."

"From the moment I saw you last evening, I knew you were a determined man."

He shrugged. "I suppose so. However, I must confess my determination is born from a fear of being idle. My family has farmed for years. Unfortunately, it bores me senseless."

"How coincidental. My father farmed near the western border of Virginia."

"Virginia? I've heard the land is rich and untamed, but that living there is nearly impossible with the savages roaming hither and yon."

"It can be," she acknowledged. "We did well enough in our dealings with the natives. My father made treaties with their leaders, and we respected one another. It was beautiful there. Untouched country with trees so high the mist settled in their branches and an abundance of game that would feed an army for a score of years."

"The place sounds like Eden." His expression turned thoughtful. "I was under the impression land grants were given by the king for service rendered. Did your father begin as a military man?"

She lowered her eyes. "No, I'm ashamed to say he didn't believe in the king's sovereignty."

His eyes darkened. "He spoke treason."

"Yes, but it doesn't matter now. He died two years ago."

"I apologize," he said and quickly changed the subject. "What did you like best about living in Virginia?"

"More than anything else, I enjoyed the solitude and freedom. A blessing I've had to relinquish since I came to live at Brixton Hall."

"Little wonder you named your horse as a reminder."

The ferry's bell rang and the craft lurched as it shifted course. Drake looked over his shoulder. "Obviously we're not to Charles Towne. Where are we?"

"We're docking at Riverwood Plantation. Its owner, Robert Gray, is a friend of the Sayers. Did you happen to make his acquaintance at the ball last night?"

"I don't believe so."

"He's a pleasant man. Last fall a storm struck and ruined many of the Grays' fields right before the harvest. Zechariah is exchanging rice for other supplies to aid him."

"Is Gray one of the rebels or is he Tory?"

Elise thought of the gunpowder and muskets being traded for rice. "I believe his politics match those of Zechariah. I don't usually pay attention to such things. Men are always preaching to us women that we shouldn't bother with politics. They say our minds are too simple and can't grasp the intricacies required to understand. They're probably right. I have enough trouble counting my cross stitch."

Elise almost choked on her words. She expected Amberly to agree with her in typical male fashion, but he surprised her.

"I don't believe it," he said. "I find that women, given the right encouragement, have no difficulty understanding any given subject. Some are even more clever than men, while the majority are more cunning."

The ferry jarred against the dock. Watching the deckhands rush to tie the mooring lines, Elise noted the cynicism in Drake's voice. She wondered what foolish woman had hurt him.

A loud crash drew Elise's attention to a crate being hauled aboard. She drew in a sharp breath. The box contained weapons and ammunition sorely needed by the patriots. French and American privateers smuggled the weapons as far as Riverwood. From there, she or Christian supervised their removal to Brixton Hall, then saw them farther upriver, and that much closer to the swamps that provided protection for the war-ravaged militia.

It was dangerous to transport munitions to Charles Towne, especially in broad daylight. Under normal circumstances she would have collected them under the cover of night. She didn't have that option today. At the ball last night, a loyal agent had warned Zechariah that the British had gotten wind of Riverwood's stash and planned to raid this afternoon. Now when the Brits arrived on Gray's doorstep, they'd find nothing stored but indigo and cotton, the very crops English merchants demanded of their Colonial brethren.

Seeing the box was safe, she released a sigh of relief, which quickly disappeared when she noticed Amberly's interest in the crate. Hoping to distract him, she entwined her arm with his and acted as though she might faint. "I declare the sun is blinding me. It's strong enough to set my skin afire."

"Would you care for a drink?" he said with concern.

"No, thank you. I just need to sit down." She hated to play the roll of insipid female, but she wanted him as far from the crate as possible. After all, he *was* English and subject to suspicion.

The ferry rocked again, announcing its departure from Riverwood. She heard the slap of water on the sides of the ferry and felt safe for the time being. The crate would be hidden away from notice. All would be well as long as they avoided the British patrolling the river.

They arrived in Charles Towne a short time later. The British-held city provided the main port for English supplies entering the Southern colonies. From the ferry's deck, Elise watched as ship after ship filled every available berth, their tall masts rising high like a forest of leafless, swaying trees. Seagulls squawked as they dipped and dived in the cloudless blue sky.

With no berth available, the ferry captain anchored in the harbor. He signaled a pair of skiffs to transport his passengers ashore. Grateful for the development, Elise viewed the situation as a blessing. With the ferry anchored away from shore, enemy soldiers would be less tempted to search the nondescript craft. Evidently the Lord had taken pity on her after all.

Elise stepped aboard the second of the smaller boats. Amberly followed and sat beside her on one of the rough-hewn benches that ran horizontally within the skiff. Seven other passengers joined them. The craft moved at speed once the oars were put to water.

The closer they came to the pier, the greater the odor.

The stink of rotting fish, unwashed bodies and overripe produce infested the wind. Elise removed a scented handkerchief from the satchel she held secure in her lap and covered her nose and mouth.

Drake leaned close. "As I said, Miss Cooper, women are often more clever than men. If not, I'd be the one with something to spare my nose from this stench."

Elise handed him the cloth, but he declined. "I'd think you'd be familiar with the putrid scents of a wharf, Mr. Amberly."

"Aye," he commented drily. "The same as a gravedigger grows used to decay."

The wharf teemed with life. British regulars lined the pier, their black knee-high boots gleaming as they paced in the sun. The racket of hollering sailors, hawking merchants and bustling pedestrians vied with the pummel of waves against the seawall.

Elise waited while a sailor tied the skiff. Drake jumped to the dock and helped her alight from the swaying craft. She moved aside and watched with admiration while he handed up the other women who'd accompanied them.

Finished with the task, he offered to carry her satchel but she refused. They walked along the pier, occasionally stepping over piles of refuse and other debris. Rough-looking sailors pushed and shoved through the crowd, their crude speech booming in her ear.

Drake slipped his arm around her shoulders, pulling her closer to his side as though to protect her from the ruffians. The action startled her. He had no way of knowing her duty to discover information for Zechariah had made her familiar with these harsh surroundings. Drake's care touched a deep chord of gratefulness within her. Other than Christian's brotherly concern, no man had ever shown her such consideration.

At the end of the pier, a congested street stretched before them. Drake asked her for the address she wished to visit, then approached a carriage for hire. He spoke to the driver for several moments before motioning for her to join him. She followed, and when he opened the door for her, stepped into the less-than-grand interior.

"Shall I put your satchel topside?" Drake asked.

"No." She sounded sterner than she meant to, but she had the letters to protect. "No, thank you. Seems everyone is in need of something these days. Luggage has a tendency to walk off on its own."

Drake finished with the driver and removed his tricorn before climbing into the coach. "'Tis the same in London. Thieves delight in robbing a body blind."

Elise tucked the satchel under the seat behind her feet. She swept back the folds of her skirt, making room for him on the worn cowhide seat across from her. The space was so small Drake's head brushed the roof. The ill-sprung hack bounced into motion, eliciting a grunt from him when he bumped his head.

She sat forward in concern. "Are you all right?"

Drake rubbed the abused spot. "Quite so, but I believe I'll be ordering a new coach built before the day is out."

Within a few blocks, the coach rolled to a stop in front of a two-story brick dwelling with a painted black door and shutters. In the side yard, a clothesline hung between Tabby's house and the one next door. A bright green dress and half a dozen white petticoats flapped in the breeze.

"It seems we're already here." He sounded disappointed. "I hope you won't miss me too much while I'm gone."

She would, for he was stimulating company. "Don't be silly, Mr. Amberly. I shall forget you the moment I leave this coach."

Hand to his heart, he said, "You wound me sorely."

She rolled her eyes, trying not to laugh. "Just don't bleed on the cushions. The driver will charge you an even greater fare, and you've already been swindled."

"How so?"

"I heard the outrageous price you settled on when we left the wharf."

"I hired the driver for the whole day."

"But you're paying him for a week."

He shrugged. "I'll not worry about the price and consider it charity. The poor man has twenty-two children and six grandchildren to feed."

"Impossible. He can't be a day over twenty."

"Chasing his grandchildren keeps him young. He turned five and seventy just last week."

Elise shook her head as she recalled the driver's boyish face. Chuckling, "You're mad, Drake Amberly."

"Aha! You called me by my name. Since you've relented, I'll expect you to use it all the more."

The driver thumped on the roof. Elise glanced up. "I believe he thinks we're too obtuse to notice we've stopped. It's no wonder considering how easily he took you for a fortune."

"A pittance, merely."

"If you're not concerned about your funds, I'm certainly not. It's my reputation I'm worried about."

He chuckled. "I should have known."

"I don't want him thinking I'm a simpleton just because of the company I keep."

He picked up her hand and kissed her knuckles. With a wink, he added, "Finally, Miss Cooper, a kind word from your sweet lips. I shall carry it with me all day." He opened the coach door and leapt out. Offering his hand, he helped her down. "I understand the ferry leaves at half past three. I'll send the driver to meet you here an hour prior."

"I can make my own way."

He waved away her protest. "I've no doubt, but why when I've already hired the coach?"

"What about you? How will you return to the wharf?"

"I have business near the waterfront. I'll walk. If you should need me, I'm meeting an associate at a tavern called The Rolling Tide."

Elise glanced away. The shock of his announcement twisted her stomach. How was it possible Amberly chose the very tavern where Hawk had died?

"The Rolling Tide, you say? May I ask what possessed you to choose that despicable place? I hear the food they prepare is nothing short of hog slop."

Thick lashes screened his golden eyes, but the black door of the house flung wide before he could answer.

"Elise, you're here! I was beginning to think you would never arrive." Tabby Smith picked her way down the house's three front steps. With a bright smile on her face and a bloom in her cheeks, she made the picture of contentment. Heavily pregnant, she looked due to give birth any minute.

"Tabby, it's so *good* to see you." The two women

embraced, and Elise turned and introduced her friend to Drake.

"It's a pleasure to meet you, Mr. Amberly." Tabby gave him a considering look. "Have we met before?"

Drake bowed respectfully and kissed the back of Tabby's hand. "I don't believe so, Mrs. Smith. I've no doubt I would remember your lovely face."

"I can see you're a charmer, sir." She winked at Elise. "You'd best watch this one or you'll be married before the summer is out."

"Tabby, please!" Elise felt her cheeks heat. She faced Drake, who didn't bother to disguise his mirth. "Don't you have business down by the wharf, Mr. Amberly?"

"The wharf?" Tabby asked with interest. "If you find yourself hungry, visit a tavern called The Rolling Tide. I hear the food there is delicious."

To his credit, Drake didn't contradict her friend. "I've heard mixed reviews, but since you recommend it, I'll partake of lunch there." To Elise, "You're quite correct, Miss Cooper. I must be on my way." He propped his elbow on the door's inset window. "I hope to meet you again, Mrs. Smith. I shall see you at the ferry, Miss Cooper. Good day to you both."

Elise waved, bereft to see him go. "Good day, Mr. Amberly."

She watched the carriage ramble down the road until it turned out of sight. A wistful sigh broke from her lips as Tabby placed her arm around her shoulders and walked her to the house. "You have the look of a woman falling in love, my friend."

Elise lifted her chin. "Ridiculous. I only met the man

last night. Besides, he's English. Other than spying on them, I have no interest in the enemy."

"Prudent, but the heart doesn't always follow the will of the mind. I was engaged to a wealthy planter when I met and eloped with Josiah. Now look at me."

Elise patted her friend's huge belly. "Yes, you're what…thirteen months pregnant?"

Tabby giggled, "Feels like twenty. What do you think your Mr. Amberly meant when he said he'd heard mixed reviews for the Tide?"

"Oh, Tabby, that's my fault." Tabby and Josiah owned The Rolling Tide. The inn had been the favored spot for her and Hawk to meet because Josiah provided a lookout and did anything else he could to help her. He'd been the one to prop the ladder by the window the night Hawk planned to turn her in. Her face scrunched with guilt. "I told him the food was terrible."

Tabby stopped in her tracks and slowly turned her head in disbelief. "You did what? How could you? I prepared the roast leg of lamb myself this very morn. My dumplings are the talk of Charles Towne."

"I know, but it startled me to learn he had business there."

Tabby patted her shoulder in commiseration. "Now I understand. But once he tries my greens and ham, he'll think you have no taste at all. Did you bring the letters?"

Elise nodded. "They're in my satchel. I wrapped them in the blankets I knitted.…"

She spun in the middle of the walk and ran to the dirt road, looking in the direction Drake had traveled. "Of all the witless… How could I have been so careless, Tabby? I've forgotten my satchel in Amberly's coach!"

Without any comment, her friend waddled up the steps as fast as her rounded body would take her. Elise ran past just in time to pull the door open wide.

"Henry!" Tabby called her servant. "Fetch the wagon. We have an Englishman and my blankets to catch."

Chapter Six

Drake jumped down from the coach. Disgust raged through him as his gaze swept over the vine-covered windows and red front door of The Rolling Tide. He'd visited the tavern once before, upon his arrival in Charles Towne. Captain Beaufort, his distant cousin and Lieutenant Kirby's superior officer, had brought him here to see the room where Anthony had breathed his last.

The thought stoked his anger until a red haze filled his vision. Perhaps he should have arranged to meet Beaufort elsewhere and saved himself from more bad temper, but in a strange way the place helped him feel closer to Anthony. Somehow it was less painful to cling to his fury than to think of his brother as gone forever.

Except for the short time Elise distracted him, he'd refused to quit his hunt for the Fox. Perhaps the girl's ability to soothe his hatred, if only for a little while, was another reason she appealed to him so much.

The carriage driver, one of Beaufort's spies, jumped down beside him.

"Your name is Goss, correct?" Drake asked.

The driver chewed the twig he'd been using to pick his buckteeth. "Aye, Your Grace, Robin Goss."

Hearing the rube use his title, Drake arched a brow in annoyance. "Captain Beaufort must have informed you of my station. However, kindly remember not to bandy that information about. For the time being I'm simply Mr. Amberly. You may address me as such, or a simple 'sir' will do. Now, I understand I'm paying you a week's wage to await me today."

A cocky grin split the driver's face and his calculating eyes lit with amusement.

Irritated by the man's shifty demeanor, Drake wondered if Goss was as trustworthy as Beaufort believed. "I have instructions for you. At half past two, you're to go to the house we departed on Church Street. Wait for the young woman I accompanied there and return her to the wharf before half past three. Wait with her until I find you. Do you understand?"

"Yup, sir, I understand. I'll follow your instructions to the letter."

Drake bristled at Goss's thinly veiled sarcasm. "You do have a watch?"

"Nope, do I look like I'm made of money?" The clodhopper jabbed the air over his shoulder with his thumb. "I'll listen for the church bells."

"Don't be late."

"Never am." The driver climbed up to his seat and positioned his foot on the brake.

Drake glanced into the coach one last time. The corner of Elise's satchel peeked out from under the bench.

He opened the door, intending to collect it, then reconsidered.

"I have a change of plans for you, Mr. Goss." With an easy shove, Drake closed the coach's door. "Miss Cooper has forgotten her satchel. Rather than await me here, return to the house on Church Street and deliver her belongings."

"Do I come back here once I'm done, or do I wait for her there?"

"Leave yourself available for her. Perhaps she and her friend will have need of you this afternoon."

The driver took up the reins. The church bells announced the noon hour. A steady flow of coaches and wagons clattered past, kicking up the thin layer of dust that covered the street's worn bricks. Robin glanced back over his shoulder. "If she don't choose to make use of my carriage, just deliver her to the wharf like you wanted?"

"Yes," Drake said. "And should you do as I've instructed without fault, I'll double your wage once you return Miss Cooper to me safely."

The spy's eyes bugged in his head. "Real pounds, none of them worthless Continentals?"

Drake took a coin from his pocket and tossed it to the driver. "Genuine sterling."

Robin chucked his twig into the street and a grin spread from one large ear to the other. "You'll have no reason for complaint. I swear it on my mother's grave."

"Brilliant." Drake watched with satisfaction as the coach leapt forward into traffic.

Turning back to the hated tavern, he gritted his teeth. A pair of drunken redcoats threw open the heavy door and stumbled out, laughing boisterously as they passed. Drake shook his head in disgust as he watched them weave their way down the boardwalk. Foxed before noon. With gadabouts like those soldiers, it was little wonder the war had yet to be won.

He caught the door before it closed and entered The Rolling Tide. The heavy portal banged closed behind him, casting the cavernous room into near darkness. He paused a moment for his eyes to adjust. A thin cloud of smoke and the aroma of roasted lamb met him before anything else.

To his right, a fire glowed in the wide, blackened hearth where a leg of lamb turned slowly on a spit. In a far corner, a man reclined with his feet atop a table, his chin to his chest as he snored into his mug. The other patrons, mostly soldiers, raised their cups for refills as two tavern wenches flitted about with pitchers of ale.

His heart ached. Anthony had bled to death in this Spartan place. Helpless fury reared its ugly head like a dragon inside him needing to release fire. The place should be razed to the ground, its every stone smashed into dust.

Forcing himself forward, he took the steps to the second floor two at a time and knocked on the door marked with a number 3, the very room where his brother died. He'd been there before, knew the coffin of a space was hardly bigger than a closet at Hawk Haven. Loosening his collar, he longed to leave, yet his duty to Anthony nailed his boots to the floorboards.

Captain Beaufort, a tall, rigid-backed military man with sandy brown hair and deep-set dark eyes, opened the door. The captain bowed low the moment the door closed. "Good day, Your Grace. It's an honor to serve you once more, cousin."

"Enough with my title, Charles. I thought you under-stood my request for secrecy. Imagine my surprise when even your spy addressed me as 'Your Grace.'"

"I do apologize, Your…sir. It won't happen again. It's just such an honor…"

Drake scanned the shabby room with its meager furni-ture and barren walls. Despite his show of deference, his cousin was the same dandy he'd always been. His unde-served air of self-importance grated on Drake's nerves. He pulled out a chair, took a seat and motioned for the captain to do likewise. "I trust you have pertinent news for me this morn?"

Beaufort puffed out his chest, obviously delighted with himself. "I believe so, Your Grace. One of my spies, a frequent contact of your brother's, met with me last night. As you know, I only suspected the Fox had connections to Brixton Hall. He confirmed the brigand frequents the plantation and may even have been at the party last evening."

"We're finally making progress." Drake began an im-mediate mental inventory of the faces he'd seen at Brixton Hall. "It's doubtful the Fox is Zechariah—"

"Indeed not," Beaufort scoffed. "He's staunchly loyal to His Majesty. Zechariah left his position in the colony's legislature rather than cast his vote for war against the Crown. He sells his crops to British troops instead of feeding the rebels and he allows his townhouse here in Charles Towne to be used as barracks for many of my officers."

Deep in thought, Drake rejected several other candi-dates. All of them were older, keen of mind but soft around the middle, hardly fit to traipse about the city in disguise. He considered the free servants, deciding on a few to watch, but rejected the slaves as prospects, since he doubted the Africans would have the necessary freedom to roam the countryside without Sayer's knowledge.

Elise came to mind, not because she might be the Fox, but because his thoughts seemed to wander in her direction with a will of their own. He savored her image, then frowned when he remembered Christian. "Perhaps it's the son."

"Again, most doubtful," said Beaufort. "Christian Sayer has a sterling reputation. He served in the Tory brigade before he fell from a horse and injured his leg last summer. I'd stake my life on the whole family's loyalty. There must be someone else. One of the freeman on the estate, a frequent visitor or another relative we haven't yet met."

"Perhaps you're right," Drake agreed, still suspicious of Christian. The puppy had looked hale and hearty to him the previous night. "Zechariah invited me to stay a fortnight. I may have to prevail upon him for the whole of it."

"Perhaps we should be honest with the Sayers," Beaufort suggested. "Tell them what we suspect and glean from them what we can."

"No." Drake moved to the window. "Before going to Zechariah, I think it best to watch Christian for a time. You may trust him, but I do not. There's something about him that seems peculiar. He displays an open personality, but there's a dark quality beneath his sunny facade."

Drake looked out over the busy street and the pair of frayed horses tethered in front of the tavern. "We'll leave this matter between the two of us for the time being."

"But sir…"

Beaufort's argument droned on, but Drake heard no more once he saw Elise and Tabby Smith arrive in a mule-drawn wagon.

Elise handed the reins to Tabby while her friend set the brake. Drake admired Elise's graceful movements as she climbed down from the wagon. Her glorious dark hair hung in a thick rope to below her trim waist and glowed in the bright daylight. He was certain she grew lovelier each time he saw her.

She seemed to be in a hurry, agitated. He didn't see her satchel and he suspected she and Goss had passed each other on the road. She started round the front of the building, as though she meant to go to the side alley, then stopped, retraced her steps, and helped her pregnant friend down from the wagon.

Drake undid the latch and pressed opened the lead glass window. "Miss Cooper," he called, just loud enough to be heard over the clatter of traffic.

Elise froze as though his voice were a gunshot. Her gaze flew to the upper story of the tavern. "Drake!"

She raised her hand to block the sun from her eyes. It surprised her to realize how much happiness lurked beneath the initial alarm of Drake catching her there. Was it possible to actually miss someone she'd seen such a short time ago? "Did you happen upon my satchel, Mr. Amberly? I believe I left it in the coach."

He raised his hand to his ear as though he hadn't been able to hear her, but she was sure she'd spoken loud enough. "One moment, I'll meet you below downstairs."

"There's no need," she assured him, but he'd already gone.

In front of the tavern, Elise balked at the door. She'd hoped to find the coach waiting outside, enabling her to retrieve her belongings and leave without Amberly ever being the wiser. She should have known better; her luck of late had been spotty at best. "You know I vowed I'd never step foot in The Tide again, Tabby. Just being here is a nightmare."

Tabby took her elbow and dragged Elise a few steps forward. "I know this is difficult for you, but you have to—"

"Do what I must. Yes, I know Tabby, but…" Her stomach rolled in rebellion. "But, I don't think I can."

"Of course you can." Tabby reached for the door's large brass knob. "How will you explain to your Englishman if you run off like a ninny?"

Tabby pulled the door halfway open. Hearty conversation spilled from inside. Elise stepped back, skittish as a calf on market day. "First of all, he's not *my* Englishman. Second, he believes I'm a proper young lady. I…I'll tell him I have Puritan beliefs. That I'd be ashamed to step foot in a tavern."

Tabby bit back a giggle. "A good Christian girl you may be, but a Puritan? He'll not believe it."

Without further ado, Tabby yanked the door open wide and, with a push, sent Elise reeling into the tavern's main room. "See? You're in."

Elise straightened. Her eyes narrowed on Tabby. "You're an evil woman, Tabby Smith. To think I thought you were my friend."

Tabby laughed. "Discounting Prin and Christian, you know I'm the best friend you've got."

Disgruntled, Elise said nothing, since Tabby spoke the truth.

A bright smile lit her friend's face. "There's my sweet husband."

Elise turned to see Josiah Smith approaching them. "Goodness, Tabby, what shall I say if Amberly realizes you're Josiah's wife? I told him the place was terrible and you claimed no knowledge of it beyond the food. Surely, he'll question our silence."

Tabby patted her arm. "I'll say nothing and I'll warn Josiah. He won't give away the game."

"There's my beautiful girl," Josiah said as he ambled forward, his leather apron stretched across his belly. After a quick greeting to Elise, he gave his wife a hearty embrace and led her toward the kitchen.

Elise envied their close bond, and wished a similar one for herself, but felt sadly convinced she'd never find that kind of love and mutual admiration.

Her heart leapt with excitement when she saw Drake at the base of the stairs. Her gaze traveled leisurely over his face, admiring his straight nose, the rakish scar along his jaw, the darkness of his sun-drenched skin.

His mouth turned in the cool half smile she'd begun to find endearing. Their eyes met and locked. Seeing the laughter in his eyes, she realized she'd been staring like a goose and he'd caught her at it. There was nothing else for her to do but hope he wouldn't mention it.

Ha! He'll probably crow all day long.

Elise tore her gaze away and brushed her damp palms in a smoothing motion down the front of her skirt. The man was driving her mad. Despite her best efforts to cover the fact, he seemed to understand how much she favored him. Against her will, her eyes slid back to his face.

As he crossed the room, she admired his inborn confidence. His piercing gaze held her as if he owned her. She felt caught but lacked the will to escape. Begrudgingly, her admiration for him grew.

Tabby returned to her. "Wake up. Do you want your Englishman to think your body has mutinied against your brain?"

"Don't be addled." Elise dug her fingernails into her palm to regain her composure. She noticed Josiah had stayed in the kitchen.

Drake reached her and enveloped her hands in his. "What a pleasant surprise. I thought I'd be deprived of your company for most of the day."

The warmth in his eyes made her feel more light-hearted than she had in years, an odd sensation to be sure, given the severity of her circumstances. "I left my belongings in the coach. I wished to fetch them back."

He reached out as though he couldn't contain the action, and brushed a lock of hair from her brow. "I assumed you would need the contents and returned the carriage to Mrs. Smith's. You must have passed it on the road."

She glanced at her friend. "I didn't see it on our way here, did you?"

"I doubt I'd have recognized it if I had," her friend admitted. "To me, one hired carriage looks the same as all the others."

"When did you send it?" Elise asked Drake.

"The church bells rang twelve just as he left."

"Was the driver to return here?"

"No, I told him to wait for you in case you needed him this afternoon. I also instructed him to deliver you to the dock in time for the ferry."

Elise felt herself soften toward him. "That was very thoughtful of you, Mr. Am—"

"Drake," he insisted.

She gave in against her better judgment. "Drake. I appreciate your kindness."

Tabby cleared her throat. "I hate to interrupt the two of you when you're so intent on one another, but we're drawing strange looks standing here in the center of the room."

At that bold reminder, Elise pulled away until Drake had to release her hand. "Then perhaps we should leave. We need to find the coach."

"That won't do," Drake protested. "I'm certain the driver will return here once he realizes you're no longer in residence. If you leave now, it's more than likely you'll miss him again."

"If he doesn't run off with the satchel instead," Tabby said as Drake pulled out a chair and shuffled Elise into it.

"Miss Cooper assures me I'm paying him well to await me today." He rounded the table and helped Tabby settle before taking a seat for himself. "I've paid him half of what we agreed. I have no doubt he'll return for the balance. It's only a matter of time before he revisits with your things."

Josiah hovered a foot away. "You there," Tabby spoke up, drawing her husband's attention. "What are you serving today? I've always found the fare you serve pleasant enough, but my good companions here have heard mixed reviews." She grinned at Elise. "However, good food or not, I'm eating for two and I suppose I'll have to take my chances."

Josiah looked affronted but played along. Obviously Tabby had taken the chance to warn him. "A pox on the liar that slandered my tavern, ma'am. It just so happens you're in the finest eating establishment in all Charles Towne. Let me fetch Louise. She'll serve you some dumplings while I prepare a platter of lamb."

Tabby shooed him away with the wave of her hand. "Be quick about it then. I'd hate to have this babe before I get to eat, no matter how bad the food may prove to be."

Elise ducked her head and covered her laughter by coughing into her hand. Josiah headed in the direction of the kitchen, muttering under his breath about the unfortunate man who'd married such a harpy.

"Well," Tabby huffed. "The service leaves much to be desired. I hope I *was* misled about the food or this place will have nothing to recommend it."

Louise, a buxom blonde, approached the table from the direction of the kitchen. She balanced the heavy tray she carried on the edge of the table and plunked a pewter mug in front of each of them.

"I'll have water to drink," Tabby said when Louise poured cider for Drake.

"Aye, mum," Louise replied, her cockney accent as thick as a loaf of bread. Elise knew the woman had arrived fresh from London less than six months earlier. Josiah must have warned Louise not to acknowledge Tabby as anyone but a common customer and not his wife. The woman ignored Elise and Tabby completely but favored Drake with a sultry promise in her wide blue eyes. She made a show of bending close so that her billowy blouse gapped open just so.

Elise narrowed her eyes and nearly gave in to the urge to pinch the flirt. To Drake's credit, she noted he did his best to ignore the eye-popping display. His restraint impressed her and her respect for him raised another notch.

"I believe I have enough," he said drily, reaching up to tip the pitcher away before his mug overflowed. "Any more and the table will enjoy quite a dousing."

"Oi!" the blonde exclaimed. "Ye're jus so 'andsome I lost ev'ry thought in me poor little 'ead."

The barmaid sloshed cider into Tabby's mug, but nearly missed Elise's altogether. "Wait right 'ere. I be bringing yer dumplin's sooner an ye can blink."

The blonde backed away from the table and rushed in the direction of the kitchen, looking over her shoulder at Drake until she ploughed into a redcoat and got a hearty shove for her trouble.

"Serves her right," Tabby muttered. "She gave me cider when I asked for water. That girl needs a good comeuppance."

Josiah returned with the platter of roasted lamb. Fresh herbs adorned the top and added to the mouthwatering aroma. "Where are your dumplings? I sent Louise to fetch them. She should have brought them out by now."

"She got…distracted," Elise answered. "I fear we'd best hurry and feed my friend. We've waited so long she's going to faint from starvation."

Josiah's eyes filled with concern as he focused on his wife. Elise felt guilty for teasing him. "Are you truly ill, missus? If so, I'll—"

"I'm fine," Tabby assured him. "Just hungry."

He nodded. "My wife is expecting and she complains of the same without ceasing. She used to be such a tiny little thing. Now she rivals my horse in size and my arms have ceased to fit around her."

Elise stifled another giggle. Tabby's look promised retribution.

"I'll go help Louise with the rest of your meal," Josiah said. "I promise I'll hurry."

"Don't forget the greens," Tabby called after him. She settled back in her chair once he waved that he'd heard her over the rumble of the other patrons. "So, Mr. Amberly, what brings you to this part of the Colonies? Are you an adventure seeker out to make a name for yourself in the war?"

Drake set down his mug. He smiled politely, but his eyes were inscrutable. "I'm here on business, Mrs. Smith. I wish to reestablish shipping contracts now that Charles Towne is free of the rebels' hold."

"Really?" Tabby replied wide-eyed. "I understood the rebels are everywhere." She leaned forward and lowered her voice. "Why, I'm as loyal as can be, but I admit I've got a soft spot in my heart for the Fox."

Elise's stomach twisted sickly.

Drake leaned forward, his interest palpable. "What do you know of him, Mrs. Smith? I've heard he's a cheeky fellow. Some inept farmer who survives on luck alone."

Elise took exception to that. "No doubt you heard such from the redcoats who've failed to catch him."

"No doubt," he said. "Do you know otherwise?"

"Goodness, no. Why would I know anything about the man?"

Tabby giggled. "Elise know anything about the Fox? How very funny."

Louise delivered a large steaming pot of dumplings and a smaller one of greens topped with ham. "There you be, sir. I 'ope it's to yer liking."

"I'm sure it will be," Elise cut in deliberately. She gave the girl a hard, meaningful look and pointed across the room. "I believe the soldiers at yonder table need their mugs refilled."

The girl pouted as she left. Elise picked up her spoon to sample Tabby's light, fluffy specialty when Josiah lumbered over to the edge of the table. He motioned toward the door, where a man stood in the shadows. "There's a hired man waiting by the door. Says he knows you, miss. Claims he has some of your belongings."

"My satchel!" Elise jumped up, causing her chair to grate on the wood floor. "I'll be right back." She shot across the room, anxious to lay hold on the important letters.

She recognized the hack driver once she got close enough to see his face. The man's buckteeth flashed into prominence as he shifted the leather case, angling it behind his back. She held out her hand. "Thank you for returning my things."

He retreated a step. "I'm thinking I deserve more than your thanks, Miss."

Her brow furrowed in confusion. "Really? How so? What is it you think you deserve?"

His suggestive glance made her skin crawl. Annoyed, she bit back a scathing retort and held out her hand. "I suggest, sir, that you keep your mind out of the gutter and give me my satchel…unless you'd rather I call my friend."

The yokel peered over her shoulder. She was certain he could see Amberly's formidable presence. The driver's leer faded into sour resignation. "I'm thinking I deserve a reward."

"How so?" Elise inquired. "You're being paid to wait the day. By rights I should be able to leave my belongings in the coach if I like."

"Your friend seemed to think this here satchel was important to you."

"Of course it's important," she snapped. "For interest's sake, how much reward do you require?"

The driver studied the tips of his fingers. His eyes narrowed to sly slits. "A hundred pounds."

She gasped. "Are you crazed?"

"Crazed? Nah. I'm thinking it's a fair sum considering how much I could get for your letters if I took 'em to the Redcoats."

Her heart picked up speed. "What on earth do you mean?"

"Just that I can read between the lines, so to speak."

"Then you must be a soothsayer, for there's nothing between the lines but parchment."

The man regained some of his boldness. "Aye, unless there's a flame nearby."

Anxiety cut through her. This shifty, obnoxious hack driver had somehow discovered the letters' invisible ink. "I don't know what you're talking about."

He shook his head, his upper lip twisted in a sneer. "Don't make the mistake of thinking I'm a lackwit just because I'm hired help. Seems we're both more than we appear. Why don't we step outside?"

"I can't." Elise sent a covert glance toward Drake, who studied them with keen regard. Tabby chatted cheerfully in an unsuccessful ploy to sway his interest from her and the driver. "My companions will question why I've gone."

The driver tugged on his earlobe and scowled. "I'm thinking I'll keep this here satchel till you can lay hold of the funds. You can tell your fancy gent I'm holding it for safe keeping."

"That won't do."

Drake stood and started toward them. Her nerves jangled in alarm. If he interrupted, would the driver call on the redcoats in the tavern and give her away? "Take the satchel to the back alley. I'll meet you there as soon as I'm able."

"You're not going to try anything smart, are you? If you do, I'll take it up with the Brits."

"I'll not try anything smart," she assured him. "I just want my case and *all* its contents. Now go!"

With a sharp nod, he left, causing her to squint when he opened the door and a bright ray of light stabbed the darker interior.

Elise headed back to her companions, dodging various patrons as they stood abruptly from their seats. Drake waited for her a few feet from their table, his expression lined with concern.

Once she reached him, Drake pulled out her chair. She remained standing, offering a shrug when Tabby sent her a glance rife with questions. "I'm sorry, but I must excuse myself for a few moments more."

Drake reached for her hand. A surge of warmth shot up her arm and traveled straight to her heart. She held her breath as his dark eyes searched her face.

"Is all well with you?" he asked quietly. His thumb brushed her knuckles in a soothing manner. "I notice you have yet to retrieve your satchel."

"Every…everything's fine. I—"

"I believe," said Tabby, pointing toward the back of the tavern, "the privies are that way. You'll have to leave by the front door since the only other passage to the back is through the kitchen."

Elise sighed with relief, grateful for Tabby's quick thinking, even if her suggestion was a trifle embarrassing. She excused herself without further comment, and wove her way back through the maze of chairs, tables and customers to the front door.

Stepping into the heat and sunshine, she exchanged the raucous laughter inside for the noise of passing wagons and carriages. The wind caught her hair as she hurried around the corner into the side alley. She wrinkled her nose at the rancid smell. Ants covered rotting food and a picked-over ham bone while rats scurried away, abandoning their decayed feasts of fruit when she stepped too near.

Rounding the back of the tavern, she remembered the large group of redcoats waiting for her the night of Hawk's death. Bile rose in her throat.

A few feet ahead, her newest adversary leaned against the brick wall, one leg bent at the knee while he chewed his thumbnail. He noticed her arrival and straightened, his insolent sneer firmly in place.

Elise stopped just out of his reach. "I've only now excused myself from my friends. I need a few moments more to collect the sum you've demanded."

He picked at his large front teeth while he mulled things over. "You happen to be in luck. I've got just a few more minutes to spare. You best hurry though, else I'll start thinking you're playing me for a fool."

"I assure you I'm not. I'll return shortly."

Without waiting for his reply, she rushed through the tavern's back door. Bright light shone through the open windows, but even the breeze couldn't dispel the room's odor of stale ale and wood smoke. Pewter dishes and a cast iron skillet sat staked on a rough-hewn table near a large bucket of soapy water. Nearby a straw broom leaned against the wall, a small hill of crumbs and dust beside it.

The other serving girl, Alice, hoisted a large platter filled with steaming bowls of dumplings to her shoulder. "Miss Cooper? What are you doing back here in the kitchen? I thought I saw you with Mrs. Smith in the tavern room."

"You did, Alice. Tell me, where is Josiah? I need to speak with him. It's urgent."

The other girl returned her tray to the counter. "I'll get him for you. Be back in a rush."

Elise watched her go, willing her to hurry. She ran to the window, her nerves carrying her there to see if the hack driver still waited.

Josiah burst through the door several moments later. "What is it, Elise? Alice says you're mighty distressed."

"We must keep our voices low," she said, accepting his outstretched hands. "I fear I'm in one of the most prickly spots I've ever tripped into."

"Tell me," he whispered. "You know I'll do everything I can to help."

She quickly related the details of the situation. "Now the weasel is demanding one hundred pounds for my letters, or he'll seek out the authorities."

Josiah looked thunderous. "The dirty scoundrel! A hundred pounds is a fortune, Elise. The Tide is prosperous to be sure, but I don't have a sum like that just lying about. If I had it, you know I'd give it to you without a qualm, but I haven't."

She chewed on her lower lip and noticed the agony in his expression. She hated drawing him into her problems at all. "Don't trouble yourself, Josiah, truly. I have no doubts you'd help me if you could."

Josiah's face lit up in sudden realization. "Perhaps I *can* help."

"How?"

"I'll have Matthew and John fetch your belongings for you."

She shook her head. "They're liable to kill him. I know he's a thief and a scoundrel, but…"

"Such an outcome would solve your problems."

She frowned, remembering Hawk. "No, I want no more blood on my hands."

"You'll have no blood at all if he goes to the Brits. Corpses don't need it."

"Josiah, please stop. I must figure a way out of this pickle with no one dying in the process."

He crossed his arms, rubbing his chin as he thought through a plan. "Does this driver know your name or anything concerning you except your appearance?"

"I don't believe so," she replied. "Even the letters bear a false signature."

"Good," he said, nodding his satisfaction. "John and Matthew will collect him—"

"But—"

He held up his hand, halting her argument. "Let me finish. I'll have the two of them collect the scum. He'll be hurt no more than a good thump on the head. We'll keep him in a warehouse near the wharf until we know you're safe. Even if he goes to the Brits once we release him, he'll have no evidence. The letters will be gone. With the lads dragging him off, he won't be able to point a finger to any involvement here. He doesn't know your name. Without conclusive proof, he has nothing."

The back door swung open. Elise jerked in surprise. Her nemesis popped his head inside. "There you are. I thought I'd have to hunt you down."

She faced him, hoping she blocked his view of Josiah. The fewer people he could identify as helping her, the better. "As you can see, I'm here. I need a few minutes more."

He stretched his neck, trying to see who stood behind her. "You've had all the time I'm willing to give you."

"You can't be serious," she argued. "You're demanding a fortune. Do you believe I carry that sum on my person? I have to be given some time."

The driver's mouth tightened into a straight line, but the tips of his buckteeth overlapped his bottom lip, giving him the appearance of a rodent. "I'll give you until the church bells sound two, but not a moment longer." As he turned to leave, his eyes assaulted her with lecherous intent. "If you don't have it by then, we'll discuss what else you've got to buy my silence. Either way, I'll be waiting in my carriage."

"Just one more question," Elise said, squelching the desire to spit in his face. He glanced at her from over his bony shoulder. "How did you learn to read between the lines?"

"That's my secret."

"Very well, but why did you suspect me and my letters?" She wanted to shake the information out of him.

"I didn't suspect you. Who would, you being such a pretty wench and all? I was looking for coin when I found them in those knitted blankets. You don't need to know any more 'an that."

He left, whistling a merry tune. Once he'd gone, Josiah growled, "I'll send the lads to meet him. The ferret'll never know what hit him."

Elise waited as long as she dared before leaving the kitchen. She offered a prayer Drake wouldn't question why she'd been gone so long. She hurried along the back of the tavern, slipping once on a mildew-covered rock. When she arrived at the front door, she inhaled a deep breath and steadied her nerves. Brushing her moist palms down the front of her skirt, she combed her fingers through her hair and adopted a serene air.

Inside the tavern, a group of men played darts. As she neared the table, she saw Louise hovering behind Drake, pitcher in hand to refill his cup if he took even the smallest sip. He seemed unaware of the blonde's attentions as he spoke with Tabby.

He smiled when he saw her, a flash of white teeth that lit up his lean face. Elise brightened in return, surprised by the sense of safety he provided.

He stood when she drew near, his conversation forgotten.

"I feared Mrs. Smith and I might need to form a search party."

She forced a giggle as she took her seat, trying and failing to hide behind her usual mask of frivolity. "Oh, I'm sorry to be gone so long, but I met up with an acquaintance and we had much to discuss." At least that wasn't a lie.

Tabby tsked her disapproval. "A sillier girl I've yet to meet. Didn't you think it rude to abandon one group of friends for another?"

"I didn't abandon you," Elise protested, thankful for Tabby's attempt to divert Drake from asking deeper questions. "What would you have me do, ignore my friend?"

"You did well enough ignoring us."

Elise smiled sweetly. "Tabby, please do remind me to push you off a pier some day."

"Ladies, 'tis a pity to see the likes of such good friends quarreling. Mrs. Smith, surely we waited no longer than a quarter of an hour. Who among us hasn't been waylaid from time to time by an inopportune acquaintance?"

Elise made a face at her friend. "Yes, who among us hasn't?"

Tabby snorted. "I should have known you'd come to her aid, Mr. Amberly. If you're anything like other men, you've already been overpowered by her charms."

"Tabby!" Elise reddened with mortification. "Please, do be quiet. Mr. Amberly's no more enamored of me than I am with him."

Tabby grinned at Drake. "I wouldn't take a wager on that, my friend."

"Nor would I," Drake said, his deep voice as stimulating as a caress. His dark eyes bored into hers and for a moment Elise sat transfixed. "But if you'd like to lose your coin, my girl, I'm game."

Tabby's laughter broke the spell. "You'd best close your mouth, Elise. Hanging open as it is, you'll draw in flies."

Elise snapped her mouth shut, her face as hot as fire. "Are the two of you quite tired of poking fun at me? Is this some sort of punishment for my taking too long at the privy?"

Tabby giggled harder, her pregnant belly shaking with mirth. Elise sighed and handed her friend a napkin. "Do stop, Tabby. It wasn't that funny."

Her friend dabbed at her eyes. "I'm so sorry. It's just… Elise…your face." She fell into another fit of laughter. "Goodness, now I'm the one who has to visit the privy."

Elise helped Tabby lever herself out of the chair in spite of her teasing. When her friend was out of earshot, Elise's gaze slunk back to Drake. "I'm sorry about that. My friend has an odd sense of humor."

He eased her hand into his larger one. "I'm sorry if you were embarrassed, but your friend is right. I'm captivated by you."

Speech deserted her. His sincerity rang true and yet her instincts assured her Drake Amberly wasn't a man given to shallow feelings or light declarations. Never in her life had she wanted to believe a man so much.

Yet she couldn't afford romantic attachments. No matter how fascinating she found him, she would have to deny the attraction. She'd learned that those she loved became pawns in Zechariah's game to bend her to his will. She removed her hand from his grasp, regretting the loss that same instant. A cheer from the soldiers playing darts erupted behind her. Drake leaned back in his chair. The tip of his finger circled the edge of his mug as he watched her from under lush downcast lashes. "I see I've spoken too soon, but I'm not a man easily dissuaded once I find something I want."

The faint sound of church bells jolted her with a reminder of her satchel. "What time is it?"

Drake extracted his watch from the pocket of his waistcoat. "Two o'clock."

She scanned the smoky tavern. Josiah was nowhere to be seen. The bell tolled a second time. Her agitation increased. Her hands balled into fists in her lap. Where was he? Had Matthew and John failed to retrieve her belongings…or was the driver on his way to the Brits with the evidence that could hang her?

Chapter Seven

"Then what happened?" Prin gasped.

Elise glanced into the mirror where she sat in front of her dressing table. Never had she felt so much relief in retiring to her bedchamber, the cloak of night putting an end to her horrid day.

In the candlelight, her sister's reflection looked back at her, beautiful dark eyes wide and anxious. Elise took a dollop of lavender-scented cream and rubbed it into her throat and hands. "Josiah came in smiling. At that point, I knew Matthew and John must have met with success. Later, Josiah confirmed it when we had a moment to speak. Amberly seemed unfazed by the need to hire another coach."

Prin sat on the windowsill. Distracted by something outside, she waved an ivory-handled fan in hopes of encouraging a breeze. "Your Englishman is plum spoiled. I thought it the first time I saw him."

Elise joined Prin at the window. Far beyond the lawn, the orange glow of a bonfire betrayed the location of slave row. Her heart ached for Prin. She knew her sister longed to be with her husband, but it wasn't possible for Prin to stay with Kane in one of the men's cabins.

"I thought you said he was dangerous?" she said, trying to distract Prin from the woeful song that carried across the darkness.

"Aye, that too."

"Well, whatever he is, he dealt with his disappointment rather well considering the sum he paid that ferret of a driver." Elise caught Prin's attention in the mirror. "Will you finish braiding my hair?"

Prin set her fan aside and began finger-combing the mass of Elise's dark tresses. "Why would your man worry what he paid? Judgin' by those fancy togs of his, he doesn't seem short of money."

"True," Elise said in contemplation. "But surely a tradesman would grumble when losing such a large sum over a hired coach. Still, he's English. They're an enigma at the best of times."

Later, Prin tucked in comfortably beside her, Elise finished her prayers and watched the flickering shadows on the plastered ceiling. The mantel clock chimed midnight. She left the bed, picking up her fan from the side table as she went. At the window, she leaned against the sill and looked out into the night, idly tapping the fan in her palm. A mosquito bit her arm. She swatted the pest and rubbed the sting.

Stars winked in the velvety sky, and the slightest whiff of smoke laced the sultry air. The nearby outbuildings stood as darkened apparitions in the yard. Farther afield, the fires no longer burned on slave row. The singing had stopped, casting the night into an eerie, silent clam. Even the trees stood motionless, not enough breeze to sway their limbs or rustle the leaves.

Elise lit another candle and glanced at the bed, where Prin's thin form made little more than a bump on the feather mattress. If only they'd been left alone in Virginia, she thought for the thousandth time. Their father's farm had burned after a bolt of lightning struck during a violent storm, but they could have rebuilt, gone on just as they had, and enjoyed a life of peace and freedom with their father's hateful presence buried in the ground.

This whole mess was her fault, Elise thought. If only she hadn't written her mother, unwisely mentioning her father's death in the tornado, Roger would never have had a chance to enter their lives and muck them up so cruelly.

"Oh, do stop, Elise," she whispered to herself. It helped nothing to fret about the past. She needed to concentrate on the present, for that was all she had. Her future was too precarious to contemplate and best left in God's hands.

Drake leaned back against the wooden bench, his arm propped along the narrow back as he chewed a sprig of mint. He'd quit the stifling confines of his room over an hour ago, hoping the fresh night air might clear his head, but he and a hooting owl remained wide-awake.

Here in the garden, the fresh scent of herbs and the sweet smell of flowers combined with the mustiness of damp earth. The gentle lap of the river should have been relaxing, but it wasn't. Thoughts of Elise kept him from sleep. Even the knowledge that he'd managed to track the Fox to his den didn't ensnare him as much as she did.

Usually a man of single-minded determination, he knew he should be devising some form of trap for his enemy, not mooning after a young woman he knew so little about. Yet today he'd admitted his attraction to Elise like an untried lad. Little wonder she hadn't taken him seriously.

Truth be told, he didn't understand his rash behavior. Past relationships had taught him to be wary in his dealings with women. He'd never had trouble attracting females, but he felt his title and fortune were his biggest draw. His wife had certainly let him know she thought so and his recent fiancée's unfaithfulness solidified the belief.

The owl hooted, and insects filled the night with chatter. Perhaps Miss Cooper had managed to dodge his every defense and capture his attention because her interest in him seemed genuine though she knew nothing of his true identity?

Whether or not that was the case, he couldn't deny he found her beautiful, witty and charming. Her mix of strength and vulnerability made him admire her and wish to protect her. He tensed remembering how every nerve in his body had jumped to attention the moment Beaufort's spy entered the tavern with Elise's satchel.

Something was amiss between her and Goss. The odd little man had disappeared after he left The Rolling Tide, and Elise seemed agitated when he queried her about the situation on the return trip to Brixton Hall.

Clearly, she doesn't trust me. He rubbed his eyes with the palm of his hand. He would just have to give her time.

He frowned. Time was a precious commodity, and he had far too little to squander. He had a few weeks at best before he wore out the Sayers' welcome, and once he found the Fox and saw the brigand hanged, he'd need to sail for home.

He clawed his fingers through his hair. The wisest course would be to leave Elise alone and put neither of them at risk of heartbreak…unless, of course, he could convince her to return to England with him.

Chapter Eight

Elise sat down for a breakfast of sausage and eggs the next morning, still tired from a restless night. Her few snatches of sleep had been filled with dreams of Drake's golden eyes. Today, she would have to be strong and establish a dividing line between them. It wasn't the wisest course of action when she considered the information she'd been ordered to obtain from him, but she had little choice if she hoped to keep her heart and emotions intact once the assignment ended.

Christian entered the dining room and locked the door behind him. "Hello," he grumbled, his level gaze making her uneasy. He broke eye contact and moved to the sideboard. "You're looking well this morning."

"And you're looking flat." Elise eyed her friend's mussed hair and rumpled clothes. His usual exuberance was muted by an obviously long night and overabundance of ale. "What happened? Were you trampled by a runaway horse?"

Christian grunted in response. He chose a plate from the sideboard and filled it with a pile of dry toast. Sitting across from her, he adjusted the candelabra and studied her with red-rimmed eyes. "How is Amberly?"

Elise lowered her lashes, shielding her gaze from Christian's scrutiny. She used her fork to push a bite of egg around her plate. "I suspect he's fine. He's out riding with Zechariah."

"Good, then we have time to talk. I can't put my finger on why, but I believe our guest is up to something quite rotten."

Elise shook her head in Drake's defense. "I don't believe so. Mr. Amberly and I have spoken on numerous subjects. He's neither said nor done anything to conflict with his claims. Why, if you could have seen the devotion in his eyes when he spoke of his family, you wouldn't question his honesty either."

He rolled his eyes. "Dearest, don't be a fool. He's aiming to gain your sympathy."

"Well, he has it. 'Tis a sad thing indeed, but his younger brother recently passed away."

"Passed away? How? Did he suffer from some malady or die in battle?"

Elise refolded the linen napkin in her lap and placed it next to her plate. "He died by means of foul play. Whether it was here or in England, I know not."

After a moment's contemplation, Christian shrugged. "Most intriguing."

"What?"

"How easily he's played you."

She scowled.

"I believe your emotions may be involved. It's made you vulnerable."

"I think you're in league with Prin to drive me mad. Ever since the ball she's been making sly innuendoes and harping on the fact she thinks I'm in love. You're both ridiculous. I've known the man less than three days, and besides, emotional…entanglement doesn't interest me in the least."

"I know." His eyes bore into hers for a moment. "However, I might be less doubtful if you sounded more convincing. At any rate, I believe Amberly means to have you. That he's not above using you for his own satisfaction, then abandoning you whenever he returns to England."

Elise wanted to believe better of Drake, to trust her instincts concerning his intentions toward her, but her mother's similar situation with Roger and Christian's emphatic warning chipped away at her hopes for the Englishman.

"I saw the two of you at dinner last night," he said.

"We didn't speak three words to each other."

"True, but neither of you could stop looking at the other." Christian paused again and his voice became earnest. "I saw the interest in Amberly's eyes the instant he noticed you at the ball and again last night. That kind of emotion will grow and grow until someone gets burned in the end. And it won't be him."

Elise looked away.

"As someone who cares for you, as someone I believe you know you can trust, I think it's only right to mention in all likelihood the man's intentions are far from honorable. Put simply, he's not going to be here long, and I don't want to see you hurt."

Elise's heart fell. Of course, Christian was right. How

could she have so easily forgotten the lessons of a lifetime? Didn't men always find a way to get what they wanted? Some, like her father, used abuse and pounding fists to force their will. Others, like her stepfather, made promise after false promise to manipulate their prey.

"You're not saying anything I don't already know."

"For shame, I hate being redundant." He finished his last slice of toast. "At the risk of repeating myself *again*— be careful."

"I assure you I will be." She picked up her cup. "Both with Amberly and Beaufort. Zechariah mentioned he'd invited the captain for a visit today."

"Not today. He's been delayed in Charles Towne. Seems one of his spies has gone missing. You don't happen to know about that, do you?"

"Why would I?"

"Oh, I don't know. From what I can piece together, the man is a hired driver last seen at The Rolling Tide."

Elise blinked with genuine surprise and quickly told him what had transpired the previous day. "I can't believe that rodent-faced driver is one of Beaufort's spies! Though it does explain how he knew about the invisible ink. How did you learn the truth about him?"

"Beaufort and I spent the whole of last night with a couple of his cronies in a mean game of Whist."

"You must have been bored to tears." She laughed. "By the look of you, I thought you'd been charming one of your marks."

A cocky grin spread across Christian's mouth. "You like believing I'm no more than a handsome rake. I try not to disillusion you."

She took another sip of tea and regarded him over the rim of her cup. "I never said you were handsome."

He ignored her last comment and rubbed his chin, deep in thought. "When you arrived in Charles Towne yesterday afternoon, who chose the coach? You or Amberly?"

"He did. Why?"

"Because when I mentioned Amberly was our houseguest, Beaufort turned strangely quiet. I couldn't fish any more information out of him."

"That in itself is an oddity."

"Indeed. I'm thinking it's mighty convenient Amberly chose a driver who just happened to be one of Beaufort's spies."

Elise had to concur. She hoped Drake was incapable of anything sinister, but she was too seasoned a spy not to be wary.

"Where did you go once you left the wharf?"

"Tabby's." She hesitated. Her heart prompted her to protect Drake, but her responsibilities lay elsewhere. "Then Amberly left for The Rolling Tide."

"You can't be serious. When did you plan to tell me?"

Elise left her seat and approached the window. Gardeners with scythes in hand clipped the rolling green lawn, refreshing the humid air with the scent of cut grass. "Now. He said he had business."

"What kind of business?"

She wrung her hands, her heart and head at odds for the first time in her life. She had to admit the evidence cast a suspicious light in Drake's direction, but a part of her insisted she give him the benefit of a doubt. "Something concerning his shipping interests."

A knock sounded, preventing Christian from asking further questions. Elise crossed the Oriental rug, unlocked and opened the door. A house slave in a simple blue dress stood there, a nervous look marring her pretty face. Knowing the young girl frightened easily, Elise smiled to put her at ease. "Good morning, Tess, what can I do for you?"

The girl's hands relaxed against the front of her dark cotton skirt. "Prin's not feelin' so well. She told me to find you and ask you to go up to your room."

"Of course, I'll go straight away." Thankful for a reprieve, Elise turned back to Christian. "I'll speak with you later."

She ran up the stairs, in a hurry to reach Prin. Her sister never complained of being ill unless she was near death's door. As far as three doors down, she heard the sound of someone retching. The upper floors of the house were nearly empty this time of morning. Only Prin remained as far as she knew. She burst into a run.

Entering the room, she gagged on the stench of vomit. Her eyes darted around the bedchamber, passing over the empty, rumpled bed and wide-open windows that provided enough breeze to rustle the sheer white curtains, but not enough to clear the smell.

"Prin?"

A slight moan drew her eyes to the corner where her sister sat on the floor, a chamber pot in her lap. Ashen beneath her mocha skin, her night rail had fallen from one shoulder and a sheen of perspiration dotted her upper lip.

Elise dashed across the room, kneeling by her sister and holding the pot as another heaving fit shook Prin's thin form. When the spasms subsided, Elise held her for a moment, soothing the dark curls from her sister's clammy forehead. "Are you feeling any better?"

"A little," Prin whispered. "I need some water to rinse my mouth."

Elise eased away to fetch the drink. "Here you are, dearest. What's made you so ill? Was it something you ate?"

Prin rinsed her mouth and spat into the chamber pot. "I don't know. I've felt poorly for the last week or so. It's been worse and worse until this morning, when I couldn't keep anythin' down."

"Why didn't you tell me?"

"You've got so many things to worry about, I don't want to be more of a burden."

"You're never a burden." Elise kissed the top of Prin's head. "I love you more than anyone. One day soon we'll be free of these lives neither of us wants to lead. In the meantime, the Lord will help us through. He promises not to give us more than we can handle and I don't want you working yourself into the ground."

Elise dampened a cloth with the pitcher's remaining water and pressed it to Prin's brow. Crossing to the bedside, she pulled a cord and rang for one of the kitchen staff. "I'm going to order you some dry toast and tea."

Prin groaned. "I don't think I can eat at the moment."

"You will in a little while. You mustn't allow yourself to become too weak." Elise took the pot from Prin's shaky fingers and set it outside the door.

Returning to Prin, she helped her sister back to the four-poster bed. She covered her with the wrinkled white sheet, then opened another window in hopes of clearing the air.

"I'm so hot," Prin tugged off the sheet. "I miss the cooler air of home. It's only July, but if the heat keeps risin' I'll be a puddle by August."

When Tess returned, Elise ordered the food and hot tea with honey.

The maid nodded and collected the chamber pot without being asked. "I'll get you a clean one of these too, Miss."

Elise returned to the bed, where she found Prin slumped against the pillows with her eyes closed. "She'll be back in a few minutes. Toast will help settle your stomach and the tea with honey will soothe your throat."

"I feel so weak, I think a wisp of smoke could carry me off."

Elise squeezed her sister's hand. "I'd catch you if it did."

Prin smiled weakly. "I know."

Another knock sounded at the door. Elise answered it, accepted the laden tray and carried it back to the bedside table. Tess deposited a clean chamber pot on the floor near the door and left.

Elise held Prin's head to help her with the tea. "Be careful, it's a little warm," she warned.

Prin took a sip, then turned her head away. "I can't drink any more."

"Try some toast."

"Not yet."

Elise settled her sister against the pillows. "You say you've been feeling this miserable for a week?"

"At least."

"Have you had a fever?"

"No."

"If I ask you a question will you be honest with me?"

Prin cracked open her eyes. "I've never lied to you in my life."

Taking a deep breath, Elise stood and leaned against the bedpost. "Could you…could you be with child?"

Prin nodded, her eyes welling with tears. "I think I jus' might be."

The muscles along Elise's neck and shoulders tightened into painful knots. Their problems were compounded. If the war didn't end before the baby's birth, Zechariah would be the lawful owner of the babe. She would be forced to buy her own niece or nephew. How she *hated* slavery! The meager funds she'd been saving to buy Kane when they left would never stretch to pay for a child as well.

Dear God, You have to help us.

"Does Kane know?" she asked, striving to sound calm.

"No. I feared admitting it even to myself."

Elise tried to offer a comforting smile. "Everything will be all right."

"How can it be?" Prin's beautiful dark eyes filled with tears, breaking Elise's heart. Prin rarely cried and always endeavored to be a pillar of strength and cheerfulness. Elise sat on the edge of the bed and gathered Prin in her arms. She rubbed her back, hoping to offer silent comfort.

Prin lifted her head and looked out the window in the direction of the slave cabins. "If not for you, I'd be out there with 'em, sleepin' in the bugs, and eatin' nothing but gruel. Much as I don't want to be there I sometimes feel guilty I'm not." She started to weep in earnest. "Oh, Lisie, Kane lives like that, and there's nothin' I can do for him. What am I gonna do when this war ends and we're free to go? How am I 'spose to take our babe and leave him here sufferin'?"

Elise wiped the tears from under her sister's large brown eyes, now red from misery. What could she say to ease her sister's pain? She could think of nothing. How could she make promises to take Kane with them? Even if Zechariah agreed to sell the burly slave, she knew it might take years to earn enough additional funds to buy his freedom. "I don't know, dearest. We'll have to pray the Lord provides a road to lead us all to liberty."

Prin's shoulders slumped with dejection. "And what if He doesn't?"

"He promises to make a way when there isn't one. We'll have to believe Him."

Prin nodded. "I know you're right. It's jus' *so* hard to believe sometimes."

"I know, dearest." She endeavored to sound more positive. "However, we *do* know a babe is a blessing. You'll need to tell Kane as soon as possible. He'll want to know. He loves you very much."

"Aye, he does," Prin said with a tremulous smile that returned some of the usual brightness to her cheeks.

Elise fetched a fresh sheet from the linen press and covered Prin. "Don't fret anymore, all right? For now, though, let's keep the child a secret from all but Kane."

A rap at the door startled Elise. "Who is it?"

"Christian," came the muffled reply. "Are you ladies decent?"

Elise glanced back to Prin, who'd pulled the sheet to her throat. "Yes, come in."

The door creaked open. Christian nodded to Prin. "You're still ill?"

"Aye, just a little."

"I hope you feel better soon." He looked to Elise. "Zechariah is back from his morning ride. He's looking for you."

"For heaven's sake, what now?" she groaned in exasperation.

"The post arrived earlier. Perhaps there's a letter for you."

Her glance slid to Prin, who appeared as though she might retch again. Elise fetched the clean chamber pot and handed it to her. "I'll be there in a bit, Christian."

"I'll tell him." Christian nodded to both of them and quietly left the room.

A few minutes later, Elise found herself standing before Zechariah's big pine desk in the library. The large room smelled of old leather books and a recent cleaning with lemon oil. A clock ticked on the mantel, the only sound in the room.

"Christian said you wished to see me."

The spymaster lifted his balding head and set his quill next to a small jar of ink before removing his spectacles. "Amberly's the one who wants to see you, Fox. What are you doing wasting half the day in bed while the man is practically frothing at the mouth for want of your presence?"

"I haven't been abed. I've… Did he ask after me?"

The old man's eyes took on a crafty gleam. She could

almost see his ears perk to attention. She wasn't a fool. Her question had been too quick and betrayed her personal interest in the Englishman. Hopefully, Zechariah wouldn't guess just how fascinated she'd become.

The spymaster shrugged casually—too casually. "He spoke of little else."

Her brow furrowed. Intrigued and flattered, she wished she could scoff at his words, but thinking of Drake's interest in her warmed her heart. "How tiresome for you."

"No, indeed. Combined with Christian's report and other news I received earlier, 'twas most enlightening."

Elise brushed a nonexistent piece of lint from the skirt of her peach-colored gown. "Are you going to share the information, or am I to root it out on my own?"

"Don't sass me, girl." Zechariah's eyes bulged with the warning. "Sit down. You're giving me a crick in the neck."

Elise pulled up a Chippendale chair and sat on the blue silk seat. "Is that better?"

"Much." The old dragon looked at her with unreadable eyes. "I've no need to repeat Christian's information. I know you had breakfast with him, and he will have told you of Beaufort's missing spy himself. Amberly is the tricky one. On one hand, he's an aboveboard fellow, a man of trade with a verifiable story who's smitten with a lovely young woman. On the other hand, he's an Englishman, and a possible aristocrat-turned-spy if your suspicions are correct."

"I believe I was wrong," she said, giving in to an inexplicable need to protect Drake.

Zechariah shook his head. "On the contrary. I've

spoken with Amberly and I think you may be right. Christian believes it, too. In fact, he thinks Amberly knows Beaufort well. If our guest *is* an aristocrat, he and Beaufort may even be related in some way. It's just a hunch, mind you, but I know the captain prides himself on his distant but lofty connections." Sayer glanced out the window. "Aha, there's Amberly now."

She moved to the window with deceptive calm. Her breath locked in her chest and her spirits lifted the moment she spied him leading his horse across the lawn. The sun glinted on his black hair, and a disturbing emotion—part yearning, part panic—settled over her.

True, he was a handsome and powerful sight in his black breeches, boots and billowy white shirt, but Drake's appeal went deeper than simple good looks. It was his core of strength that drew her, his humor and gentle care.

"Why are you standing there gawking, girl?" Zechariah's knowing laughter made her cringe. "Go catch him."

He followed her rapid flight to the door. "Christian is on his way to check the muskets you smuggled yesterday. Amberly looks as though he's turning on that same path. It wouldn't do for him to discover them. I'll depend on you to provide a distraction."

Chapter Nine

Drake led his borrowed mount, Valiant, toward a sandy path that ran along the gently lapping river. A breeze blew from the east, ruffling his hair. Black clouds warned of a storm's rapid approach. He'd heard of the fast-moving rains that swept over this part of the South Carolina coast. With the humidity high and the temperature rising, he'd be grateful if a good soak brought respite from the heat.

He followed the trail into a copse of tall oaks dripping with musty Spanish moss and edged by a thick growth of spiky, fan-shaped shrubs.

Thunder rolled in the distance. Valiant neighed and stamped his hoof, spraying sand and sending a lizard skittering into the undergrowth. Drake stroked the horse's sleek gray muzzle while he studied the surrounding area. He meant to find a divergent path or hidden means of travel that might aid the covert operations of the Fox. Kirby had scouted much of the plantation's rice fields and outer acreage the previous day. To Drake's disgust, the lieutenant had found nothing suspicious.

Drake's brow furrowed with frustrated anger. The narrow trail seemed to stretch out before him into another dead end, but he was certain there had to be something to give the brigand away. He only had to find it.

Three days had passed since his arrival at Brixton Hall. Three *more* days the Fox had been allowed to live unpunished while Anthony lay in a grave. It galled him that neither he nor any of Beaufort's spies had made any headway in locating his prey. The trail grew colder by the hour.

Lost in his thoughts, he reached out and plucked a leaf from a nearby bush. Spring green, it reminded him of Elise's lovely eyes. A twig snapped behind him. He turned and saw her peering around an overgrown shrub. For a moment, he wondered if his will had conjured her up. Obviously caught staring at him, she blushed and lowered her lashes before flashing him a beguiling smile.

He tied Valiant's reins around a low branch and met her halfway as she walked toward him. Before either of them spoke, he drew her into his arms, as if it were the most natural thing in the world for him to hold her.

Elise didn't resist, though she knew she should. It felt wonderful to abandon herself to the bliss of simply being with him, to forget the troubles that plagued her life if only for a few moments.

Watching him as she had been for the last several minutes, she'd realized she might try to deny her feelings to Prin, the Sayers, or even herself, but this Englishman fascinated her. The awareness terrified her, waged an internal war that confused as much as stimulated. How could she have fallen into the trap of wishing to be with this man when every instinct she possessed warned freedom should be her ultimate goal?

Drake brushed a light kiss across the top of her head. "Good morn, sweet. Seeing you here has turned this already fine day into sheer perfection."

His words warmed her heart. "Sir, you're a shameless flirt."

"Hardly, love, I simply state the truth."

Thunder rumbled again and Valiant whinnied nervously in protest of the portentous sound. Elise had been intent on Drake and hadn't noticed the darkening sky. She suddenly wished she could hide. "I *hate* storms. You need to fetch Valiant. We're in for a downpour. We should head back to the main house before it hits full force."

The black, fast-moving clouds drew Drake's attention. "I don't think we'll make the house before the deluge begins."

A loud clap of thunder drowned out her reply. Her heart lurched with fear even as the first fat drops of rain hit the dusty path.

"Elise, don't fret. Come with me. I'll return you indoors."

He reached for her hand just as another deafening blast of thunder boomed like a cannon above them. In her mind, she saw her burning home. She heard the screams of loved ones, smelled the horrible stench of scorched flesh and bone. Pure fear propelled her into action. "No time! The slave cabins are around the next bend."

Drake rushed to collect Valiant. He leapt into the saddle, then leaned down to pluck her up and deposit her in front of him. Elise clamped her arms around Drake's waist. She ducked her head and pressed her cheek to the center of his chest, drawing comfort from the steady beat of his heart. At Drake's command, the horse sprang forward in an agitated race for escape.

The storm intensified. Bright bolts of forked lightning split the raging sky. Wind whipped through the trees and the rain struck like cold, sharp needles on Elise's exposed skin. Desperate to calm her terror, she prayed for mercy, begging God to help them reach cover.

Drake reined Valiant to a halt outside the first structure in a long row of rustic cabins. He helped Elise dismount, jumped down beside her and set Valiant free to find his own shelter. Lightning flashed overhead and thunder crashed around them. A slave woman, her head wrapped in a kerchief, opened the door and bustled Elise inside as if she knew her well.

Inside the hovel, wind whistled through the parchment-thin walls, but at least the cabin provided a meager haven from the storm. Drake slammed and bolted the door against the wind. He ducked his head to keep from bumping it on the slated ceiling. In one quick glance he noted the dirt floor, simple table, bench and rolled mats along the wall. Disgusted by the rough treatment the slaves endured, he turned to find a dozen sets of large, wary coffee-colored eyes peering at him from the next room. Wanting to relieve the women's anxiety, he started to offer his thanks for their shelter, but the door closed abruptly, leaving him and Elise alone.

Violent thunder shook the cabin. Elise spun to face him, her soft lips curved in a wobbly frown.

Drake gathered her close. Her arms locked around him

as though she worried the wind might pick her up and steal her away.

When her trembling subsided, he lifted her chin. "Elise? How do you fare?"

"I'm so glad you're here with me," she whispered. "I never feel safe, but when I'm with you all the fear fades away."

"You can stay with me forever if you wish."

She pressed her cheek to his chest. Outside lightning flashed and the wind howled. Its cold fingers rattled the shutters. She shivered against him.

He held her tight, enjoying the way she fit against him. Never before had he felt as though a woman had been made just for him.

Outside, the storm continued to rage, but Elise no longer noticed. Her world had shrunk to include just the two of them, and her senses revolved solely around the man who held her with such protective care. The first man who'd made her feel secure. The first man she'd ever loved.

Ice spread through her veins. She didn't want to love Amberly. He'd said she could stay with him forever, but he couldn't truly be hers. Hadn't Christian warned mere hours ago that Drake would soon leave for England? If she didn't start using her head, she would be left with nothing but empty arms and a shattered heart.

She pulled away, a lonely ache forming in her chest that same moment.

"What is it, sweet?" Drake reached for her hand. "Come back to me. Don't go."

"I'm sorry," she whispered. "What must you think of me?"

"That you're the most intriguing woman I've ever known."

"Silly, you mean. I know it's childish to fear storms."

"I don't think you're silly. Tell me why you're afraid."

Elise clasped her arms around her middle and fought the temptation to lean on a person other than herself or Prin. She wanted to open up to him, to share a deeper bond, but what could she say that wouldn't spur more questions and the revelation of her darkest secrets? She wanted to trust him, but in reality he was little more than a stranger.

"Tell me, sweet."

Wind whistled through the shutters. The strength to fight him drained away. What would it hurt to tell him just one event in her past? She took a deep breath and related the story in a dull voice as if it had happened to someone else. "Two years ago my father's farm was hit by a terrible storm. Lightning struck our home and burned it to the ground. Most of our slaves, all people I held dear, died trying to escape or extinguish the flames."

Her throat constricted until her voice became a rough whisper. "That same night we suffered through all manner of violent weather. A tornado passed over and destroyed the outbuildings, including the slave cabins. Many of our people were found in the ensuing weeks, their bodies mangled as though the winds had carried them away and dropped them from a height."

He urged her to sit on the rough-hewn bench and took the seat next to her. His arm wrapped around her shoulders, he tucked her close against his side. "My darling girl, I can't imagine what you must have suffered. I'm glad you've found safety here with the Sayers."

She swallowed the bitter taste of denial. She could never tell him just how unsafe it was for her at Brixton Hall. Without examining her need to do so, she moved closer to him, like an orphan finding shelter on a bleak night. "You said you want to know my secrets. Few know this one. Indeed, I shouldn't tell you if the truth be known, but…once the war ends, I plan to leave Brixton Hall for good."

He frowned against her brow. "Why? Are you very unhappy here?"

The storm began to relent. Muted voices drifted in from the next room as she allowed her silence to speak for her.

He brushed his lips against her temple. "You're not planning to leave alone, are you? If so, 'tis foolish to entertain such dangerous notions."

"I'm not surprised you'd think so, but I don't believe it is foolish. I've relied on myself since that horrible night. If the Lord made a way, I'd leave Brixton Hall today, but I have nowhere else to go."

He stroked her hair and kissed the top of her head. "Why do you wish to leave? Are the Sayers cruel to you?"

"No."

Drake's tone turned chilly. "Is the puppy pestering you?"

"Puppy?" she asked, confused. "You mean Christian?"

"If he is, it will be my pleasure to persuade him otherwise."

"There's no need. Christian is my friend, not my dilemma." Bemused by Drake's unexpected display of irritation toward Christian, she wondered what her friend had done to encourage Drake's dislike.

"Sayer had the nerve to warn me off you the night of the ball. I didn't care for his presumption."

Aha. She smiled against his damp shirt. "No, I don't believe you would."

He grunted, then said seriously, "If you want to leave, come with me. I'll keep you safe."

Hope bloomed inside her…then wilted. "And be what, your mistress?" She laughed with ill-concealed contempt. "Never. I promise you, I won't ever be any man's strumpet."

"I'm glad to hear it." Long moments passed with only the rain dripping off the trees outside to mark the time. He'd meant to offer marriage. He realized the prospect was sudden, but why wait when he'd found a woman he could truly care for? He didn't care if she agreed because she wished to leave the Sayers; at least she wouldn't have chosen him for his wealth and title. He knew she was as drawn to him as he was to her. As far as he was concerned anything else could be dealt with and he would have a lifetime to convince her to love him.

"You said the Sayers are good to you."

"They're kind enough." She glanced to their linked fingers, and eased her hand from his grasp. "But I wish to be away from here, to have a home of my own."

"How do you plan to accomplish your goal? What of funds? If you refuse to be a mistress, how will you afford a home with no husband to secure one for you?"

"That's why I'm still here." Bitterness crept into her voice. "Brixton Hall is like quicksand. I'm up to my chin in it and no one cares."

"*I* do." Her face registered her distrust. He took both of

her hands in his. "What can I do to make you realize I have only the best intentions toward you, Elise? What can I say to make you realize how quickly and completely I've come to care for you?"

She bit her lip. Her eloquent eyes spoke of her inner struggle to believe him.

"I don't want you for a mistress. I want you for my wife."

Elise couldn't mistake his sincerity. Her heart began to race. For one brief moment she allowed herself to forget the suddenness of their situation and to imagine spending a lifetime with him. The vision made her lightheaded. She wanted to throw her arms around his neck and shout, "Yes, yes, yes!" Instead, she willed her pulse back to normal and shook her head, determined to stay planted in reality. "You'd marry me because I'm unhappy at Brixton Hall? You…you can't just decide to wed a person on a whim."

"Who says it's a whim?" He shrugged as if they were discussing the most tepid topic, but his eyes were intense, expectant. "Can't you tell when a man has fallen madly in love with you?"

Her heart did a peculiar little flip, then almost stopped beating altogether. Blood rushed in her ears. She couldn't have heard him correctly. But no, she'd heard him quite distinctly. He loved her? Her own declaration of love sprang to her lips, but she bit her tongue. She couldn't leave with him. It would be cruel madness to encourage him when she was chained to Brixton Hall.

She swallowed the painful lump in her throat and reached up to brush a soft black curl off his brow. "I wish

I *could* marry you, Drake, but I cannot." He started to speak, but she forestalled him by pulling away and placing her fingers over his lips. "Let's talk of it no longer."

"Don't change the subject, woman. You can't deliver the news you wish you could marry me, then forbid me to speak of it. I won't have it."

"Then we have nothing left to say. I won't discuss marriage any longer."

His expression proclaimed his displeasure. Clearly, he wasn't used to being rejected. "You're the most obstinate female imaginable."

"So I've been told." She traced his angular jaw and the long scar along his jaw. She hated the idea of him experiencing the least bit of pain. "What happened here? Did you fall?"

He released a frustrated breath and clawed his fingers through his damp hair. "No, if you must know, nothing so mundane. My younger brother, Anthony, had a ferocious temper. He was always trying to best me at fencing. I was seventeen at the time and refused to let him win. One day, unbeknownst to me, a young lady he fancied came to watch our practice. Naturally, I won."

"Naturally," she mocked, poking fun at his arrogance.

He laughed. "Cheeky girl. As you can imagine, Anthony's pride was on the line. He flew into a rage, deciding to take off my head in the process. Fortunately, he missed my jugular and nicked my jaw instead."

"He sounds like an animal." His mouth tightened and she realized her faux pas. She wouldn't like it if someone spoke ill of Prin. "I'm sorry. I shouldn't condemn a man I didn't know."

"No matter. Anthony's temper was his worst quality, but he had a sharp sense of humor as well. I wish you could have known him."

A horse whinnied outside and Elise jerked in surprise. She'd forgotten the world beyond the cabin, and she resented the reminder. "I don't want to go, but perhaps we should head back to the house. Zechariah and the others will soon notice our absence and wonder what's happened to us."

"I suppose you're right, although the idea of someone finding us here does hold some merit."

"How can you think so?"

"Simple, my girl. If I claimed I compromised you, it would put an end to this game of fox and hound we're playing. All I'd have to do is sit back and wait while *Zechariah* convinced you to wed me."

She tried to laugh, but his reference to her as a fox made her quail. "Sadie and the other fine women of this cabin would vouch for my good name. Besides, do you really want a wife who must be forced to wed you?"

His jaw clenched. A flash of some unnamable emotion crossed his face before he could bury it behind a glib facade. He stood, straightened to his full height and wrenched open the door. "Good heavens, no. I had such a wife and it's not a circumstance I'd care to repeat."

Stunned by his announcement, Elise stared at the cabin door he'd shut on his way out. A spasm of unreasonable hurt pierced her chest. She saw how much her thoughtless comment wounded him. Obviously he held deep emotions for the woman who'd been his wife.

His wife.

He'd had a wife. Why the knowledge stung, she didn't understand. He was a full-grown man. Of course he'd had a life before meeting her, but the thought of him in love with someone else cut to the quick.

A knock on the connecting door drew her attention. Sadie peered around from the next room. "You be all right, Miss Lisie? I knows you afraid of them sto'ms."

"I'm fine," she assured the older woman, "Thank you for loaning us your room." With a hug and a wave to the other women, she left and hurried to find Drake.

The rain had stopped and the sky was blue again. Raindrops glistened on the leaves and pine nettles before dripping to the drenched earth. She breathed in the fresh, sweet air, hoping Drake hadn't wandered off too far without her.

When she found him checking Valiant's saddle, she heaved a sigh of relief. He didn't bother to look up from his task and she ended up addressing his back. "Drake, please forgive me. I had no idea I'd be reminding you of hurtful memories."

He paused in stroking the horse's satiny neck. Somewhere in the trees overhead, a bird chirped for its mate. "There's nothing to forgive, Elise. You didn't wound me. My wife died years ago. Her memory is no longer a cause for grief."

She wasn't convinced, but his manner shouted his unwillingness to discuss the topic further. Renewed tension stretched taut between them. If not for the singing birds and the croak of a bullfrog nearby, they would have been stranded in silence.

He grasped the reins. "We should be on our way."

"Yes, I suppose we must." As they walked along the path, she watched him from under her lashes. He'd retied his shoulder-length hair at the nape of his neck with a cord of black leather. In spots, the dampness of his thin cotton shirt stuck to his thickly muscled back and arms. Truly, he was splendid, exceptional to look upon, and the gentlest man she'd ever met. Forced or not, the woman he'd wed would have been an imbecile not to adore him.

He turned his head and winked at her. Caught staring at him yet again, she pretended not to see his smug expression, and lifted her chin. The sharp movement caused her loose hairpins to rebel and several of them slipped free, sending the damp mass of her hair in a tumble down her back.

She heard him chuckle and saw him stoop to retrieve the mutinous pins.

She tried to arrange her hair into some semblance of order, but the pins refused to hold. "I never could do much with my own hair." She brushed several thick strands back from her face. "Do I look presentable in the least?"

Elise caught her breath as Drake appraised her. His eyes were the color of molten gold in the sunlight and she wanted to bask in their warmth all day.

"You look stunning, love." He took her hand and entwined their fingers, golden-brown and creamy-white. "I could admire you forever."

She laughed nervously as they rejoined the path that led to the main house. "You must be addled."

"Hello there!" a voice called out. They turned to see Christian meandering up the shaded trail.

Her friend was perfectly dry except for his sodden riding boots. His dark brown hair ruffled in the light breeze. He must have passed the storm in the shed near the dock. She'd forgotten he was so close by, that she'd been sent to ensure Drake didn't discover him inspecting the weaponry she'd brought up from Charles Towne the previous day. She grimaced inwardly. Drake was making her lose her concentration as well as her heart.

"Hello, Sayer." Drake eyed Christian with a mix of impatience and irritation. "How did you happen to sneak up behind us and miss the downpour as well?"

Christian shrugged, though he glared at their entwined hands. "By having the wits to go inside, Amberly. There's a small shed near a dock upstream. Too bad neither of you had the same good sense. Why didn't you head back to the house when you heard the storm's approach?"

"We did start back." Elise stepped in to diffuse the male aggression. "But we didn't make it."

"Obviously, Elise. You look like a drowned rat."

"You must be blind," Drake said. "Miss Cooper couldn't help but look like a spring morning even on her worst day."

"If you say so, Amberly." Christian laughed. "So where did the two of you ride out the storm?"

"Sadie's cabin."

Christian smirked. "In a pinch, I suppose Sadie is an acceptable chaperone."

Elise narrowed her eyes and tamped down the urge to box her friend's ears. "Where's your mount, Christian? It's difficult to believe you *intended* to soil a fine pair of boots."

"Of course not. I had to let Apollo find his own shelter when the storm hit. The sorry beast didn't bother to return."

"Intelligent animal," Drake said cheerfully. "We had no such trouble with good Valiant here." With eyes only for Elise, he said to Christian, "Don't let us keep you, Sayer. We'll meet you later, up at the house."

Chapter Ten

Drake shut the door of his bedchamber, stripped off his shirt and removed his leather boots. A maid had straightened the room. The four-poster bed was neatly made and a vase of purple wildflowers graced the nightstand.

Reclining atop the covers, he crossed his arms behind his head and allowed his mind to wander. The thought of Elise made him smile. Was it possible God hadn't forgotten him after all? For the first time in years he offered up a prayer of gratitude.

"There you are." A feminine voice carried through the closed door from the hallway. "I was worried sick on account of the storm. I went huntin' for you, but Zechariah chased me back up here."

"I'm fine." He recognized Elise's voice. "I'm sorry I worried you."

"You don't look fine. You look like you took a tumble in a mud puddle."

"Why thank you, Prin."

Drake chuckled as the ladies moved out of earshot. When

he'd left Elise in the garden, her hair in disarray, her cheeks flushed, he'd thought her the loveliest woman he'd ever seen.

Thinking about a lifetime with Elise, he realized he was happy about the institution of marriage for the first time in his life. Nay, he was ecstatic. Her shock when he'd proposed had matched his own, but once the words were out he had no wish to take them back. His first marriage had been by the king's command. Diana had never forgiven him for not being the man she loved, a French marquess she'd met at court.

At nineteen, he'd hoped for more than a lonely arranged marriage. He'd tried to warm to her, but Diana had wanted no part of him. Their union had been one of cool politeness underscored by her disdain for the whole affair. She'd insisted on living in London while he chose to remain at Hawk Haven. When she'd died of a fever in the fifth year of their marriage, he'd barely noticed her absence.

Older, wiser and far more jaded than any twenty-four-year-old ought to be, he'd refused additional attempts by the crown to shackle him a second time. He'd ceased tormenting himself with the hope of learning why God had taken most of his family and forgotten him, and his prayer life had dwindled to nil.

Only the need for an heir had spurred him to consider matrimony a second time. The fact that Penelope's dowry included a strip of borderland he'd long been interested in acquiring for his estate had added to her appeal. When he'd first met her, his former fiancée had seemed to have all the qualities a perfect duchess would need in abundance: impeccable breeding, outward beauty and a fine social standing. It wasn't until a month before their wedding that he'd begun to hear the rumors. Finding her in the arms of another man and discovering she'd only agreed to his proposal due to pressure from her family to wed a duke had been a blessing in the end. With his anger and embarrassment now cooled, he was grateful he'd learned the truth before the marriage. Had he wed Penelope as he'd planned, he never would have known love with Elise.

Thank You, Lord, for bringing Elise into my life.

Years had passed since he'd last spoken to God, but those few words acted as a ray of warm sunlight on his frost-bitten soul. He realized just how much he'd missed the peace that came with daily prayer and a grateful heart. *Forgive me, Lord, for shutting You out of my life all these years.*

The clock on the mantel signaled he should dress for dinner. He leapt up, eager to return to Elise. For the first time in his life, he was certain he'd met a woman who was interested in him as a man and not a duke. She may have turned down his proposal, but he'd seen her regret in doing so.

Drake grinned. He wasn't a man who took no for answer once he'd made up his mind. He crossed to the wardrobe and removed the best set of clothes he'd brought with him. Tonight, he'd begin his campaign to win her in earnest.

He whistled a jaunty tune as he poured water in a basin and began to shave.

Once dressed, he left his chamber and headed for the dining room. Darkness had fallen. Crystal sconces along the hall and down the stairwell glowed with candlelight.

The closer he came to the first floor, the stronger the aroma of fresh baked bread, spices and roasted meats became. His stomach growled with hunger.

When he entered the dining room, he found servants lighting the candles in the chandelier above a table set with fine bone china. A maid put the finishing touches on the flower centerpieces, bobbed a curtsy and scurried from the room.

Drake turned to go, deciding to wait for his dining companions on the veranda farther down the hall. Outside, the night was balmy, the stars and moon bright in the satiny black sky. Crickets chirped and an occasional lightning bug sparked in the distance.

He pressed his palms against the rail and enjoyed the tranquil quality of the place. It had been months since he'd felt relief from his grief. That he possessed any at present was due to Elise's influence. Simply looking at her made him jubilant, but the driving need to find Anthony's killer tempered his happiness. He couldn't come to terms with his brother's death until he found the Fox.

"Good evening, sir."

Drake whipped around to face his cousin, Captain Beaufort. "Charles, what do you mean by sneaking up on me?"

"I called to you, but you were lost in your thoughts, Your Grace."

"Quiet, man!" Drake lowered his voice to an annoyed whisper. "How many times must I remind you not to call me that. Do you want me to end up the bait for some colonial ransom-seeker?"

"My sincerest apologies, Your…er, sir. It's such a departure from propriety, so unnatural, I find it taxes my memory to call you aught but your title."

Drake ground his teeth in frustration. "I shan't remind you again, Charles. Another slip and I'll see you swabbing decks for the next twenty years."

Beaufort's eyes grew round as an owl's. "But, sir, I'm in His Majesty's army, not the navy."

"True, Captain, but I own a fleet of ships that I insist be kept spotless."

The captain gulped. "I understand, sir. I won't blunder again."

"See that you don't. Now, tell me why you're here. I thought you'd been delayed until tomorrow."

"I've sent Lieutenant Kirby to search for a man I've lost."

"Who?"

"The carriage driver who drove you yesterday. His name is—"

"Robin Goss."

"One and the same," Beaufort confirmed. "He disappeared after I spotted him outside The Rolling Tide yesterday afternoon. He didn't meet with me last evening as planned. I've ordered inquiries, but nothing's turned up. I'm hoping Kirby will have more success than I and learn something of his location."

Drake considered Beaufort's revelation. "I wondered what happened to the man when he didn't return to us. Elise chided me. She suggested I'd overpaid him and he'd run off with my coin to retire in Jamaica."

Beaufort gasped. "Miss Cooper dared to chide you, sir?"

Drake leaned against the rail and a fond smile quirked

his lips. "Indeed, she did. Truth to tell, I find I enjoy being teased by her."

"I understand," the captain said with a sly grin and a wiggle of his bushy blond eyebrows. "Miss Cooper is a beauty even if she is a dunce. She'd make a fine mistress and provide you with a merry time while you're here in South Carolina."

"Actually, Captain, she's a stunning woman with a quick wit and sharp intelligence. I've no intention of making her a mere mistress. I hope to make her my wife."

Beaufort's eyes bugged. "Forgive me, sir, I mean no disrespect, but your *wife?* Isn't that a bit…sudden?"

"Perhaps, but I'll be leaving Charles Towne as soon as my business is concluded. I refuse to take a chance of losing her."

"But she's a colonial miss, sir. It's not right for someone of your…er…for someone like you to marry someone so common."

"On the contrary, Captain. There's nothing common about her." His gaze turned frigid. "She's perfect for me and I shall wed whomever I wish. I dare anyone to suggest otherwise."

Christian Sayer hastened into his father's study. He shut the door with a firm shove that set the candle flames to flickering. "I have news you're not going to care for."

Zechariah scrambled to his feet. "What is it, boy? Spit it out."

"I overheard Beaufort and Amberly just now. I thought to make introductions and engage them in conversation before dinner, but it seems they know each other well. The door leading to the veranda was ajar and I arrived just as the captain referred to Amberly as 'Your Grace'."

"I can't believe it!" Zechariah plopped back in his chair, a look of stunned disbelief straining his round features. "Elise guessed rightly. He *is* an aristocrat."

"He's a duke," griped Christian. "We might as well have the Prince of Wales under our roof!"

Deep in thought, Zechariah rubbed his chins. "I'm sure we can produce results from this."

Christian held up a staying hand. "Wait, you haven't heard the rest."

"There's more?" Zechariah gasped.

"Aye, he has designs on our Elise as well."

The old man's eyes narrowed. "How so?"

"I heard him tell Beaufort he wants to wed her."

"You're jesting! If he's a high and mighty duke, you've got to be."

"No." Christian sat heavily in a leather chair near the fireplace. "I heard Amberly clear as a fire bell. He said he hoped to make Elise his wife."

"Well, I'll be," Zechariah said in amazement. "If she could be persuaded... Just think of the possibilities! Amberly may be privy to the most sensitive information. As his wife, Elise would be in an superb position to supply us with it."

Christian shook his head. "You've recovered fast enough. I thought you'd be reeling from shock."

"Nonsense, my boy." Zechariah tapped his temple with his index finger. "Shock forces the mind into action. Complacency makes it slow as molasses."

"She won't do it, you know. She's far too principled."

Zechariah's eyes burned with a crafty light. "I think she will. She's smitten with Amberly. You only have to see them together to know it."

"That may be," Christian conceded irritably, "but then you have the problem of persuading her to spy on her husband. If she cares for him enough to chance marriage, she'll be loyal to him. You'll lose her for us altogether."

"Elise is a girl of good sense. Her main goal is to see Prin free. If this business with Amberly comes to fruition, I'll simply concoct a new bargain with her. If she marries Amberly and agrees to give us information, I'll release Prin into her care."

Christian stood to leave. "You have it all worked out. I hope your plan doesn't ruin you or bring harm to Elise."

"How could it?" the spymaster said smugly. "Elise is too adept a spy to be caught. Besides, she'll be a duchess. Amberly will have the means to protect her if she's discovered."

"And when will you inform her of your plans?"

Zechariah blew out a candle and stood to leave with Christian. "I believe I'll have a word with Amberly after we sup. I need to see where he stands on the matter first. It would be foolish to put ideas in the girl's head before we know His Grace's true intentions."

Chapter Eleven

"Amberly, I'd like a word with you," Zechariah said as he snuffed his cheroot in a small pewter tray. A plume of smoke rose from the smoldering remains of rolled tobacco, adding to the haze and pungent odor that lingered in the parlor.

Drake stood as Zechariah heaved himself to his feet. Beaufort smoked a clay pipe near the open window. Curiously, Christian Sayer displayed none of his usual acerbic wit. He sat near the unlit fireplace, his feet on a stool, his eyes hooded as though he contemplated a matter of dire consequence.

"Not here." Zechariah waved Drake toward the open French doors. "In my study across the hall."

Drake followed the older man into the opposite room and waited for Sayer to light a candle before he took a seat in a padded wingback chair. "How may I be of service, sir?"

Zechariah sat behind his desk and lit an additional trio of candles. His chin dipped to his chest. Rolls of fat ringed his neck, giving him the look of a turtle peering from his shell. He studied his clasped hands for several ticks of the mantel clock, then eyed Drake with a shrewd gaze. "I trust you won't think me forward for saying so, Amberly, but I believe there's an attachment forming between you and my ward, Miss Cooper. I wish to know your intentions toward her."

Drake's brow arched in surprise. Had his admiration for Elise been so obvious? "I have the best intentions. I wish to marry her, in fact."

"You've asked her then?"

"I've broached the subject."

"What was her response?" Zechariah queried. "Yea or nay?"

Drake stomped down his irritation. He wasn't used to being questioned like a schoolboy, but Sayer was Elise's guardian. If—no—*when* she agreed to marry him, it would make life easier if he had the older man's consent. "As yet, nay. However, I plan to erode her defenses until she has no will but to answer in the affirmative."

"I see." Zechariah chuckled as he shifted a stack of papers. "You're a bold one, Amberly. I can't say you're the first suitor intent on wooing our fair Elise, but I believe you'll succeed where all the others have failed."

"Your words are encouraging, sir. May I ask why you believe so?"

Zechariah leaned back in his chair, his amusement apparent. "Because, my dear boy, you're the first man she's fancied in return."

Drake kept his face straight, but his pulse leapt within him. "I'm pleased to hear it."

"Yet, as her guardian," Zechariah inspected his fingertips, "I have to see to her well-being."

"Most certainly. Let me assure you I have her best interests at heart."

"Perhaps, but what of your circumstances, Amberly? Are you in a suitable situation to provide for Elise's needs, to ensure her happiness? Or do you plan to stow her away in one of your ships and subject her to the rigors of sea travel?"

"No, she'll not be floating about the high seas," Drake replied, a touch wary of his host's probing questions. "I'm quite capable of caring for my own. I guarantee that as my wife Miss Cooper will want for nothing."

"And what is your living situation in England?" Zechariah asked nonchalantly.

Drake lowered his eyes and brushed a wrinkle from his linen sleeve. His interest turned toward the window, where a breeze brought in the faint beat of drums. He hadn't noticed the pagan rhythm until now. He regarded Zechariah, who waited patiently for an answer. Why did he have the feeling there was an ulterior motive lurking beneath the old man's questions? "I am as well off as anyone, I suppose. Wealthier than some, less so than others."

"An ambiguous reply, Amberly. I'd wager you're better off than most."

Drake studied the man with a carefully blank expression. "I wouldn't know. I'm not privy to other people's financial affairs, sir."

Zechariah picked up a pipe and lit the tobacco. After several deep drags, he eyed Drake through the smoke. "And if this marriage were to take place, how quickly would you like to see it happen?"

"Once she agrees, I wish to marry as soon as it can be arranged. My business here is almost complete, I believe, and I would like to return to England the moment it's concluded."

Fleeting surprise rippled over Zechariah's plump face. "Your business is almost finished? Have you signed your shipping contracts then?"

"Not as yet, but I have leads and prospects." Drake stood and strolled to the window. He smelled a fire, but couldn't see one. Leaning against the frame, his eyes searched the darkness for the origin of the drums, but he saw nothing except a sky full of stars and the shadows of swaying trees.

"I'm glad to hear it. I've been giving your terms some thought." Zechariah set down the pipe and scratched his shiny pate. "I'd like to hire your fleet if we can come to a more reasonable price."

Drake's business instincts rushed to the fore. "And what is reasonable?" he queried suspiciously. "Half my original offer?"

Zechariah hooded his sharp gaze. "Would you take it?"

"Do you suppose me a fool, sir?" One of the candle flames flickered and died. "That's what I'd be if I let my services go for so paltry a sum."

"Paltry? You must be joking. Half your price is more than full for most other shipping ventures."

Drake shrugged as though it mattered not to him. In truth, it didn't. He had little use for the money. He'd lifted the price to discourage anyone from serious consideration of his offer. If his terms were accepted, he'd have no subterfuge in his hunt for the Fox.

"I couldn't possibly convince my captains to risk their lives for less than ninety-five percent. As you must know, English ships are the favorite prey for privateers and Frenchies."

"I know the risks, but you drive a hard bargain, Amberly. Suppose I used my influence to garner Elise's consent to wed you? Would you offer me a discount then?"

"You can't be serious," Drake said, his ire pricked. How dare the old man treat Elise as though she were nothing more than a head of cattle to barter? "I'll only accept Elise if she comes of her own accord. I was married before, you see, to a woman who wed me for numerous reasons other than myself. It was an unhappy union, not one I care to repeat."

"I see." Zechariah steepled his thick fingers and rested his chin on them. "What happened to your wife?"

"She died of a fever several years ago."

"And there's been no one since?"

Drake bristled at his host's audacity, but capped his annoyance. He usually asked the questions. It was a novel experience to be on the receiving end of someone else's interrogation. "No one serious. I told myself I'd never remarry. As the years passed, the sentiment faded. I engaged myself to another woman, a neighbor's daughter. I found her morals clashed with my own and broke off with her shortly before I left England."

"Seems right fickle of you, boy. What could she have done to deserve such coldness on your part? Am I to understand you'd discard Elise if you found she disagreed with you?"

Drake refused to explain the circumstances of his

severed engagement. It was none of the old man's affair. "On the contrary. I don't believe Elise could do anything I wouldn't forgive and forget."

Sayer smiled coolly. "Hmm…I wonder."

At the slave cabins, a bonfire raged. Flames roared high into the night sky, filling the air with the smoky aroma of burning pine and dry leaves. Laughter flowed freely and the tempting scent of roasting boar made Elise's mouth water. Drums beat a frenzied pace, enticing a good number of Brixton's African population to dance with wild abandon.

Elise sat on a stump in the shadows, a child on each knee. An older girl, Mary, stood behind her, braiding her hair. Elise had volunteered to sit with the children while their parents enjoyed a rare hour of merriment.

Prin and Kane had walked into the woods to talk about the baby and share some privacy. Elise expected them back at any time. She'd have to return to the house soon. Zechariah wanted to speak with her at midnight.

She pushed the thought to the back of her mind. Her meetings with her spymaster had grown tense of late and she wanted to enjoy a few stolen moments before returning to face him.

Looking down at the little ones in her arms, she smiled at their sweetness. The youngest child, a baby girl of six months, gnawed on her little fist, while eighteen-month-old Jed clapped disjointedly to the pounding drumbeat. Elise bent her head and nibbled playfully on his neck, laughing when he squealed and giggled.

"Miss Lisie, I can't braid your hair if you bend your head like dat," Mary complained.

"I'm sorry, precious." She sat up straight. Mary was a solemn child and Elise knew the girl performed even the simplest tasks with the seriousness of a grave tender. "I won't move again until you're finished."

She closed her eyes and allowed the drumbeat to pulse through her. Little Jed smoothed his finger over her cheek, drawing her attention to his impish grin. She smiled back. She loved children, but somewhere along the way had given up hope of having her own. For one fanciful moment, she allowed herself to imagine being the mother of Drake's child. Would a child of theirs have his silky black hair and deep, golden eyes? She wished it could be so.

Elise blinked and kissed the top of the baby's head. She had no reason for this emptiness in her heart. She'd been content with her lot and clear in her purpose until Amberly had insinuated himself into her life. Soon, she would have a niece or nephew to spoil. She assured herself that when the time came any misplaced longing for a child of her own would disappear.

Mary dropped the completed braid against Elise's back and the tip brushed her tailbone. The little girl leaned forward and rested her chin on Elise's shoulder. "I'm all done, Miss Lisie. Who's dat man starin' at you over there?"

"What man?" Elise twisted in the direction Mary pointed. Drake stepped from the shadows a few feet away. The fire's orange glow shimmered on his skin. Her chest tightened, and it was all she could do not to smile like a simpleton.

His straight white teeth flashed in a charming grin as he strode toward her. "I'm surprised to find you here, my love."

Tenderness washed through her. "What are you doing here, Drake?"

"I heard the drums and came to investigate. I've been enjoying the view."

"Yes, the dancers are quite something, certainly different from what one usually sees in the sedate drawing room of Brixton Hall."

He crouched before her. His gaze slipped to where Mary peeked over her shoulder. The child ducked behind Elise and whispered a hurried goodbye before she ran toward the row of cabins.

"I wasn't talking about the dancers," he said. "You with babes in arms is one of the most delightful views I've ever encountered."

A blush rose to her cheeks and she was grateful for the dark. "You have a knack for flattery, sir. Did you learn the art in school?"

He chuckled. "Of course. I made the highest marks of anyone."

Jed jumped off her lap before she could reply. She tightened her arm around the baby, who had fallen asleep, and watched as the little boy thrust himself at Drake. Drake accepted the child with ease and settled him on his hip. He found a nearby stump to sit on, and seemed not to notice when the child's busy fingers demolished his neatly tied cravat.

"Jed likes you," Elise said, pleasantly surprised he hadn't pushed the boy away.

Drake's long dark lashes lifted, exposing his magnetic gaze. "If only you liked me half as well."

She could drown in those eyes of his and be content. She

sought a witty reply, but none came to her. Instead, she chose the truth. "I fancy you a great deal more than I should."

He grinned as if he'd guessed as much. "Then marry me. We're drawn to one another. There's nothing that stands between us to keep us apart. I can provide for you—you've nothing to fear."

His intensity sent a shiver down her back. His words threatened the future she'd planned for herself and Prin. How would he react if she told him of her sister? Would he be horrified like her neighbors would be if they knew she claimed a slave as kin?

She swallowed tightly, teetering on the brink of following her traitorous heart. She wanted to trust him, but didn't know how. "You don't miss a single opportunity to press your case, do you, Mr. Amberly? What is your rush?"

"I shall be leaving for England as soon as my business is complete. I refuse to consider returning without you."

The prospect of never seeing him again made her chest tighten with dread. "*Would* you leave without me?"

"Will you force me to?" In a driven tone he added, "How can I be more clear in my intentions, Elise? I want you for my wife, my love, the mother of my children. What say you? Will you have me or reject me?"

At the thought of saying no, a sharp, desperate pain sliced through her heart. Oh, how she wanted to say yes, but how could she? She had to stay out the war or lose the chance of ever freeing Prin.

A loud cheer rose from the dancers near the bonfire. Grateful for the distraction, she pretended great interest in the commotion. The roasted boar had been taken from the spit. She looked back to her would-be husband and noticed Jed chewing on a section of his shirt. "He's teething. You may want to stop him or you'll soon have a hole in your fine linen."

Drake glanced at the boy as though he'd forgotten Jed sat in his lap. Gently, he removed the cloth from the child, who immediately began to cry as if his life were ending. Elise stood, careful not to jostle the baby, and beckoned the little boy as he fled Drake's lap. She handed the baby to Drake and knelt to console the overly tired Jed.

Picking up the little boy, she cuddled him while he cried into the curve of her neck. "The children really should be abed. They've been awake all day," she whispered. Glancing up, she squelched the need to giggle at the sight before her. Drake, infant dangling from his large hands, reflected an expression of unvarnished panic.

"Do you need assistance?" she asked, holding out her free arm to relieve him of the baby. Drake complied in an instant, obviously eager to be rid of the squirming being. Tenderly, she cuddled the whimpering infant while trying not to laugh. "I take it you have little experience with babies?"

Drake dragged his fingers through his hair. The flames shimmered over his high cheekbones and those dark eyes of his shone with self-mockery. "You've found me out, sweet."

She smiled softly. "Are you averse to them, then?"

"My own or other people's?"

"Do you have your own?"

"None as yet." He grinned at her meaningfully. "However, to answer your question, I am fond of children."

Elise glanced at the baby girl she held and smiled. "Based on your smooth handling of this one, I would never have guessed."

"Go ahead and mock me, sweet. Once our own children arrive, I'll become an expert child-handler."

Surprise widened her eyes. He spoke as though they were already wed. Her lashes dipped to shield her study of his lean, sculpted face. She had no doubt he would be an ideal parent: strong, protective, dependable. The exact opposite of her own sire. "It's been my experience that men avoid child-rearing as though it were a disease."

He shrugged. "Some may, but I look forward to spending time with my offspring."

"Does that sentiment extend to changing their soiled diapers as well?" Elise teased.

"I said I plan to be with them, not change them. There will be plenty of nursemaids for that."

She chuckled and was about to reply when a rustling in the woods drew her attention behind her. Hand in hand, Prin and Kane picked their way through the brush. Kane, a giant of a man, was unmistakable. Black as pitch, his slick, bald head reflected the firelight that revealed his contemplative expression.

"Prin, I'm over here," Elise called out, relieved to see her sister in much better sorts than when they'd left the house an hour ago.

Prin waved in acknowledgment and gave Kane a quick kiss goodbye. She wove her way around stumps and fallen limbs to join her. "I didn't know you was still here, Lisie. I thought ol' man Sayer was of a mind to give you a talkin' to."

"Prin," Elise said with a slight nod in Drake's direction. "I told you I'd wait here for you. Did you forget?"

Leaning forward, Prin picked up Jed. The little boy sighed in his sleep, but didn't wake when she draped him over her shoulder. Her gaze darted toward Drake and her eyes flared when she saw him. Her manner instantly more servile, she tipped her head in greeting and curtsied before taking the baby from Elise's arms. "I'll take these little bundles to their kin and be waitin' for you to leave, Miss Elise. Jus' let me know when you're ready."

Choosing to ignore Prin's big grin and knowing laughter as she walked away, Elise turned to Drake. He stood and offered his hand to help her up. "Your maid, I presume?"

"Yes, Prin has been with me a long time and she's very dear to me. *If* I were to consent to wed you, she'd have to come along. I would never consider leaving her here at Brixton Hall."

He reached out and stroked her hair. "Whatever you wish, Elise. However, consider she won't be able to remain a slave if she returns with us to England. She'll receive a wage for her labors and the freedom to decide if she stays in our household or seeks out other employment."

"That's fine by me," she said, trying to contain her joy. "I have no doubt she'd wish to stay with us."

"Will Zechariah free her into our employ?"

Elise's thoughts raced. Would her spymaster allow her to end their agreement? Would he consider releasing Prin? For a moment, she allowed herself to hope and squashed the practical side of her nature that warned she dreamed for too much. "I don't know."

"Perhaps he might consider allowing me to purchase her. We can free her once we make for England."

She regarded him with amazement. His generosity astonished her. No one had ever been so kind to her. To spend the large sum it would take to purchase Prin, only to turn around and relinquish it was... "You would do that for me?"

His thumb caressed the back of her knuckles. He moved closer. His scent of leather mixed with spices filled her senses. She longed to wrap her arms around him and hug him tight.

He must have read her thoughts. With a gentle tug, he pulled her deeper into the shadows, farther away from the fire's shifting light and the revelry of the merrymakers nearby. He tucked a wisp of hair behind her ear and brushed her cheek with his fingers. His gentleness made her heart ache.

"Elise, I would do much more for you if you allow me to know your wishes. That you seem overcome by such a trifling thing makes me wonder ever more heartily of your situation here. What must I do to make you realize that *my* wishes include making you happy for the rest of your life?"

Without thought, Elise melted into his embrace. His arms banded about her, holding her close. How much time passed she didn't know and didn't care. She should return to the house, but even the shortest separation from the man she loved was becoming unbearable. Zechariah could wait a few more minutes. She rested her cheek against his chest. "I want to be your wife, Drake."

He leaned back, a look of hope etched on his handsome

features. "Did I hear you correctly, sweet? Are you consenting to my proposal, or just toying with me?"

She laughed and nodded, suddenly alive with so much happiness, she thought she might take flight. "You heard me, sir. But there is a difficulty I must see to before we can announce our intentions."

His brow furrowed. "A difficulty? How so?"

"Trust me," she said. "Please, trust me."

He nodded. "I do, but—"

"Good." She pulled away before he could say more. The separation wrenched like a physical pain. "Now I must go."

"Wait." He pulled her back for a soft kiss that left her grinning all the way back to the Hall.

Elise rapped on Zechariah's study door and waited for his command to enter. Once inside, she glanced at the French mantel clock. The tapered candles flanking the porcelain piece illuminated her tardy arrival.

"Where have you been?" Zechariah looked up from his work, his cheerfulness enough to rouse her suspicion.

"With Prin." She refused to elaborate and came to stand before his desk. "Why did you wish to see me?"

The spymaster waved her into a seat. "Tonight has been most fortuitous, m'dear."

"Truly, how so?" she asked, a bit wary. To her recollection, she'd never seen Zechariah so light of heart.

"Christian has uncovered some magnificent news on Amberly."

"Wonderful," Elise adopted a conspiratorial tone. She hoped her acting ability would stand her in good stead, though the protective instincts usually reserved for Prin rushed to the fore. "I'm very impressed. For my part, I find Amberly to be the most hard-shelled individual I've ever met."

Zechariah leaned back in his chair and folded his hands over his wide girth. "You were right, Elise."

"I was? How so?"

"He *is* an aristocrat." Zechariah beamed like a beacon. "In fact, he's even more. He's a high and mighty duke. Christian heard Beaufort refer to him as 'Your Grace.' Amberly rebuked the man and reminded him not to use his title. It all makes perfect sense, you know. The man's arrogance is a palpable thing. His wealth, his disinterest in negotiating for better shipping terms all point it out as truth. No real man of trade would be so unwilling to compromise his price."

"A duke? Why…he's practically royalty." Stunned, Elise thanked God she was sitting down. Otherwise, the sting of shock would have laid her low. As it was, she grew weak with dismay. Her stomach swirled in sickening waves of disappointment and heartbreak.

She couldn't possibly wed Drake now. Not when she'd spent years committing treason against the very crown he counted as family.

Humiliated, she bit her lip and pretended to swat a fly from her lap while she blinked back hot tears.

The old man startled her back to attention when he slapped his knee and chortled, "Imagine the funds we could winkle from the British if we offer a duke up for ransom."

She forced a smile. "Just think of it."

His mirth faded. "You don't seem as impressed as I thought you'd be, Elise. Perhaps my other plan will be more to your liking?"

"What other plan?"

He studied her until she squirmed. "My plan involves you more than anyone."

"Me?" She sat forward in her chair. "What am I to do now?"

Zechariah hauled himself from his chair and lumbered to the open window. One of his silk stockings sagged around his ankle, but he seemed not to notice. Easing himself onto the window seat, he sighed and leveled her with a thorough glance.

"You know, my dear, I love this land and hope with all my heart it will be a fine nation one day. 'Tis why I'm often so narrow of purpose and act in ways that may seem cruel when I force you to my will. In truth this war is only a game. As in chess, the craftiest player will rule. One move may make all the difference to which side wins or loses."

Elise nodded and worried at her lower lip. What he said was true. She knew he wasn't an evil man, just determined to aid the cause and see the Colonies set free of England's tyranny. She didn't begrudge him his sentiments because she shared them. It was his constant manipulation she detested, and the unnecessary way he used Prin as a weapon against her that she abhorred.

"To that end, I'm going to ask you to do something you may find objectionable in the extreme," the spymaster continued.

Fear crawled up her spine. "What is it?"

"I wish for you to wed Amberly."

She sucked in air and almost choked. "You what?"

"Let me finish." He held up his hand as if he expected a verbal comeuppance. "He's smitten with you. I confirmed it earlier when I spoke with him after we dined."

"You didn't!" She felt her cheeks heat with embarrassment.

"I know you're taken with him, so don't act affronted. Hear me out."

Elise couldn't deny his statement, yet seethed in silence. The high-handedness of her spymaster appalled her. So what if she wished to marry Drake? After years of his manipulation, Zechariah's plan rankled her to the marrow. He couldn't know for sure that she loved Amberly, yet Sayer had the nerve to ask her to sacrifice the rest of her life for his purposes.

"I ask that you espouse the man and convince him to remain in Charles Towne. The war situation is critical. The British have been routed from the Carolina interior, but their grip on Charles Towne grows ever tighter. Who can guess their next move? As Amberly's wife, you would be in the center of Charles Towne's British society. Think what beneficial information will be discussed in such close and exalted company."

"How can you imagine so? Have you forgotten that Amberly has gone to great pains to deceive us all, to make certain none of us learned his true station?"

Zechariah rested a hand on each of his knees and leaned forward. "Captain Beaufort knows his true identity. I must assume other important Brits do as well."

"And if I agree, you seriously expect me to spy on my husband? Surely, you know me better than that, Zechariah. My sense of loyalty would never allow it."

The spymaster rubbed his jaw in the palm of one beefy paw. "I feared you might say as much."

"Well, at least you give me some credit," she scoffed.

"Oh, I do, my dear. 'Tis the reason I'm willing to strike a bargain with you."

The craftiness in the old man's eyes made her heart twist with dread and fear.

Chapter Twelve

Elise stood before the mirror, admiring her wedding gown. The dress was the loveliest creation she'd ever seen. Cut in elegant lines, the pale green silk did wonderful things for her skin. The square lace-edged neckline suited her oval face and made her neck appear long and slender. She hoped Drake would be pleased when he saw her.

He'd returned to Charles Towne only this morning, so there had been no chance for them to speak in the week since she'd last seen him. She'd tried to keep busy in his absence. There'd been more than enough to do. She'd thrown herself into wedding preparations, visited friends and gone on long walks around Brixton Hall. Hours had been spent riding Freedom, praying she'd made the right decision.

Every time she remembered what she'd agreed to, her palms began to sweat and her lungs constricted until she couldn't breathe. She swallowed thickly, remembering the choice she'd made between principle and practicality. Her conscience rebelled at having to spy on Drake, but

Zechariah's offer to free Prin now instead of waiting until the war's end had muted her protests. That, and the fact that if she declined his offer to report any unusual information, he promised to send Prin to an upriver plantation notorious for the mistreatment of its slaves.

How else was she to view the situation than as an answer to prayer? She'd spent long hours begging God for a way to see Prin, the baby *and* Kane set free. Her marriage insured Prin and the baby's safety. Now all she had to do was convince Zechariah to let her buy Kane.

She prayed Drake wasn't plagued by second thoughts concerning their marriage. She'd had none once she admitted he was her heart's choice for a husband. Even the distrust of men she'd learned from her father and stepfather's cruelty could not dim the hope she harbored for her future with Drake.

But Drake *was* a duke. As much as she loved him and wanted a life with him, she couldn't fathom his insistence to marry her, a colonial girl, when he could have any woman he chose. That he wanted her for his wife seemed incredible.

The soft strains of a violin filled the high ceilings and large open space of St. Michael's church. Anticipation raced through Drake as he waited in the wings to take his place at the altar. Today he would wed. He was as excited as a lad on Christmas day. He'd never been so nervous or so hopeful about his future.

The week he'd been parted from Elise had stretched like an empty eternity, but he'd had much to attend to. Besides paying Zechariah an outrageous sum for Elise's maid and horse, he'd secured the special marriage license, overseen the preparations for a rental house that would afford them the necessary privacy owed a newly wedded couple and written his solicitor in London announcing his nuptials. His primary concern revolved around safeguarding Elise's welfare. If anything happened to him she would be well provided for and free to do as she liked without the Sayers' charity.

He'd also doubled his efforts to hunt down the Fox. His informants inhabited every corner of the city, spreading the word that his reward for the spy had tripled. The Fox would eventually make a mistake and be caught, or someone greedy enough would turn him in.

If anything, Drake was more determined to avenge his brother and see the matter done. He looked forward to returning home with his bride and starting a family. Hawk Haven needed reviving, and Elise was just the woman to see it done.

The church's pipe organ boomed to life. The intricate notes throbbed, rattling the delicate stained-glass windows that cast colorful patterns on the polished wood floors. Footsteps sounded behind him. He turned to see John Kirby and Charles Beaufort rushing his way.

"Are you ready, sir?" the captain asked.

"I've never been more so, Charles. John, do you have the ring?"

The lieutenant patted the pocket of his new vest. His fingers delved into the brown wool and extracted the circle of gold. "Right here, sir. I'm honored you've given me the chance to serve as your best man."

"Yes, especially since Lord Anthony would have been your choice if not for his untimely demise," said Beaufort.

Drake lost some of his exuberance. "Yes, my brother's presence is missed today most of all."

Beaufort smoothed his blond wig. "You know it would have been my honor to stand in his stead if it weren't necessary to keep our relationship a secret, sir. However, I'm happy to lend my presence here to ensure you have at least one family member to witness your union."

Drake straightened his navy waistcoat and slipped on the matching jacket. He clasped Beaufort on the shoulder, refusing to have his good mood marred by his cousin's awkward attempts to earn his favor. "Come, cousin, I'm to wed. I have no wish to wait a moment longer."

Taking his place at the front of the church, he held his breath as Elise floated down the center aisle, a vision in light green silk and creamy lace. Until he'd been separated from her, he hadn't been aware of how alone and empty he'd been. Just one look at her replaced his loneliness with joy.

As he took Elise's hand and spoke his vows, he thanked the Lord for the gift of her. Humbled by God's mercy and kind forgiveness, he marveled at how blessed he felt for the first time in years.

Chapter Thirteen

Pealing bells announced the wedding ceremony's conclusion. Outside the pristine white church, the sky was a clear watercolor-blue blemished only by a few inky clouds on the horizon. Elise purposely ignored them. Since the day she and Drake had spent trapped in Sadie's cabin, the threat of a storm no longer cast her into the throes of panic.

The bells stopped chiming. The wedding guests' laughter and conversation filled the churchyard. Elise regretfully left Drake's side and made it a point to speak with each of her friends and neighbors in attendance.

An hour later, she found Tabby chatting with Christian near a redbud tree. After hugging Tabby, she reached up to give Christian a peck on the cheek, but he wrapped his arm around her and turned his head just in time to plant his lips on hers.

She yanked free, a touch embarrassed by his gall. With a tight laugh, she thumped him in the ribs. "What are you about, you silly man?"

"I wanted to see Amberly's reaction." A mocking smile

turned his lips. "I believe I see smoke shooting from those ducal ears of his."

Elise heard the cold, sarcastic undertone that belied her friend's teasing manner. She turned her head sharply to scan the yard for Drake and found his gaze fixed on her. A scowl marred his brow. She offered him a smile, hoping to ease his displeasure.

When Drake smiled in return, she glared back at Christian. Until now, she hadn't realized her friend disliked Drake to such an extent, though she should have guessed.

Christian despised the English in a way that she had never completely understood. She loved liberty, embraced the hope America would one day govern herself, but she had never fully abhorred their mother country. Christian refused to tell her why he harbored such hostility, but she believed it had something to do with the untimely death of his mother. That Drake was both English and of noble birth made him a double target for Christian's antipathy.

She reached out and squeezed his hand in warning. "Be kind enough to remember that he's now my husband, Christian. I'll expect you to be civil, if not downright cordial."

Christian grunted. "You expect too much. The thought of you with that English popinjay makes me want to puke."

"Now there's a pretty sentiment on my *wedding* day," Elise said flatly. "Drake is not a popinjay. He's a wonderful, caring, loving man, who—"

Tabby hooted with laughter and clapped Christian on the back. "Listen to how protective she's become. You might as well keep your rancor to yourself. It's clear she's defected to the enemy."

"What are you implying, Tabby? I assure you I'm as a loyal as ever," Elise whispered, bristling with indignation.

"I didn't question your loyalty, my dear. I know you married for Prin's sake, not because you've turned Tory all of a sudden."

"The irony is rich, is it not?" Christian said mildly. He brushed a fly from his coat's honey-colored satin sleeve. "The rebel and the duke. I'm sure Amberly would love to know his wife is the mysterious—"

"Oh, do hush," Elise snapped. Her gaze darted to where her new husband spoke with Zechariah across the trimmed green lawn. Her eyes locked on Drake's handsome face. Her heart did a queer little flip of excitement and her breath faltered in her chest.

Tabby waved her palm in front of Elise's eyes. "I do believe she's been transported to another world."

Elise laughed self-consciously and turned back to her friends. "You're a terrible lot. Your baiting is most unfair."

"Hardly," Christian mocked, his tone as dry as a stone. "I can think of a great many things that are more unfair."

Tabby stepped in before Elise could rebut with a waspish reply. "What is wrong with you today, Christian? One would think you're a jilted suitor. Look at her face. You've wounded her, and for no reason. Elise has done nothing wrong. She's been true to her convictions, but she's a woman with limited choices. Like all of us, she wants to pursue a life of happiness and see her loved ones safe. In similar straights, I'm certain you'd act no differently."

Shamefaced, Christian nodded. Tabby entwined her arm with Elise's and led her away.

"Thank you, Tabby. At times, Christian can be such a mule."

"There's nothing to thank me for. Men usually forget they have more choices in this world. Sometimes they need a reminder, is all."

In deference to Tabby's delicate condition, they walked slowly, allowing Elise the chance to take in the scene surrounding her. Laughing children chased each other around the stately white church. One of them had brought a kite, and a handful of boisterous boys were busy tugging it free from an ill-placed pine.

"I wish Prin could have been here," Elise said quietly.

Tabby patted her hand. "It's to your credit that you care for the girl so well, for I know no other who would admit to such a relation. But your neighbors might have found it unseemly to have a slave present as a guest."

"I don't give a fig for their opinion on that score," Elise snorted.

"But you should," Tabby said sagely. "Consider how Prin would feel if she put in an appearance only to be shunned by others in attendance. As it is, she's safe and sound, tucked away at my house for the next few days. You need a day or two alone with your husband."

Elise bowed her head for a moment. "You're right, of course. People can be cruel. It's just…it's just that I'm nervous about…about tonight."

"Tonight?" Tabby exclaimed much too loudly for comfort.

"Lower your voice," Elise hurried to say. "Do you want me to die from mortification?"

Tabby flashed a wicked grin. "With a man such as your

new husband, I doubt you'll die from mortification. More like you'll die from happiness. In fact, if I weren't as big as a Holstein and so in love with my darling Josiah, I just might be jealous."

Elise didn't have a chance to comment. A group of matrons stopped to chat and congratulate her on catching such a fine figure of a man. While the ladies shared sewing tips and recipes, Elise nodded and responded at the appropriate times, but Drake owned her attention. Each time she stole a glance in his direction, she caught him with his shimmering eyes alight and watching her. The magnitude of his love engulfed her from clear across the churchyard and her own tender feelings echoed in reply.

The church bells tolled five. Drake broke away from his conversation with Zechariah and headed her way.

She watched him stride across the lawn, a little stunned by the depth of her emotion for him. How he'd managed to consume her life so quickly confused her, but there she was, thankful to God, indeed grateful, that such a splendid man had been sent her way.

When Drake reached her, he kissed the back of her hand, sending a stream of warmth up her arm that didn't stop until it infused her heart.

"It's time to leave, my love." He didn't give her an opportunity to protest. Instead, he guided her to the church's wrought-iron front gates. Cheers and a shower of white rose petals and rice followed them into an awaiting coach.

The coach rocked as Drake stepped up and took his place on the padded bench across from her. His lean, muscular frame dominated the rich interior. The scent of spice that clung to his skin mixed with the smell of the coach's new red leather seats.

Drake smiled, slow and smooth. His golden eyes roamed over her, reflecting the pride and pleasure he took in looking at her. "You're finally mine."

His voice reminded her of warm honey. Her mouth ran dry. With nerves stretched tighter than a sail in a blustery gale, she glanced out the window. She was Drake's wife now. By law, his possession to do with as he willed. She chewed her bottom lip and lowered her gaze to her clenched hands in her lap.

As eager as she was to be his wife, the situation filled her with fright, for she despised the idea of being owned— even by Drake. Ironically, her marriage had assured Prin's freedom while relieving her of her own.

Drake rapped on the coach's hardwood ceiling. Through the window she heard the driver cluck his tongue, spurring the team of matched grays into immediate motion. She leaned out the window, waving a last farewell to their guests.

The coach turned the corner. Her friends were out of sight. With nervous hands, she smoothed the front of her pale green gown. The well-sprung coach cruised along Meeting Street. She ran her hand over the smooth leather seat. Lifting her lashes, she flushed when she saw Drake studying her with an intense, unreadable expression.

"What's troubling you, Elise? You seem agitated. Are you having second thoughts about marrying me?"

"No, not really." The assurance stuck in her throat. "Are you?"

He seemed to relax, as though he'd been fighting a

battle within himself and finally won. Why he should be uneasy, she couldn't fathom. It was she who faced the unknown. He'd been married before.

"On the contrary, our marriage pleases me to no end. The only thing that would make me happier is if you take off your wig."

"What?" She blinked in confusion. "Why?"

"I want to see your hair. I believe I've developed a most intoxicating fascination for it and I haven't seen it for a whole week."

His heated gaze singed her, released a flurry of nervous butterflies in her stomach. Instead of protesting, she reached for the pins that held her wig in place. One by one, she slipped them from the hairpiece and placed them in the pale silk purse dangling from her wrist.

The atmosphere hummed between them. Her hands trembled as they removed the wig and set it on the seat beside her. She removed the skullcap holding her wig in place and shook out her heavy tresses until they curled about her shoulders and flowed down her back. "Does that please you?"

"Everything about you pleases me," he murmured.

A deep rut in the road sent her lurching forward. His strong hands encircled her waist before she could slam back down on the padded seat. Before she knew what he was about, he tugged her onto the seat beside him. He wrapped his arm around her shoulders, anchoring her to him as equal currents of love and devotion swirled through her.

The coach slowed to a stop. With a low growl of irritation, Drake lifted his head, a dark frown marring his brow at the interruption. They couldn't have reached the house he'd rented already. He was about to query the driver when the sound of muted but insistent voices alerted him to something amiss.

"Where are we?" Elise asked.

"I don't know as yet. If we're not underway in a moment more, I shall have to inquire." He brushed the window curtain aside and leaned out to take in the scene. A duo of British regulars and their sergeant waited on horseback along the city street, while another regular held the horses' reins.

"I don't care if it's the king 'imself," the sergeant barked from his saddle. "A fancy coach doesn't mean you can pass this way without the proper identification. We don't allow you colonial dogs in this section of town if we can 'elp it."

"But, sir," the driver protested. "I—"

"Allow me, Artie," Drake reached into his jacket pocket and withdrew a packet of neatly folded papers before handing them in the direction of the offending officer.

The redcoat released the horses and snatched the papers from Drake's extended hand. He passed them to his superior, who untied the documents and started to read. After a few tense moments, the officer lifted his eyes, his face devoid of his former insolence and as pale as the parchment he held in his shaking grasp. "I…I do *sincerely* apologize, Your Grace!" He jumped down from his saddle and bowed, nearly losing his black helmet in the process.

The other three soldiers lost their bored expressions the moment they heard Drake's title announced. The two on horseback bounded to the ground. In unison, all three bowed so low they almost toppled over, then snapped to attention in a way that Drake would have found comical under different circumstances.

Keenly aware Elise was in hearing distance, Drake fixed the sergeant with a cutting stare and extended his palm. "My documents, if you please. I trust I'm English enough for your tastes to carry on into this part of the city?"

"Yes, yes, of course, Your Grace." The soldier thrust the documents back to Drake as if they'd suddenly caught fire. "I do apologize for interrupting your journey, sir."

Within moments the coach leapt forward. Drake scowled as he slid his identification back into his breast pocket. "I'm sorry you were subjected to that sort of odious behavior, sweet."

"I'm used to those types of remarks, Drake. Some of His Majesty's soldiers are quite courteous, but the greater number of them are overbearing as that little snipe." She pulled back the lace curtain and looked out to see they were turning toward the heart of British Charles Towne.

Sliding the cloth back into place, she cocked her head and studied her new husband. It had bothered her sorely that he'd kept the news of his title from her.

"Why did the sergeant call you 'Your Grace'?" The coach lurched over a particularly large rut in the road and Elise reached for a leather strap near the window to maintain her seat. "Drake? Is there something important you haven't shared with me?"

Chapter Fourteen

"Drake?" Elise prodded over the clatter of horses' hooves. She held her breath, waiting for him to admit the truth. What a relief it would be to no longer have to hide her knowledge of his aristocratic status. "*Is* there something you should tell me?"

Her fingers bit into the silk-tufted side panel as the coach bounced over another rough patch of road. She'd almost abandoned hope of receiving an answer when he pinned her with a level stare.

"I must plead guilty, sweet. There is a matter in which I've been less than candid with you."

Her lips compressed. She lifted her chin, hoping she appeared sufficiently annoyed by his evasiveness. "And yet you've assured me I can trust you."

"You needn't concern yourself on that score. I'd never harm you on purpose," he promised. "What I've been remiss in sharing concerns my place in society, not me as a man."

"That sounds ominous." She aimed for a light note that would encourage a quick account from him.

"Hardly." His long fingers scraped back the soft black hair from his furrowed brow. "The long and short of it is that I possess a title, lands and the wealth bequeathed to such a heritage."

Though she'd anticipated his announcement, hearing the truth fall from his own lips sent a frisson of panic through her limbs. Somehow it hadn't seemed real that *her* Drake was a high and mighty lord of the British realm.

Quite suddenly he seemed like a mysterious stranger, foreign to everything she believed and held dear. With a delicate cough, she cleared her tight throat. "The soldier referred to you as 'Your Grace?'"

He tipped his noble head. "The fifth duke of Hawk Haven at your service, *Your* Grace."

She flinched as though he'd cast a slur upon her name. Light pierced the window lace, creating a silvery, speckled pattern that ebbed and flowed with the swaying coach. The curtain whipped in the breeze and she reached out to straighten it, grateful for something to fix upon besides his dark looks and her darker thoughts.

Elise knew she should exhibit some kind of emotion— joy, dismay, even anger for having such important information withheld from her—but at the moment her emotions were a torturous web of confusion.

The liberation she'd expected upon hearing his confession eluded her. A crushing weight settled on her shoulders and a perverse sense of guilt churned her stomach. How could she accept his confidences when she harbored so many secrets of her own?

"My situation is a trifle complicated," he continued. "I

hoped you would view your new status in light of the honor it is. But, I dare say, you appear less than gratified."

"I'm sorry. I'm a touch overwhelmed." Reminding herself that he *would* see the gift of a title as an honor, she fiddled with the ivory lace that edged her light green sleeve. "When were you going to share this news with me? Surely, it would have been more fitting *before* we wed?"

His eyes shifted to the window. "It may have been more opportune, but I had my reasons for silence."

"I must confess, I'm faint with curiosity. Why would you wish to keep something so important from me?"

"I wanted to be assured you wed me for no other reason than you cared for me alone."

"I do care for you," she was quick to assure him. "But if you're a duke, how can you wed *me,* a simple colonial girl?"

His expression softened. "You're anything but simple, though I *have* wondered why you play the simpleton on occasion."

She shrugged. "Most men prefer a woman of little brains."

"I don't. I prefer you just as you are. Don't ever hide yourself from me, Elise."

She nodded even as guilt washed through her. She'd never felt more of a liar. How she wished she could tell him all her secrets, but her loved ones' safety hung in the balance.

As the coach rumbled through the streets, he sighed. "Where was I?"

"You were explaining why you didn't tell me you're a peer."

"Ah, yes. My first wife married me because the king desired an alliance between my family and hers. She was in love with someone else and resented me from the first day of our marriage. As you can probably guess, there was no warmth between us. After she died, I was hard-pressed to notice she was gone."

Elise sat forward and took hold of his hand. Drake was a proud man. She knew it cost him to admit what must seem like a monumental failure in his eyes. "She didn't deserve you."

His grim smile said otherwise. "I should have tried harder."

"It takes two to try," she whispered.

He nodded and released a wary sigh. "Last year, I acquired a fiancée."

She gasped. "What happened?"

"I found her with a lover. She had agreed to wed me at her family's insistence—for my fortune and title."

"You must have been devastated!"

He shook his head. "Not in the least. My pride was bruised and I was angry, but not hurt. I'd sought to wed her for my own less than heartfelt reasons, though I would have been faithful and trustworthy."

"The girl must be an imbecile." She snorted. "Both of them were. I don't see how any sane woman couldn't help but love you."

He smiled, his white teeth flashing in the coach's dim interior. "Are you sane, then?"

Her cheeks flushed. "I was until I met you. Now, I'm just crazy about you."

"And I adore you," he assured her with more honesty than she'd ever encountered. "For the first time in my life I've found love."

Her heart swelled with tenderness and her throat closed with emotion. "It's the same for me, too."

He bent his head to kiss her, but the coach began to slow and rolled to a stop. Drake flashed a wry grin. "Barring the possibility of additional overzealous redcoats, I believe we've arrived at the house I arranged for our use. We'll be residing here until we make for England."

Elise peered out the window for a better view of the whitewashed brick three-story townhouse. Aged magnolia trees provided shade in the trimmed front yard, and potted white roses flanked either side of the gleaming red front door. "And how long might that be?"

"God willing, not much longer," he said. "I've been absent from Hawk Haven for half a year. My sister will be anxious to see me."

"Why must we remain in South Carolina at all?" She tried not to sound overeager, but she wouldn't feel completely safe until she and her family were far away from everyone who knew their secrets. "Why not sail for London as soon as possible?"

His sculpted face turned hard as flint. "Soon, sweet. I'm not quite finished with a few business matters here in Charles Towne."

The driver opened the coach door, eyes averted to the road. Drake jumped down first, then raised his arms to help Elise alight.

The moment Drake's hands encircled her waist, her nerves jangled in giddy alarm. Without pause, he swept her into his arms. The air whooshed from her lungs in a hearty, startled laugh as she looped her arms around the strong column of his neck.

His joy palpable, he raced up the brick walk to the front door. The door swung wide as though welcoming them of its own accord. The scents of roses, herbs and roasting beef greeted them. They were inside the wide entryway before Elise looked over Drake's shoulder to see who'd opened the door.

A stout woman of about three score or more thrust the door closed, casting the front hall into twilight. Her broad smile made her eyes mere slits above her weathered apple-red cheeks. Wiping her hands on her apron, she bobbed curtsy after curtsy while she spoke in brisk German.

"What did she say?" Elise whispered from her lofty height in Drake's arms. "I didn't understand."

Drake grinned down at her. "This is Frau Einholt, the housekeeper. She's welcoming us to our new home. She said there's a light repast ready for us to enjoy whenever we like, and the trunks you sent from Brixton Hall have been unpacked."

He paused, listening as the robust woman chirped with animated enthusiasm. "She's congratulating me on my fine choice of bride."

Elise smiled and thanked the housekeeper for the compliment. The beaming woman curtsied again, obviously understanding some English even if she didn't speak it.

When Drake answered in German, Elise waited for the translation, but none came. He'd started up the curved staircase before she asked, "What did you tell her just now? I know it was something improper. The two of you shared a most mischievous laugh."

They reached the second floor and he placed her on her

feet. "She wished us good fortune, long life and a house full of sons. I thanked her, 'tis all."

Elise eyed him with playful suspicion. "There's something more. I'm sure of it. What else did you tell her?"

Drake chuckled. "It's ill indeed when a new wife distrusts her husband."

She tried to sound stern. "Tell me what else you said, Drake Amberly."

He didn't answer. Instead, he caught her to him, pressed open a door behind him, and pulled her into a large candlelit chamber. "I merely mentioned we plan to begin work on filling the house full of sons tonight."

Chapter Fifteen

The next morning Elise dressed and left the room to join Drake downstairs for breakfast. Her cheeks heated when she recalled Drake's tenderness as he'd made her his wife. She'd never felt more cherished. With a grateful heart she thanked the Lord for letting them find each other. It truly was a miracle when she considered their opposing circumstances.

Drake met her at the bottom of the stairs. The riding crop he held suggested he'd been to the stables. His billowy white shirt open at the neck revealed a hint of bronzed throat. His golden eyes searched her face with tender concern. "Hello, sweet. How do you fare this morn?"

"I'm most well," she said, a little breathless. "And you, my dearest husband?"

His smile warmed her heart. He took her hands in his and brushed his lips across her knuckles in a gentle kiss. "I've never been happier. I knew you were the woman for me that first day we sailed for Charles Towne."

"So soon?" she asked in surprise. "How did you know?"

He led her across the hall to the morning room and seated her at a table laden with fresh bread, cheese and fruit. "When a man's been searching for his match as long as I have, he knows her the moment he spies her."

The word *spy* sent a shiver of fear down her spine. Some of her merriment dimmed. A pessimistic voice in her head reminded her that Drake loved Elise Cooper, the ward of a Tory plantation owner, not Elise Cooper, the patriot spy. What would he do if he ever discovered her past as the Fox? Would he understand and move on with their lives, or would he see her treason to the crown as an unforgivable betrayal and set her aside?

"Elise?" Drake knelt on one knee beside her chair. "Did I say something wrong?"

Her gaze slipped to his face and his concerned frown. Thick dark lashes fringed his questioning eyes. The thought of losing him formed a painful lump in her throat. She cupped his cheek with her palm, determined to cast off the haunting questions and do her best to make him happy.

"No, you've said everything just right."

He stood and pulled her to her feet. "Good, because I have one more gift for you before we eat."

"Another gift?" She ran her thumb over the back of the smooth wedding band he'd given her to mark their marriage. "But I don't have one for you."

He nuzzled her neck and nibbled her ear. "I want you, nothing else."

Her gaze softened as she traced the sculpted line of his

lower lip. "You really are the most wonderful man I've ever known."

His eyes glowed with love. "Come, sweet, your gift is outside." He held out a hand to her and led her down the wide hall and past the sitting rooms. She might as well have been floating, she felt so light and happy. He held the back door open as she emerged into an open-air courtyard of curved brick walkways and a circular center garden. Fresh, fragrant herbs, including her favorite, rosemary, perfumed the warm summer morning.

A stable stood across the courtyard some distance away, and the faint whinny of horses drifted across the expanse toward them. Drake led her onward. The earthy smell of horses and hay grew stronger the closer they came. Once inside, Drake lit a lantern, illuminating the stable's spacious interior. Drake's shiny new coach sat to the left. Huge bales of hay stood stacked to the beamed ceiling, and various articles of horse tack hung along the walls.

Drake's pair of matched grays stood in individual stalls next to each other, but it was the bay gelding toward the back that brought tears of happiness to her eyes. "Freedom? You're giving me Freedom?"

He shrugged fluently. "I know you love him. Seemed a bit of lunacy to leave him behind."

Elise shrieked with joy and threw her arms around Drake's neck, squeezing him tight.

Freedom whinnied and kicked at the door of his stall. She crossed the sandy floor and reached out to stroke his forehead. The onslaught of happy tears tickled her nose. "Hello, my dear friend. I thought I'd lost you."

The horse nickered and pressed the side of his head into her palm.

Drake moved close behind her and settled his hands on her shoulders. "I believe he missed you, too."

Elise melted into Drake's embrace. "How did you convince Zechariah to sell him? When I tried to buy him, he wouldn't hear of it."

Drake kissed the top of her head, and stroked her hair. "You're not as persuasive as I am, apparently."

"Drake, how much—"

"Truth be told, Sayer seemed almost desperate to be rid of you. When I told him I refused to consider marriage without the horse included in the bargain, he seemed quite eager to part with the old boy."

She gave him a watery smile and sniffed. "I couldn't ask for a more perfect gift."

"Then why the tears?"

"I don't think I've ever been this happy. Thank you," she whispered, standing on tiptoes to give him a kiss. "Thank you with all my heart."

"Isn't Moira the most beautiful child you've ever seen?" Tabby chirped with maternal pride. "It's hard to believe she's seven weeks old."

"Indeed, it is," Elise said, cradling the Smiths' new arrival. "Such wide blue eyes and what perfect, cherubic cheeks. She's a darling. Don't you agree, Prin?"

Prin turned from the window of Tabby's parlor, where she'd been watching the quiet street. The blue-and-yellow striped curtains fluttered into place as she moved toward the unlit fireplace. "She's sweet as maple sugar, that one. You and Mister Josiah should be peacock proud."

"We are." Tabby beamed. She scooped the baby from Elise's arms and sat in a nearby rocking chair.

Elise leaned back on the settee and patted the seat next to her. "Come sit with me, Prin. There's plenty of room for us both."

When her sister joined her, Elise gently squeezed her hand in encouragement. She knew that along with feeling ill from her pregnancy, Prin longed for Kane. A cloud of melancholy followed her sister no matter how much she tried to be strong and act as if nothing were wrong.

"You know," Tabby said to Elise, "you've been married nearly two months. Folks will be expecting you to be with child before too long."

Elise's cup clattered as she returned it to the saucer. "It's too soon, surely."

Tabby and Prin shared a telling glance.

"After weeks of marriage with your dazzling husband," Tabby teased, "I can't believe you've not considered the possibility."

"I try not to think about it," Elise said, her unease with the topic difficult to conceal. "I may not have a choice, but until I know Prin and I are completely out of danger, I'd rather not have to consider a babe."

"That's wise," Tabby agreed as she ran a fingertip along her daughter's cheek. "I don't think there's anything I wouldn't do to keep this precious girl from harm. But as you say, you may not have a choice."

The discussion struck a chord of fear in Elise. If she became pregnant, Zechariah would have one more weapon in his arsenal against her. He'd used her love for Prin enough times in the past to convince her he wouldn't be above using her child. She could hear his threats in her mind. "Elise," he would say, "bring me this information or I may be forced to turn you over to the British. Think. What will your child do without his mother?"

"Elise?" Tabby intruded her troubling thoughts. "Is all well with you? Why, you look positively violent."

"Do I?" She pasted on a smile. "I'm fine, really. Just a little tired."

Her friend giggled. "Not been getting enough sleep, eh?"

Prin set her cup aside and studied Elise with concern. "Perhaps we should be headin' home?"

"Don't leave yet." Tabby stood and placed her sleeping daughter in a cradle dressed with frills and white lace. "Zechariah will be arriving soon. He wishes to speak with you."

Elise bit her lower lip. She'd been avoiding her spymaster and wished to continue in that vein. While at a dinner party a fortnight ago, she'd learned news that might be of interest to him, but her loyalty to Drake made her loath to share it. "Why didn't you tell me, Tabby?"

"He asked me not to." She tucked baby Moira in one of the blankets Elise had knitted for her. "I thought it strange, but then supposed there must be a reason."

A light knock sounded on the door and a servant stepped through once Tabby called him in.

"Ma'am, Mr. Sayer is here to see you."

"Thank you, Henry. Show him through."

A few moments later, Zechariah waddled in. After he

performed a shallow bow, Tabby motioned him into a chair, which barely held his girth once he rolled into it.

"Prin," Tabby said. "Let's you and I take the baby and our tea tray to the garden. The oaks will give us plenty of shade to escape this dreadful heat."

Prin waited until Elise nodded her approval before picking up the tray and following Tabby into the hall. Henry followed and closed the door.

Zechariah studied Elise, his gaze as sharp as a well-honed dagger. He leaned forward and rested his hands on the ball of his walking stick. "You look fit enough, girl. Marriage seems to agree with you."

She folded her hands in her lap and held his gaze without flinching. "Yes, it does."

"That lad you married is treating you well, then?"

"Very well indeed."

There was a slight pause as Zechariah inspected his shoe's square, brass buckle. "You may not believe this, m'dear, but I've been most concerned about you."

Elise's brow rose in cynical inquiry.

"You may think I enjoy manipulating your life, but such is not the case. I—"

"Forgive me, Zechariah, but I've been the subject of your machinations more times than I can count. You've conspired against me so often I find it hard to believe you have a true care for my welfare."

"'Tis why I'm here, Elise. I have news you'll wish to hear." He tapped the tip of his walking stick against the floor, giving her time to snatch in several breaths. "Actually, I've come for two reasons today."

"I'm surprised you haven't come to call before now."

"I might have, but you've been avoiding me since you wed. Don't think I haven't noticed. It's a shame I had to trick Tabby into helping me or I doubt I'd be seeing you today."

Elise reddened, but didn't deny it.

Zechariah cleared his throat. "You've had ample time to retrieve information to aid the cause. I'm here to collect it."

Elise jumped to her feet, her bountiful green skirt swirling as she swung toward the open window. "I have little to tell you."

"Some is better than nil. Spit it out, and be quick about it. If you think to break our bargain I'll be forced—"

"To call in the British," she sneered with ferocious bite. She wondered if she'd ever be free of that particular threat. "I'll have you know I do have news I'm willing to impart. Not because of your threat, but because contrary to what you suppose, I love this land as much as you. From the beginning, I would have freely shared the knowledge I gleaned, but you chose to dangle Prin's freedom over my head and use threats to bend me to your will."

"By what other means could I be sure—"

"Be quiet," she snapped.

To her surprise, he fell back in his chair, sputtering and indignant, but eventually silent.

"Before I share what I've uncovered, I'm adding to our bargain." She straightened her spine and thrust back her shoulders in a silent dare for him to refuse her. "I wish to purchase Kane from you."

"Impossible." The old man shook his head, setting his jowls to flapping.

"'Tis a simple transaction, why is it impossible? I'm willing to pay you double his worth."

His gaze slunk to the floor. "I may have need of him yet."

Elise narrowed her eyes, savvy to his ways enough to suspect he'd planned something reprehensible.

"You think I don't know about him and Prin or the *illegal* marriage you arranged for them. But I assure you, girl, I know everything that happens on my plantation."

She threw up her hands. "I can't believe it! You intend to bargain with his freedom in order to bend me to your will at some future date?"

"I know you and your soft heart," he admitted. "If Prin longed for him enough, you'd do whatever was required to get him for her."

"You're despicable." Her upper lip curled in disgust. "Always playing with people's lives as if they're pieces in some game."

"On the contrary. I'm just determined," he said without remorse. "But that's neither here nor there. You've mentioned you have news. I believe the war situation is desperate enough for extreme measures. My contacts tell me Washington is stalemated with Clinton in New York and Cornwallis is like a plague of fire weaving his way through Virginia. Share your information and I'll have Kane, his freedom papers signed and sealed, sent to you this eve."

Hope sparked in her chest. She lifted her chin. "How can I be certain?"

"You wound me, child. You may not like my methods, but when have I ever lied to you?"

He hadn't that she knew of. "I have your word?"

"Aye." He held out his palm. "You have it. Your information in exchange for Kane's freedom."

Wary, she shook his hand. "At dinner a fortnight ago, I heard it mentioned that General Clinton has called Cornwallis to leave the southern colonies altogether and aid him in New York. It seems Clinton fears Patriot forces plan to attack before the onslaught of winter."

"It will take weeks for Cornwallis to march to New York."

She shook her head. "No, he and his army are to wait in Yorktown for the British fleet to transport them north."

Zechariah slapped his knee suddenly and hooted with excitement. "Do you know what this means, my girl? Lafayette is camped in Virginia. If I can send word to him and his army there, he can notify Washington and Rochambeau's combined forces farther north. If the armies converge—"

"We might win a major battle this year."

"God willing, we might capture Cornwallis's whole army and win the war." His eyes began to twinkle with excitement. He levered himself to his feet and made his way for the door. "Good day to you, Your Grace." He grinned as he reached for the brass doorknob. "I knew wedding you off to Amberly would bring us a bout of luck."

"Wait. You said you had two items to discuss with me. So far, we've spoken of just one."

"Ah, yes, I forgot. The Fox is in trouble."

"The Fox is dead," she said adamantly. "He ceased to exist the day I married."

Zechariah clamped his hands behind his back and

rocked on his heels. "That may be, but it seems he has a persistent admirer who refuses to let him rest in peace. Several months back I received reports that an individual was offering a reward for the Fox's capture. At the time, I thought nothing of it. After all, who among the British wouldn't like to see the Fox hang? But, a short time ago, just a few days before your marriage, in fact, it seems that original sum was tripled."

"Tripled?" she asked curiously. "What was the original amount?"

He paused. "Five hundred pounds."

"Five *hundred?* You must be jesting!"

"I wish I were, my dear, but there it is. Whoever is hunting you means serious business. Fifteen hundred pounds is enough to make any man consider.... Why, even I was tempted to turn you in for such a fortune."

Elise dropped into a nearby chair.

"Don't go all female on me, girl. You've lost every scrap of color. I'm not likely to do it, you know. At least, not without good reason."

Robin Goss shivered in the moldy dampness of his warehouse cell. Rats squeaked in the dark, and their scurrying feet scratched along the wood floor. He bellowed in frustration as he strained against the rope around his wrists, but the dank rag in his mouth muffled the feral sound.

He cursed the day he'd found the woman's traitorous letters in his carriage. His last remaining hope was that he would someday escape, hunt her down and make her pay.

A key rattled in the lock. Disgusted by the stab of excitement that lanced through him, he realized he'd been held in this pit long enough to appreciate the sight of any human face, even one of his hated captors.

The door swung wide. One of his kidnappers, the one he'd heard called "John," entered carrying a lantern and tray of steaming food. A homespun mask covered his face. Black gloves protected his ham-sized hands. The smell of mustard greens, bacon and cornbread briefly cloaked the smell of rotting fish, making his mouth water.

"How's our pris'ner, this fine night?" John snickered under his breath as he dropped the tray on the table. "I'm thinkin' you must be hungry considerin' I'm late this eventide."

Robin tried to swallow. He was starving. His eyes followed the movement of the dishes as John laid them out on a rickety bench, the cell's only piece of furniture.

John crouched before him and removed the gag. Robin heaved in a lungful of salty air. "Can I eat?" The words burned over his parched throat.

"'Course, but there'll be no exercise tonight," John said, untying the ropes that bound Robin's wrists and ankles. "I'm wantin' a pint before I head home to the missus."

"Sorry to be such an inconvenience," Robin muttered. "Let me go and I won't bother you again."

John grunted with laughter. "Don't be daft." His huge hand jabbed toward the food. "Now, eat up a'fore you lose your chance."

Robin stood slowly, his leg muscles tight from sitting in one position on the hard floor all day. He eyed his captor, studying the big man, wondering, not for the first time, if he could take him in a fight.

"Don't even think it," John warned, patting the pistol that bulged in his pocket. "Matthew is waitin' just outside the door. He's armed heavier 'an me and hankerin' to shoot himself a traitorous spy."

"I'm not the traitor," Robin sneered. "These colonies belong to King George. I'm doing my part to see they stay that way."

John's nostrils flared with obvious fury. "Well then, it does my heart good to know you're tied up in here where you can't do more damage. Now, eat the food and shut your stupid mouth! I got no patience for your Tory prattle."

Robin shoveled the food with his fingers while he fumed. Each hearty mouthful fortified him a little more. He washed the meal down with the provided mug of ale. "I need to relieve myself," he told John. John stretched and ambled toward the door. "I'll count to thirty. You'd best be high and dry by then."

Raising his hand in a mock salute, Robin waited for his captor to leave before he positioned himself by the door. Ole John had grown lax. He'd never left him untied and alone before. When his captor returned to bind him this time he was in for a nasty surprise. Once he escaped, Robin promised Captain Beaufort would get an earful.

"…twenty-eight, twenty-nine, thirty." John shouted as he burst through the door, his pistol at the ready.

Robin pounced from the corner. His arm wrapped around John's thick neck, snapping it so quickly the man didn't have a chance to cry out. John wilted to the floor, dragging Robin with him. The pistol bounced on the planks. Robin yanked his arm from around his captor's neck, grabbed the pistol, and rolled to his feet.

Matthew burst into the room, brandishing his own weapon. Robin fired. Matthew yelped. When the smoke cleared, Matthew was on his knees, gasping for breath, a look of stunned horror on his ashen face.

Robin spared a moment to watch Matthew's lifeblood drain from the hole in his chest. He couldn't help smiling. He was free again after months of rotting in this pit.

Matthew slumped face-first to the floor. Robin stepped over the dead man and raced out the door.

Chapter Sixteen

Robin Goss pushed his way through the jostling crowd of the smoke-filled Ax and Hammer tavern. The Scottish barkeep, Michael MacClean, set down the stein he was drying and eyed him with suspicion.

"Don't you recognize me, Mac? It's Robin," he yelled over the fiddle music and raucous conversation that threatened to dislodge the rafters.

"*Robin?* Robin Goss?" the barkeep hollered as though blinders had been ripped from his eyes. "I didna' recognize you with that bedraggled mane hidin' yer face. Where you been, laddie? It's months since I saw you last."

Robin's buckteeth bit into his lower lip. His fingers clenched the sticky counter. "Rebels nicked me off the street and stowed me in a warehouse not three blocks from here."

"Those filthy traitors!"

"Aye, they were, but they've seen the light," Robin said darkly. "What's the date, Mac?"

"The twenty-ninth of September." The Scot glanced at the mantel clock. "For another few hours anyway."

"Two stinkin' months." Robin wiped his bearded chin with the back of his filthy hand. His confinement had given him plenty of time to recall the day he'd been kidnapped, the traitorous female spy he'd uncovered, and her accomplices at The Rolling Tide, including its owner, Josiah Smith. He had no doubt that she and Smith were behind his imprisonment.

Killing John and Matthew had only whetted his appetite for vengeance. Hatred burned in his belly until the need to strangle the wench threatened to tear him in two. "They kept me locked in that rat hole over two rotten months!"

"I believe you." Mac stepped back, picked up a towel, and began to dry a stoneware plate. "Nothin' else would explain why you look so beastly and smell vile enough ta make yer mother cry."

Robin's lips compressed in vexation. "Keep your sweet talk to yourself and pour me a drink, old man. I'm so dry I've got sawdust clogging my veins."

Mac slid him a pint, sloshing foam over the mug's pewter rim.

Robin took a long swig of the bitter brew. He leaned back against the counter as he looked over the sea of English revelers. Sailors jigged to the Irish fiddles while a group of army officers gambled in the protective shadows of a corner table.

Robin cocked his head, studying each officer through the lantern light and smoky haze.

"Who you lookin' for?" Mac boomed over a bagpipe that wailed in competition with the fiddles.

"Captain Beaufort," Robin shouted. "I went to his office

across the way, but he's quit for the night. I thought I might find him here."

Mac shook his head as he handed a barmaid a tray full of overflowing mugs. "I havna seen him in nigh a month."

Robin drained his tepid ale, but it did little to quench the rage in his belly. He slammed the empty mug onto the bar and turned to leave.

"Have a care, laddie," the Scotsman warned, staying Robin with a tight grip on his wrist. "That'll be two pence."

Shaking free of the barkeep's tight grip, Robin warned him off with a level stare and jammed his hand into his grimy pocket, remembering too late he was poor as dirt. "I'll have to owe you, Mac."

The barkeep's eyes narrowed with anger. "And will you be askin' yer pa for funds then?"

"No." Robin's voice landed with finality. His father had told him to put his education to use. He wasn't to return to Lowell Plantation until he'd made something respectable of himself. Becoming a Tory spy, disguised as a carriage driver, was a far cry from what his patriot father considered acceptable. "I'll get Beaufort to lend me a bag of coin."

Mac guffawed. "He won't be handin' out silver unless you become one of those Fox hunters of his. You've been away, so you may no' have heard—the ransom's tripled. Fifteen hundred pounds is enough to make the soberest of gents tipsy with the want of it."

"Fifteen hundred pounds!"

"Aye. You heard me right, laddie."

"And no one's found the scum yet?"

"No one." Mac picked up another mug to dry. "You'd

think that amount o' money would spark some clever soul into finding the vermin, but from the whispers I've heard, the leads have all dried up. Most think the Fox has left Charles Towne altogether. Perhaps gone to Williamsburg or the swamps to aid that other sly one, Francis Marion, and his militia of rebel slime."

Robin's imagination teemed with possibilities as he stroked his matted beard. Could the spies he'd uncovered at The Rolling Tide somehow lead him to the Fox? Could he watch Josiah Smith, wait him out until he learned enough of the tavern owner's secrets to force him to his will? For fifteen hundred pounds, it was worth a try.

A current of elation danced through Robin, bringing a sudden, hateful smile to his lips. The promise of combined retribution and revenge spurred him to the tavern's iron-hinged front door. Over his shoulder, he shouted, "I will repay you, Mac—with interest. I just need a little time."

Alone in the parlor, Elise attempted to read her well-worn Bible. The rays of the late afternoon sun flooded through the windows behind her, illuminating the yellowed pages, but her mind refused to concentrate and the words blurred together.

Dropping the book on her lap, she spread her hands over her flat stomach. Tabby's banter yesterday had made Elise admit the truth. She was with child. Last month she'd missed her monthly and now she was a week late again.

Joy flickered to life deep inside her. She was carrying Drake's child. A soft smile turned her lips as she imagined the tiny hands and feet knitting together within her womb. Even the threat Zechariah posed to her happiness couldn't snuff out the wonder lifting her spirits.

"Hello, sweet." Drake strode into the room as though her thoughts had called him home. His exuberant energy brought the large, airy parlor to life. Tall and strong, he lacked only an earring and cutlass to personify a pirate she'd once read about. Black breeches and leather riding boots molded the muscular length of his calves. The embroidered neckline of his stark white shirt highlighted the swarthiness of his skin and silky black hair. He was a dessert for the senses and he simply stole her breath away.

He deposited a leather satchel on the mahogany desk near the door and poured himself a drink. The smoldering look in his honeyed eyes told her how glad he was to see her.

"I must say, Your Grace, you look tempting enough to eat."

She rolled her eyes, but couldn't stop the smile that spread across her lips. Sliding the Bible onto the table beside her, she blushed under his affectionate perusal.

He tipped the glass in her direction. "What were you reading?"

"My Bible."

His brow furrowed in surprise. "What passage?"

"Romans eight. It's one of my favorites." Her hand caressed the worn leather Bible. "I find it's a true comfort in times of trouble to know no matter where I go or what I do, I can never be separated from Christ's love."

"Are you troubled, Elise?"

"Not when you're here," she said with a smile. "And what of you? Do you have a favorite passage?"

He turned thoughtful. "I supposed of late, it would be the story of the prodigal son. When I was younger, I trusted in the Lord. After my sour marriage and the untimely deaths of my parents and older brother, I stopped believing in God's mercy. Then I met you, and I've had much cause to thank Him ever since."

The knowledge warmed her. "I'm glad I've had a part in bringing you back to your faith."

"You've brought about a good many things in my life."

Touched that he should think so, she blinked back sudden tears. "Just promise me you won't turn your back on God again if something should happen to me in the future."

His cheerfulness faded. "I refuse to think of my life without you."

"Please promise me," she insisted.

He nodded. "I promise."

"Thank you." She smiled brightly. "Now, tell me where you have been all day. You were sorely missed."

He leaned against the mahogany cabinet behind him and regarded her with a spark of mischief in his eyes. "'Tis good to hear. A man *should* be missed by his wife."

She plucked at the gold fringe of a pillow she held and watched him from under her lashes. "I didn't say *I* missed you."

His brow arched with mock severity. "How in the world did I acquire such a lippy duchess?"

"I don't know." She grinned. "Good fortune?"

His rich voice took on a husky timbre. "Indeed, the very best."

Sweet affection filled her senses. She'd been more than blessed to wed such an excellent man. The terror she'd had of marriage thanks to her mother's misfortune with Roger was well and truly gone, buried under the onslaught of Drake's constant love and attention.

She patted the seat beside her. He prowled toward her like a man intent on ravishment. Her heart hammered against her ribs in anticipation of his touch.

As he brushed aside the layers of her skirt and petticoats, he claimed his share of the plum-and-gold-striped settee. "To answer your question, I've spent an unfortunate day in Beaufort's witless company."

She wrinkled her nose in distaste. "You told me he's your cousin, but if he irritates you, why must you spend so much time with him?"

"Before we wed, I mentioned that I'm hunting for someone while I'm here in the Colonies. Beaufort is supposedly aiding me. The longer I'm here, I grow less and less certain."

"Ah." She laced her fingers with his and brushed her thumb across his knuckles. "Who is the unfortunate soul you're looking for?"

His expression turned dark, almost savage. "My brother's murderer."

She gasped. Sympathy welled up inside her. Through their talks she'd learned how much Drake loved his family, how protective he was and how serious he took his duty toward them. She twisted in her seat and cupped his cheek with her palm. "I'm so sorry. You told me you'd like to find the culprit, but didn't say you were looking for him here. Tell me more. Perhaps I can help in some way."

He stretched out his long legs and crossed them at the ankles. "There's nothing you can do, sweet, and frankly, I refuse to dwell on the miscreant any longer today. I have more enjoyable things in mind. Come here."

Eager to obey, she swayed into his arms. He smelled of warm spices and sunshine. Beneath her palm, his heart picked up speed. His arms banded about her, pulling her close as though he'd been waiting all day just to hold her.

A sharp rap on the door made Elise jump. Prin burst into the room.

"Lisie, I… I'm sorry." Her sister reversed course, yanking the door closed as she backed out in embarrassment.

"Prin, wait!" Elise struggled off Drake's lap.

Prin peered around the door, a look of apology in her huge brown eyes. She massacred a curtsy and bowed for good measure. "I'm sorry. I thought you were alone. I jus' wanted to let you know that me and Kane are headed to the market. It's late, but Frau Einholt says she's needin' some cornmeal if we can come by any. Did you want me to fetch anythin' special for you?"

"I need nothing at the moment." Elise looked to Drake, who studied Prin with narrowed eyes. "Do you, darling?"

Drake declined and Prin hurried to leave. When the door clicked shut, Drake called Elise back to her place on the settee beside him. Something in his manner was different. She couldn't put her finger on what, but she suspected it had to do with Prin.

His arm tightened around her shoulders and tucked her close to his side. "Something intrigues me, Elise. I hope you can help me puzzle it out."

The room's mellowed light made it difficult for her to see his expression. She drew a pillow back onto her lap and hugged it to her middle. "I'll always aid you whenever I can."

"It has to do with your maid."

"My maid?" she braced herself. "What would you like to know about her?"

Quite deviously, as if he thought she wouldn't notice, his fingers eased one of the pins from her hair and then another. "There. That's better."

He sounded so pleased with himself. She shook her head in amusement, causing the thick skeins to tumble around her shoulders. She'd grown used to his obsession with her hair. Since the first week of their marriage, she'd given up on having it arranged in a decent style if Drake was within arm's length.

"Now, about your maid," he continued. "I'd like you tell me the truth about her."

"The truth?"

"Yes, the truth." He stroked her hair. "Mind you, I haven't seen her often, as she seems to hide from me, but I have noticed a marked resemblance between the two of you, except for her darker skin and curly hair, of course. Is she somehow a relation? It strikes me that she's much too familiar with you and rarely behaves like a maid if she believes I'm absent. When she does stumble upon me, she regards me as if I'm his majesty's master of the whipping post come to whisk her away for a sound lashing."

Elise didn't know whether to laugh or cry, but the time had come to tell him the truth about Prin. "She's my half sister, and you might as well know, the giant trailing her about is her new husband. They were married in secret the week before you and I met. Zechariah allowed me to buy

Kane yesterday. They're expecting a child this winter." The words flowed with more ease than she'd imagined, lifting the heavy weight of one of her secrets from her shoulders. "I apologize if Prin's made you uncomfortable. She doesn't know how to behave around you. She loves you for making me happy, but neither of us knew how you'd react to the truth. I've wanted to tell you a hundred times—"

"Then why didn't you?"

She searched his face, but could read nothing in the lean, hard lines of his expression. She grappled for the right words, tried to explain without making him angry. "Can't you guess? I've never known anyone to understand my feelings for Prin. Even Tabby was scandalized when I first told her. It's as though no one sees beyond the shade of her skin. She was a slave so I'm expected to ignore our sisterhood, forget she's the one person I've loved and depended on all my life.

"Our family's past is ugly," she continued. Embarrassed, but determined to admit the full truth, she left his side, afraid to see his reaction. "Prin's mother belonged to our father. She was his housekeeper and he forced her to be his mistress. Prin is four years older than I. When we were children she protected me from father's…unpleasantness."

His silence greeted her confession. She glanced up to find his reflection in the looking glass. Fury glittered in his gaze before he stood and turned his back on her. She clutched the pillow she'd brought with her from the settee like a shield; afraid she'd misjudged how he'd react.

She shouldn't feel betrayed, she reminded herself.

She'd been the one to keep secrets. It wasn't acceptable to claim a slave as a relation. Why, when no one else had ever understood her loyalty and love for Prin, did she expect Drake to feel any different? Worse, he was a duke. His family tree stemmed back to Creation, mingled with royalty and most likely had nary a hint of scandal in its branches.

She turned and studied his back. Poker-straight, his legs braced and his hands locked behind him, he took a deep breath before he faced her. His ire emanated in waves. She cringed. All her past experiences with this kind of anger had resulted in a beating or a tongue-lashing. She set down the pillow and backed away, primed to escape.

Drake must have guessed her intention. "Where are you going?"

"I'm not blind to your fury, Drake. I won't stay here and allow you to unleash it on me."

He could not have looked more stunned if she'd punched him in the nose. "You must be joking. I would never raise my hand to you. I think, however, I've finally hit upon the truth as to why you didn't confide in me about your sister—you still don't trust me."

"Not true!" she protested. "I do, but—"

"Don't think I haven't noticed there's a part of yourself—a secret self—you keep hidden away from me." He dragged his fingers through his hair, his shoulders stiff with tension. "I am more than angry, I am furious, but not with you, you silly woman."

"Not with me?" Her throat convulsed over a jagged lump of shock. "Then who?"

He shook his head as though he couldn't believe he'd

wed such a simpleton. "Your father, your neighbors, anyone who has ever caused you the slightest amount of pain." His fist slammed into his open palm. "I'd like to crush them all."

Disbelief held her in thrall. Never had anyone been outraged on her behalf. With the greatest care, he pulled her against him. His voice dipped low and brushed along her nerves, soothing her as though she were still the child who'd hid in fear from her father's drunken rages.

"Elise, there's nothing you needn't tell me. I want to know your every thought, your every dream. I would do battle for you, fight for you until my dying breath."

Snuggling against him, she basked in his embrace while her thoughts lined up like opposing armies within her head. He could make promises because he didn't know her darkest secrets. She trembled at the thought of him discovering her past and turned her back on the mental promptings that advised her to confide in him. Her love for Drake was too precious to risk losing with a confession that, she reminded herself once again, would soon be moot.

"I'm glad to hear it," she whispered, warmed by his declaration that he would fight for her. "Our child and I couldn't bear to live without you."

"You would never have to, I..." He stopped, blinking in stunned amazement. "What child?"

She looked up into his face to judge his reaction as she pressed his palm flat against her stomach. "This one," she said softly. "The one we're expecting in about seven months' time."

His delight was immediate. Joy reflected in his eyes, his smile, the gentle, almost reverent way he clasped her to him. "My life improves each day you're a part of it. Thank you, my love, for making me the happiest of men."

Elise sat at the opposite end of the dining-room table, too far away for Drake's liking. He wanted her within arm's length, close enough to touch her at all times.

He picked up his goblet, admiring how her green eyes were bright and lively, her soft cheeks rosy with happiness.

The knowledge that she carried his child filled Drake with enormous pride and a primitive need to protect her. Love, hot and fierce, rippled through him, growing with each beat of his heart. She was everything to him. A gift from God to heal his jaded soul and bring his heart to life again.

Wanting to please her, he'd shunned convention and insisted Prin and Kane join them for dinner that night. They'd just finished their coffee. Prin had begun to relax, another blessing from the Lord. Her fidgeting had resulted in only a few minor spills—nothing that soaking the starched white tablecloth in lye soap for a week wouldn't fix.

Drake turned to Kane. "So, my good man, now that you're free, how do you plan to earn your way and support my lovely sister-in-law here?"

Elise stilled. Prin went round-eyed with curiosity, whilst Kane's hand shook as he set down his sterling silver spoon, careful not to clang it against the delicate rim of his fruit bowl. Squaring his shoulders, the former slave spoke with quiet dignity that didn't quite conceal his worry on the matter. "I don't rightly know, suh. I been a slave all my life. I worked the Sayers' fields since I was a child and for the last five years, I managed 'em under the overseer's guidin' hand. Thanks to Miss Lisie and Prin, I knows how to read and write a little. I can do sums in my head and on paper, but—" he looked Drake straight in the eye "—I don't know a white man in the whole south who'd hire a black man when he could buy hisself one."

"You may be right," Drake leaned back in his chair. He stole a glance at his wife, amazed by her strength of character and generous nature. He suspected there were few who would bother teaching a slave how to read. "I suppose it's a good thing I'm English. I have a proposition for you."

Confusion marked Kane's weather-worn black face. "I'm sorry, suh, but I don't take your meanin'."

"I'd like to offer you employment. Not here in Charles Towne, you understand, but in England. My wife and I will be returning to my estate in Oxfordshire as soon as possible. I hope you and Prin will accompany us there. Once we arrive, I'd like you to train under my estate manager, Peebles. If you agree, you will assume his position when he retires in two years' time. The wages are excellent and a comfortable house is provided on the grounds of the estate."

A huge smile split Kane's plump lips and he was already nodding his head in eager acceptance, but Drake continued. "While we remain here, I'll expect you and your bride to honeymoon, of course. I sent my man this afternoon to inquire about renting one of the houses flanking this one. I know my wife won't be happy if her sister isn't close at hand. As a belated wedding gift, I'd like to pocket your expenses whilst we're all waiting to leave South Carolina. What say you? Is that acceptable?"

Kane's smooth head pivoted to find Prin, who had huge tears rolling down her cheeks.

"Yes, suh. Thank ya, suh. That's mighty generous of ya, suh." Gratitude radiated from Kane's stunned dark eyes. "Mighty, mighty kind."

"No need to thank me," Drake said. "We're family."

Kane's smile wavered. A proud man himself, Drake understood. "Don't think of this as charity, for it isn't. The honeymoon is a belated wedding gift. The rest I wouldn't offer if I didn't believe you capable of making a success of the position. I've seen the Sayers' crop fields. They not only rival those of many English estates, they surpass some. I'd like to put your knowledge to use at Hawk Haven."

Kane gave a solemn nod. Drake knew he'd just earned the giant's undying loyalty, but it was the love reflected in Elise's delighted expression that pleased him most.

Frau Einholt entered the dining room. Atop the silver tray she carried lay a crisp white note sealed with a blob of red wax and the stamp of the letter *B*.

Drake took the missive, broke the seal and began to read:

> *Sir,*
> *It is with a glad heart that I send you word. Our efforts to locate the Fox, though fallow until now, have begun to bear fruit. As of a few moments ago, one of my most trusted sources, the carriage driver you met in Charles Towne, has returned as though*

from the grave. He claims he has reliable informa-
tion concerning the whereabouts of our mutual foe.
My contact assures me the rebel spy will be ours
within one week's time.
  Your diligent servant and most faithful cousin,
  Beaufort

"Drake?" said Elise. "Is everything well?"

He looked up, taking in her innocent face and the question puckering her soft brow. "Everything is superb, my dear." He placed the corner of Beaufort's missive in the candle flame nearest to him and watched it burn until the heat forced him to drop it in his bowl for the servant to remove. "The note is from Beaufort. He assures me the noose is tightening around the throat of my nemesis. Anthony's murderer should be bagged by week's end."

Chapter Seventeen

The hall clock chimed noon just as Elise made her way to the downstairs parlor. A messenger awaited her. Dressed in a white gown embroidered with lavender flowers, a lavender stomacher and yards of white petticoats, she hoped she looked cool and fresh—the exact opposite of how she felt.

In the week since she'd told Drake of her condition, she'd begun to suffer slight bouts of morning sickness. So far, though, today was the worst. Cold chills skimmed over her skin. Moisture broke out on her upper lip. She'd already retched twice, and a third trip to the chamber pot loomed large in the foreseeable future.

Plastering a smile on her lips, she entered the parlor. The messenger's sour stench turned her delicate stomach. She pressed a hand to her mouth and waited for the queasiness to pass. "I…I apologize for your wait, sir. I'm a bit under the weather this morn."

He raised his head. She fell back a step, caught off guard by the man's venomous, yellow eyes.

"No matter, ma'am. I'm only here to deliver this missive from your friend Mr. Smith."

She reached for the extended note, leery of touching the grimy fellow. "What's your name, sir?"

The messenger's mouth tightened ever so slightly. "Brody, ma'am."

His name didn't sound any warnings in her memory and she was certain she'd never seen his skeletal face before. She turned her attention to the message. Breaking the wax seal, she unfolded the stiff white stationery and scanned the tremulous script.

> *I have grave news which I must give to you and only you. You are my last hope. The Dragon and Wolf are not to be found. I beg you. Meet me at quarter to nine at our usual rendezvous. It is a matter of life and death.*
>
> *Yours,*
>
> *J*

Elise crumpled the starched paper in her bloodless fingers. Dread seeped into her heart as she quickly deciphered the message. Josiah needed her to meet him at The Rolling Tide later that evening concerning a matter of life and death. Zechariah and Christian weren't to be found. Something was terribly amiss. Josiah knew she'd ceased spying as the Fox. He wouldn't call on her without enormous cause. He'd put his life on the line too many times to protect her. She wouldn't ignore his cry for help.

She set aside her misgivings and focused on the eerie messenger. "Tell Mr. Smith I'll do as he bids."

* * *

In a fine mood, Drake rapped once on Beaufort's door and entered the Captain's dockside office. Bright midday sun glinted on the polished pine floors, momentarily blinding him. As his eyes adjusted to the light, the harsh smells of fish and salt from the nearby wharf assaulted his nostrils.

"Your Grace." Beaufort scrambled to his feet behind a corner desk piled high with stacks of crumpled papers and unopened envelopes.

Drake strode to the window and adjusted the shutters to block out the glare before commanding a seat on the ball-and-claw-footed sofa. "I've just returned from my ship, *The Queen Charlotte.* After receiving your assurance on the Fox's capture sometime this week, I'm having her readied to sail."

Beaufort collected a set of crystal goblets and a bottle of port from a nearby cabinet. He offered Drake a drink, but Drake declined. "So soon to quit America? How I envy you, sir. Is your wife reluctant to leave her homeland?"

Drake shrugged. "As a matter of fact, she seems more than eager to be on our way."

"Strange," commented Beaufort. "Christian Sayer gave me the impression she rather fancies Charles Towne."

The bottle clinked on the rim of a glass as the captain poured himself refreshment.

Drake leaned back in his seat. "I've grown to quite like the place myself. 'Tis lush country even if it is hot as blazes and everything is rather primitive compared to

England. In truth, I find its relaxed attitudes a pleasant change from the formality of London and even Hawk Haven, for that matter. With fewer servants milling about, privacy abounds."

Beaufort returned to his chair and drank from his own glass. "As a newly wedded man, I'm positive the chance to be alone is much appreciated, eh, Your Grace?"

Drake was in too grand a mood to take offense at his cousin's flat attempt at wit. "Indeed, Charles, I'm the happiest of men. My wife pleases me more every day. Have I told you I'm to be a father in the spring?"

"Brilliant news, Your Grace!" The captain raised his glass in congratulations. "Perhaps Anthony's death is a blessing after all."

Drake's good mood vanished along with Beaufort's mirth. He watched his cousin pale as Charles realized how tactless he'd been. Drake gritted his teeth. "Enlighten me to your meaning, Captain."

"I meant nothing disrespectful. Just that if Anthony had lived 'tis unlikely you would have met your lovely wife."

Muffled cries of the gulls outside filled the tense silence. "I prefer to think of it as God returning good for evil."

"I couldn't agree more, sir." Obvious in his attempt to return to Drake's favor, Beaufort picked up an open letter from his desk. "It seems there's even more good fortune in store. I received this letter minutes before you arrived. Robin Goss has done it. He says we must meet him at The Rolling Tide at nine this evening. The Fox will be ours tonight!"

* * *

When the clock chimed seven, Elise dressed with the rain and danger in mind as she prepared to leave for The Rolling Tide. Fortunately, her sickness had receded after lunch and no longer plagued her.

Word arrived from Drake earlier in the afternoon, explaining that business would keep him away until the next morning. As she tied the laces of a black wool dress over black petticoats, it struck her as coincidental, his being away the very night she would have had to make an excuse to leave, but she wasn't one to question good fortune in tight circumstances. Instead, she laced up a pair of sturdy boots, slipped a loaded pistol into her skirt pocket, and sat down at her writing desk.

When she finished a message to Zechariah she called for Prin. "Is my coach ready?"

"You asked for it, didn't you?"

Elise didn't acknowledge her sister's surly tone. Dear Prin was *not* happy. "I need Kane to carry this correspondence to Brixton Hall. He must wait until he can give it to either Zechariah or Christian, no other."

Arms crossed tight across her chest, Prin's face creased with unease. "I don't like this whole business, Lisie. I don't like it one bit. I want you to stay home and for once take care of yourself instead of everyone else."

Elise set aside her own reservations and patted her sister's hand in reassurance. Pressing the envelope into Prin's palm, she gave her a tight hug. "Don't be such a handwringer. Josiah's asked for my help and I'm not about to withhold it after all the times he helped me. Just do as I ask, please, and all will be fine."

"You know I will," Prin grumbled.

A short time later, Elise dodged the rain and stepped into the waiting coach. As it bounced into motion and gained speed, rain drummed on the roof and blew against the lead glass window.

Outside The Rolling Tide, the coach rocked to a halt. Elise opened the door herself and stepped down, splashing in a puddle on the street. Cold water soaked her boots and the hem of her skirt, making the layers of her clothes cumbersome and difficult to maneuver. She reached up, gave the dark shape of the driver a handful of coins and instructed him to wait for her around the corner.

For several long moments, she observed the tavern from a covered doorway across the street. Smoke poured from the chimney and mingled with the mist rolling in from the harbor. Josiah must have trimmed back the ivy. Light coursed through the front windows and illuminated the slick, wet street. Fiddle music spilled from the doorway as an occasional patron came or went, but she noted nothing out of the ordinary. Even the number of redcoats seemed less than usual.

Taking a deep breath, she waited for a carriage to pass before sprinting across the brick street and into the dark alley that led to the tavern's back door. Rain doused the front of her dress and poured from the wide brim of her hat. Skimming her fingers along the alley's rough brick wall to guide her, she saw nothing in the darkness, only heard the scurrying of rodents as they fled her swift steps.

When she reached The Tide's back door, she yanked it open and rushed inside the kitchen, savoring its instant warmth. The cockney barmaid, Louise, sliced a ham before the blazing fireplace.

"Louise," Elise said as she removed her hat and shook it under the eaves outside. "Where's Josiah? I'm to meet him in a few minutes' time."

The barmaid ceased her work and wiped her sweaty brow with the back of her hand. "'E's above stairs. Said to tell ye 'e's waitin' for ye in the last room to the right."

Elise thanked the blonde as she crossed the kitchen and darted up the tavern's back steps. She ignored the peculiar feeling that all was not well, but considered that she hadn't spied in months. Most likely she was out of practice and her nerves more jumpy than normal.

At the landing, she turned to the right. Simple pewter sconces lit her path down the empty hall, past the room where Hawk had died. The faded memory of that cursed night rushed to the forefront of her thoughts, dousing her with guilt.

Dear God, how she hated this place and its painful memories. After tonight, she would *never* return here. If Josiah needed her, he'd have to make arrangements to meet her somewhere else.

When she arrived at the designated door, she tapped out three soft knocks, the signal she and Josiah had agreed upon long ago.

"Come in," she heard him call through the door. Slowly, she lifted the latch and pressed open the portal. It was dark in the small room except for the slice of light cutting in from the hall behind her.

"Josiah?"

Her friend sat behind a small square table, his face in

shadow. He seemed tense and rigid, when she knew him to be a relaxed sort. "Why are you in the dark? Shall I fetch some candles?"

He hesitated over the simple question. "No…there's no need. I have some here."

With the tips of her fingers, Elise shoved the door inward, broadening the scope of light. She winced when she saw her friend's battered countenance. Purple bruises and fresh cuts covered his face and throat. He looked as though he'd fought a berserk mule and lost. One eye swollen shut, tears sliced paths through the dried blood on his cheeks.

"What happened to you?" she gasped as her concern pulled her deeper into the small room.

A heavy hand grabbed hold of her, yanking her forward. The door slammed, trapping her as the room went black. Arms, thick and hard as mighty oaks, banded about her, crushing the breath from her lungs before she could scream. Panic paralyzed her for a timeless second. Josiah had betrayed her!

Disbelief and terror churned her stomach. What would they do to her? Fear for her unborn child chilled her heart. She tried to scream for help, but a second captor shoved a rag into her mouth and tied the ends behind her head.

A forceful slap burned across her cheek. A pair of fists pummeled her ribs, and knocked the wind out of her. As she gasped for breath, tears of pain pricked her eyes, but she shook her head and squeezed them tight to stem the flow. Whoever these monsters were, they wouldn't make her weep!

Forcing her brain to function, she kicked her legs in a

ferocious attempt to break free. Her heels found her attacker's shins, his instep, his knees, but the brute might as well have been fashioned from steel.

In the dark, Josiah begged piteously for her forgiveness. "I had to do it, Elise! They threatened to murder Tabby and Moi—"

"Shut up, you mangy dog!" a hoarse voice commanded. A moment later the sound of something heavy met human flesh with a sickening thud. Josiah grunted and fell silent.

White-hot fear seized Elise. She was trapped by an unknown number of adversaries, bagged by enemies violent enough to threaten an innocent woman and child be slain for their purposes.

Her cheeks throbbed where she'd been hit. Her bruised ribs ached. Behind her someone struck flint. A spark of fire glowed to life.

Elise's gaze flew to the table, where she saw Josiah knocked cold, tied and leaning forward in his chair.

"Give me a lantern," one of her captors demanded. Glass pinged against metal. The light bloomed. Four simple-hewn chairs and the small table where Josiah slumped made up the furnishings in the otherwise stark room.

The hulk behind her slammed her into a seat. Another man tied her. She kicked at him with all her might. He grunted several times as her feet found their target, but he wouldn't be stopped until her hands were bound tight behind her back, and each of her legs was lashed to the chair.

Elise straightened her spine as much as the thick hemp rope allowed. She focused on the framed landscape hanging on the far wall, desperate to clear her thoughts, but fear clawed through her brain. What if these ruffians had somehow learned Drake's true identity and planned to use her as bait to snare him? Just as bad, what if he found her missing and searched for her only to end up hurt or killed? Her imagination tortured her.

Please, dear God, please, she prayed. *Whatever Your plans for me, please protect my husband!*

A man in a simple white shirt and rough tan breeches placed himself between her and the wall. "Look at me, Fox."

A river of relief flowed over her. These lunatics wanted her, not Drake. Perhaps he would stay safe.

"Fox? I don't know—"

The man laid a fisted blow to her jaw. Bright spots of light danced in her vision. He struck her again with the back of his hand. Warm blood trickled from the corner of her mouth.

"When I give you an order, you best do it quick," her captor growled. "Now, look at me, wench. Don't you recognize me?"

The man was deranged. Elise would give him no cause to strike her again. Quickly lifting her gaze, her eyes widened in horrified recognition.

"Robin Goss, at your service, ma'am. I'm happy to see you remember me. For certain, I could never forget *you,* Fox. I have yet to thank you and Mr. Smith properly for my stay at the wharf. Two months is a long time and requires that I show you a great deal of gratitude."

His fingers threaded painfully into her hair. With a violent yank, he jerked her head back and lowered his face to within an inch of hers. His rotten breath spread across her face and invaded her nose, making her gag in reflex. "If you promise not to scream, I'll remove the rag."

Eager to get the putrid cloth out of her mouth, she nodded.

"Once I'm done showing you my thanks," he said, untying the gag, "I plan to give you to your *worst* enemy."

With the rag gone, she dragged fresh air into her lungs. She ran her thickened tongue over her split bottom lip and tasted blood. Her words slurred. "My *worst…?*"

"Oh, yes. I suppose you can be forgiven in thinking I'm him, but there's one more. Someone willing to pay fifteen hundred pounds for your sorry hide."

Something in his words rang in her memory, but her limited powers of concentration gave her no chance to dwell. A pair of men moved from behind her. Brody's shifting image she recognized. He'd brought her Josiah's message earlier that day, but she'd never seen the human mountain next to him before.

"Meet my lads." Goss's fleshy lips parted in a smirk that revealed his rodent teeth. "But then you've met Brody, haven't you?" He waved his palm in the direction of the mountain. "This here's Clancy."

"For—forgive me when I say it's no pleasure to meet you."

Goss backhanded her across the face. "I expect better manners from a *lady,* even if you are nothing but a filthy, traitorous spy."

Head spinning, ears ringing, Elise could no longer concentrate. She knew his words should mean more to her, but consciousness seemed like a luxury she could barely hold on to. One of her eyes was swollen shut and her vision blurred in the other.

Pain became her one sensation as what seemed like fist after fist rained down in stunning blows. The dim light began to fade. Sound came to her as though from a distance. The netherworld beckoned.

They're going to kill me for certain.

Her mind fought against the agonized haze overtaking her and savored the vision of Drake for a moment of sweet solace. A sob caught in throat. She couldn't bear to leave him.

Using the last ounce of her energy, she squirmed in the chair, but escape was futile. Another slap across the face brought a wave of darkness. Believing she'd met her end, she prayed one last time for forgiveness. As she lost consciousness, her heart broke on the thought she would never again see her husband.

Chapter Eighteen

The swiftly moving coach wasn't traveling fast enough for Drake as it splashed through the dark, narrow streets. A keen sense of anticipation gripped him until he thought he might leap from his skin. He snapped open his filigreed pocket watch and held it up to the small interior lantern. A few minutes more and he'd have the Fox by the throat.

Thunder rumbled ominously. Cold air blew in through the partially raised window and whipped the curtains. Drake shut the window and pulled his cape closer around him. His gaze shifted to his cousin fidgeting in the opposite seat. "Pray, Charles, why so down in the mouth? Are you worried Goss has somehow led us false?"

Lantern light flickered over Beaufort's glum face. "Oh, no, Your Grace, I've a touch of indigestion, but it shall pass. My spy knows if he leads us astray, the reward is forfeit. It's not a risk he's willing to take, nor does he need to. He found the Fox's weakness, you see, a friend and frequent contact willing to turn Judas."

A bolt of lightning struck overhead, washing the coach's

leather seats and tufted velvet walls with a moment of clear, white light. He thought of Elise and worried the storm might frighten her. He would be overjoyed when he could return home to keep her safe. "I'm eager to have this business over and done."

Beaufort nodded. "Unless the Fox manages to flee again, we'll have all we need to condemn him."

Drake's eyes narrowed. "Is his escape a concern, Charles?"

"I don't believe so, but the Fox is a wily creature. He escaped your brother once, and Robin Goss is not the clever chap Lord Anthony was." The captain swallowed nervously. "I have redcoats surrounding the tavern. They'll follow us once we go inside to give us aid if need be."

As the coach driver slowed their breakneck pace and reined the horses to a halt, Drake wiped the foggy window with the lace curtain and pressed the cloth out of the way behind a hook.

Beaufort leaned forward, scanning the front of The Rolling Tide. "Aha! There. You see it? They've just lit a light in the second-story window. That's our signal, sir."

"Then let us delay no longer." Drake's heart pounded with the thrill of the hunt. Finally, he would avenge Anthony's death. He bounded from the coach, ignoring the sting of cold rain on his face.

Inside the tavern, his quick pace led him through the maze of occupants, past carousing sailors and a drunken fiddle player who smelled as if he'd soaked himself in rum. Taking the stairs two at a time, he glanced over his shoulder to see Beaufort huffing his way up the steps several paces behind him. Four redcoats, one of whom

Drake recognized as Lieutenant Kirby, followed farther behind the captain.

When Drake reached the landing, he didn't hesitate until he passed the room where Anthony died. Righteous fury fueled him onward. As he drew closer to the room that held his nemesis, the unmistakable thud of heavy blows meeting human flesh and the low, mewling cries of a trapped victim penetrated the red haze of his anger. A few steps from the door, he tasted victory.

"That's enough, Brody," a vaguely familiar voice said from inside the room. "We only get the full reward if the Fox is turned in alive."

"We got in three or four licks, is all. She could take another half dozen and live to tell the tale," a second voice argued.

Drake's hand froze on the doorknob. *She?* He hesitated, listening. The voices were muffled by the door. Perhaps he'd misheard?

"I said *enough,* Brody. Any more and you'll break her bones. Use Smith for punchin' practice. It won't matter if he gives up the ghost."

"While he takes Smith, how 'bout I have a little fun with the wench?" a third, deeper voice asked.

"Not enough time, Clancy," the first voice said. "That lummox Beaufort'll be here any minute."

"Lummox?" Charles hissed behind Drake. "Goss is nothing but a weas—"

"Quiet!" Drake insisted.

"He's bringing the soul who's offering the reward." Robin laughed. "Can't wait to see the surprise on his face when he finds out the Fox is a wom—"

Drake thrust open the door, cutting off Goss, who whirled sharply to see who entered.

"You!" Goss choked. Blood fled his face, leaving him as gray as a gravestone. "Anyone but you!"

Drake ignored Goss's horrified exclamation. His gaze flew about the room, looking for the woman Robin claimed to be the Fox. Surely Anthony hadn't been killed by a female? And even if such a circumstance were somehow possible, what kind of woman would perpetrate so vile a crime?

Two oil lanterns cast enough light for him to see the spare furniture and the battered hulk of a man slumped over the table. With the windows closed the smells of blood and sweat permeated the hot, stuffy room. From the corner of his eye, Drake saw Goss's henchmen close ranks in front of a second trussed individual hidden in the shadows.

"Get out of my way," Drake growled as he shoved a human mountain from his path.

"Wait!" Robin shouted. It was too late. Drake recognized Elise's luminous hair the moment he saw her bowed head. Stunned disbelief robbed his body of breath. What was she doing here? Numbed by the sight of his battered wife, all feeling drained from his limbs until overwhelming pain roared back with a vengeance.

She didn't move. Terror warned she might be dead. Begging the Almighty for mercy, Drake staggered forward and dropped to his knees in front of her chair. He laid a shaky hand on her chest and felt the rise and fall of her shallow breaths. Relieved beyond measure, his eyes closed on a prayer of thanks.

Behind him, an argument ensued between Goss and Beaufort. The captain ordered the spy and his henchmen to sit, then brought in the redcoats to enforce his command when the angered trio rebelled.

Drake ignored them all. A dozen questions buzzed in his head, but nothing mattered in that moment save Elise. Not his pride, not his quest for vengeance. His whole being focused with frantic intensity on his wife as he gently tucked a bloodied strand of hair behind her ear.

With the greatest care, he tested her jaw and found, by some miracle, it wasn't broken. He lifted her chin, wincing when he saw the dark bruises forming on her precious face.

Frantic with worry, he ripped off his white linen cravat and dabbed at the blood streaking her cheeks and cut, swollen lips. He held her head to keep it from lolling while his other hand untied the ropes that bound her to the chair. Freed but unconscious, she sagged against him and would have slipped to the floor had he not held her tight against his chest.

As he gathered her into his arms and stood, a new kind of rage brewed within him to rival the intensifying storm outside. How dare these filthy animals abuse his duchess!

He turned toward the shouting behind him. Kirby and three other redcoats held Goss and his comrades at bay with weapons drawn, while Beaufort stood over them like an affronted rooster. "You've done it this time, Goss. I've heard enough—"

"But she *is* the Fox!" the spy shouted.

"Don't be a fool," Beaufort scoffed. "Her Grace is as much the Fox as I am."

Drake refused to consider the possibility of Robin Goss's accusation. The whole idea of Elise being the Fox struck him as absurd. There must be some other explanation.

"Cease your bickering!" With great care, Drake adjusted Elise in his arms. "Captain, I want these men arrested and taken far beyond my sight."

A chorus of alarmed protests rose from Goss and his duo of cutthroats. Robin leaped to his feet. "On what charge?"

One of the redcoats silenced him by slamming the butt of his musket into the spy's middle. Drake took perverse pleasure in watching Goss double over and drop to his knees, moaning in agony.

Beaufort quickly obeyed Drake. "Lieutenant Kirby, arrest these men on charges of kidnapping and attempted murder. I believe one of the prison barges will have plenty of space to host them."

The three men spewed obscenities and fought like fish trying to escape a net, but the redcoats made quick work of subduing them and prodded the prisoners out the door.

"What about Smith?" Beaufort asked.

In his concern for Elise, Drake had forgotten the tavern owner. He glanced down at his wife, who'd grown paler during the last few moments. There was no time to dwell on Smith. "Convey him to my home, but put a guard at his door. This man must have lied about my wife and betrayed Elise into Goss's clutches. I should like to know the reason."

Downstairs, Drake left the tavern by way of the back door. He hunched his shoulders against the cold driving rain and held Elise close to keep her as dry as possible. A stiff wind snatched at the edges of his cape as his expeditious steps took them around the brick building to his waiting coach.

Quick to help him, the driver opened the door. Drake placed Elise on the velvet bench as if she were a piece of priceless crystal.

Climbing in, Drake shook off his wet cape before taking the opposite seat, then lifted her onto his lap. He held her tight with one arm while he covered her with his cape, hoping the warm lining would fight off the chill.

"Your Grace?" Beaufort popped his head inside, water dripping from the brim of his hat. "I've stowed Smith in a hired carriage. We'll follow you back to the townhouse."

"Fetch a physician on your way," Drake ordered. He cradled Elise close, her heated forehead pressed against his jaw. Already her skin grew hot with a rising fever. "Make haste, there's not a moment to lose."

"Stop your pacing, young man." Doctor Hardy glared over the rim of his spectacles. "You're becoming a distraction."

Drake raked his fingers through his hair as he swung on his heel. A sharp retort born of anxiety teetered on the tip of his tongue, but he bit it back. Elise's care was his main concern. If he was disrupting the doctor, he'd position himself in the corner and wait stock-still if need be.

Heavy of heart, Drake watched Elise where she lay with a deathly pallor in the four-poster bed. Prin had washed her battered face and applied an herbal salve to her chafed wrists, but there'd been no time to cleanse her hair and it was still caked with blood. After building a fire to keep her warm, he'd exchanged her black garb for a fresh dressing gown. There was little else he could do to fight his feeling of uselessness.

Sick with worry, he rasped, "Will she recover?"

Doctor Hardy, a severe fellow with a disapproving manner, looked up from checking her pulse. "It's too early to tell. I've examined her, and fortunately her bones are undisturbed. These cuts and bruises on her head and face will heal in a few weeks, but we'll have to wait and see if her brain has suffered any ill effects."

Drake swallowed the lump in his throat. "And the child?"

"I've no way of knowing if your wife is damaged internally. As of yet, there's no evidence she'll miscarry." The doctor replaced his instruments into a worn leather bag. "Perhaps the next time you lose your temper, you'll refrain from releasing it on your lady."

Incredulous, Drake found himself speechless for the first time in his life. "You don't think *I*—"

"The law may not frown on a man chastising his wife, and I have no wish to come between you, but when tempers rise, you must remember that self-control is the order of the day. Your lady is too delicate to take this kind of abuse."

The physician had his mind made up. Gritting his teeth, Drake called Prin to see the doctor out.

Drake crossed the room to the footboard and gripped the smooth mahogany rail. His gaze touched on Elise's beaten face and a sharp lump of emotion gathered in his throat. Where she wasn't bruised or cut, her pale skin blended with the white sheet and pillows behind her.

His chaotic thoughts were nearly unmanageable. The doctor was right. Drake may not have abused her, but he'd not been home protecting her as he should, either. Elise had wanted to leave for England weeks ago. With his obsession for revenge, he'd made her stay. Now he might lose her and their child.

Torment swirled around him. Grief and helpless frustration bit deep. He sank to the edge of the bed and took her hand in his. Ropes had made her wrists raw, and the glossy sheen of the foul-smelling salve Prin applied earlier glistened in the candlelight. Raising her slender fingers to his lips, he blinked excess moisture from his eyes. He hadn't wept since he was a boy, but his heart was shattering from the tightness of his chest.

A soft knock sounded on the door. He quickly wiped his cheeks. "Come in."

Prin entered carrying a cup of steaming coffee. The aroma churned his stomach. Cool air from the hall streamed through the open door, causing the fire to dance in the hearth.

"I thought you might need this."

Drake took the cup, but set it on the side table untested. "Do you think she'll be all right?"

"I'm believin' the Almighty will see her through. She's been treated worse and survived it." Prin's eyes shone with unshed tears. "She may look as fragile as a dove, but she's stubborn as a mule and tough as an ox."

"What do you mean, she's been treated worse? How? Who?"

Prin straightened the edge of the bed sheet. "I don't know what Lisie told you 'bout our pa, but he was a vile man with no good qualities I ever saw. He'd drink like a pack of sinners on Saturday night, then get mean. I did my best to protect her, but sometimes, he'd catch her and I couldn't do nothin' to stop him from hittin' on her."

Drake shook his head, wondering what kind of barbarian would beat an innocent little girl.

"Then there was that ruckus last winter, but it wasn't near as bad as this."

An alarm bell went off in Drake's head. "What happened?"

Prin's face turned anxious. Clearly she'd spoken out of turn and regretted it. She crossed to the pitcher on the writing desk. "I think we best keep water going down her if we can. I'll get a clean cloth. We can keep it moist and wet her lips if nothing else."

"What happened last winter?" he persisted. "Did one of the Sayers abuse her?"

"It's not my place to say."

He'd come to the end of his patience. "I'm making it your place. What happened?"

Prin shifted nervously. "She was in a tussle with a man who tried to kill her. She fought with all her might and he ended up dead."

Lightning flashed in the window. In an instant all the questions he'd sought to deny crystallized into one clear, horrifying picture.

"You're not lookin' so good, your Grace."

He ignored her. "Where did this happen—The Rolling Tide?"

"How did you know?" she asked in surprise. "Did Elise tell you 'bout it already?

He closed his eyes, absorbing the agony that sliced through him like a bayonet. "No, I'm afraid she never did."

"Then how did you know about her troubles at the Tide?"

"Captain Beaufort mentioned it some time ago." Drake allowed the silence to linger as he gathered his wits. His gaze slid toward the bed where Elise lay in frightening stillness.

Worry, shock and betrayal vied for precedence in his mind. The one woman he'd believed in most deserved his faith the least. His hands clenched into fists of indignation. How could he have been so gullible? He deserved a flogging for his blindness. "How long has Elise been the Fox?"

"I…I can't say." Prin backed toward the door. "You'll have to talk to her 'bout that when she wakes up."

Drake had suffered one too many blows in the last few hours to forego issuing threats if necessary. "Prin, answer me or you and Kane gather your belongings and go."

Prin froze. Surprise etched her mocha features. "Would you really cast us out?"

"If you force me to it." He crossed his arms over his chest. Tension vibrated under his skin. He leaned against the cool windowpane where rain beat against the glass.

She nodded, her face solemn as if she'd learned a valuable lesson concerning his character. "I was a fool. I never guessed you'd be so heartless."

His laugh was cold and grated with bitter irony. "I

believe this business has duped us all in one way or another. I want the truth. *Now.*"

Chin quivering, his sister-in-law sat heavily in the wing chair before the fire. As she wrung her hands, she spoke to the mantel and avoided looking in his direction. "She's been a spy since the winter before last."

"To whom does she report her findings?"

"I don't know."

Embers crackled in the fireplace. Drake didn't believe her, but he let the lie pass. His suspicions pointed toward the Sayers, despite Beaufort's assurance they were loyal to the crown. No matter, he would find out eventually. "Why did she resort to espionage? Is she really such a traitor she would risk her life for so futile a cause?"

Prin buried her face in her hands as though she'd suddenly come to the end of her tether. Rocking back and forth in the chair, she fought back sobs until she broke down and wept. When she lifted her head, tears streamed from her pleading eyes. Drake refused to soften. "Answer me!"

She wiped her cheeks with her palms and sucked in several deep breaths. "She's a patriot who believes in liberty, but…but mostly she spied to save *me.*"

Chapter Nineteen

"It's been two days, sir. I suggest you pray. She's in God's hands now."

Through the pain piercing her skull, Elise heard the cryptic announcement as though a thick portal stood between her and the speaker. Something smelled foul, like lard mixed with herbs. She remembered the beating. Her mind snatched at disjointed memories of Goss and his henchmen, but the images swirled together in a gruesome haze. Sharp blades of agony sliced her skull and limbs, preventing the slightest movement. Her tongue felt thick against the walls of her lacerated mouth, making it impossible for her to speak.

"There must be something else you can do. You're supposed to be the best surgeon in the city!"

Drake's voice penetrated the fog. She wanted to reach out, console his obvious distress, but her arms felt as though someone had bolted them to the bed.

"I can't lose her."

The despair in Drake's voice broke her heart. She tried to reassure him, but the darkness beckoned, and she was too weak to fight its call.

Drake prowled the solitary confines of the bedchamber, willing Elise back to consciousness. His concern for her outweighed his feelings of anger and betrayal. After three ghastly days to ponder Prin's disturbing revelations, he was ready to climb the walls. Exhausted by the vigil he'd kept at his wife's bedside, he stayed close nonetheless. Leaning over her supine form, he ascertained her breathing for the hundredth time. He reached for a cloth and dipped it in cool water to wet her lips.

In his heart, he ached for her, cursed the hardships she'd braved to create a better life for herself and Prin. He admired her loyalty, a quality he'd never known in any other woman, but her role in Anthony's death tormented him. He feared without the Lord's help his faith in her might never recover.

Elise fought to open her eyes, but her weighted lids declined to obey. As she came to wakefulness, she listened for some indication of where she might be. A window must be open. She could hear the faint chirping of birds. The lightest of breezes brushed her sensitive cheeks, chilling her heated skin.

A dull ache pulsed through her limbs, her jaw throbbed and her head pounded. She wiggled her toes. The fingers of her right hand moved, but those of her left felt crushed. She couldn't fathom how, but she thought it might be broken.

"Elise?"

Drake. Anxious to see him, she found the will to open her eyes. As she struggled to focus, his dear face swam into view. He looked haggard, unshaven. His brilliant golden eyes were dull. Had he lost weight? She tried to smile, but the muscles of her face were stiff and sore.

"Thank God you're awake!" He brought her left hand to his lips, and she realized he'd been holding it all along.

"Are you well?" she asked in a reedy whisper.

"I?" He swallowed thickly and raked his fingers through his hair. Strain pinched his mouth and lined his eyes. "You're the one who has given us all a fright."

She licked her scabbed lower lip. "Our child?"

With great care, he lifted her head and held a glass of water to her lips. "The child lives. Just as you will."

She heard his determination and clung to it. Using all her strength, she lifted her hand to clasp the back of his. "I…I love you." She wanted to say more, but her eyelids grew heavy and slid shut as weariness claimed her.

Drake dismissed the guards from Josiah Smith's door and strode into the guestroom. He found the rotund tavern owner in a clean white nightshirt, lurching about the comfortably appointed room in a state of palpable distress. The man's head was bandaged and his round face battered, but at least he was on his feet, Drake thought bitterly. More than he could say for Elise.

Smith's face lit with fear the moment he saw Drake. He slumped on the edge of the bed. "How is she?"

"Little you care, Smith. My wife fares far more ill than you, apparently."

Josiah's hands shook until he clutched the rumpled sheets on either side of him. "Will she be all right?"

Drake chose to ignore the man's concern. He nodded. "No thanks to you and your loose lips."

"I had no choice!"

He bit back an infuriated growl. "I'm waiting to be enlightened on that score. How much were you paid to betray the Fox?"

Josiah sighed in resignation. "You know the truth about her then?"

Drake inclined his head.

"I'd never betray Elise for coin. I had to protect my family. Robin Goss and one of his minions broke into our home. They threatened to murder my wife and child if I refused to lure Elise into their net."

"Where is your family now?"

Josiah hedged. "I've been told they're safe."

"Ah, I assume that means you've talked with Prin."

Smith's silence was an affirmative answer. He stumbled to his feet, his face crimped by the pain of his movements. "I need to see about their welfare myself."

"Beaufort's men are posted outside your door and yonder window. There's little you can do to escape."

"I can try. Wouldn't you do the same in my position?"

"I wouldn't be in your position, Smith. I know how to be loyal." Drake paused at the door. His fingers gripped the frame as he regarded Josiah with scorn. "Do you happen to remember a spy known as Hawk?"

"Aye, I remember the pompous scoundrel well. He was an arrogant fool with a hateful sense of humor. Elise was the only person with any patience for him. I believe she considered him a friend." Josiah's face contorted with disgust. "The greedy Judas sold her out for silver. His betrayal nearly broke her. She hasn't been the same since he died, but if you ask me, he deserved what he got."

Unable to tolerate another moment in the colonial's company, Drake turned to leave. "I suggest you rest and rebuild your strength, sir. As weak as you are, you'll offer no sport when they hang you."

A fortnight later, Elise sipped her hot tea in contemplative silence. Prin had warned her that Drake knew about her previous life as the Fox. Though he hadn't mentioned it yet, she was convinced he despised her. Before he'd quit visiting her a week ago, the accusation in his eyes had been enough to make her tremble.

With a sigh, she ran her palm over the slight mound of her belly, thanking the Lord for His mercy toward her child. After the beating she'd endured, she knew how fortunate she was the baby lived.

Turning to face the window, she fortified herself with a breath of crisp autumn air. Since the night of her clash with Goss, she'd regained her strength bit by bit, but this morning was the first she'd felt recovered enough to confront her husband.

Her chamber door opened. Prin entered the room carrying a fresh set of candles to replace the spent ones beside the bed. She grinned. "Except for that sad frown, you're lookin' mighty fine this mornin', Lisie. Them yellow bruises are still faint round your eyes and along your jaw, but at least you don't look like a kicked raccoon anymore."

Elise cast off her doldrums and offered a smile for her sister's sake. "That's good to hear. I think I'll be healed before the week is out."

"I doubt it," Prin said matter-of-factly. "Sit forward and let me plump your pillows."

She did as Prin bid, grimacing when her movement shot a twinge of pain through her ribs. "Where is Drake?"

"Probably in that study of his downstairs. He don't come out much."

"What do you suppose he's doing in there?"

"Broodin', I expect." Prin shrugged. "He holed himself up the afternoon he talked to Josiah. Didn't come out for 'bout a week. Now, at least, he sometimes goes ridin' on one of them fine horses of his."

Tears misted her eyes at how much he must be hurting. *Please, Lord, don't let this mess cause him to turn his back on You again.*

"I wonder what he and Josiah discussed?" she said.

Prin shrugged. "I'm not sure. That same day I was told not to speak to Josiah anymore. I'm not even allowed to take him his food. Frau Einholt does that now. By the way, you best be careful what you say to that one. She acts like she don't understand much English, but more than once I caught her with her ear to a door."

Elise made a mental note to be careful around the housekeeper, then steered the conversation back to the Smiths. "Josiah must be distraught about Tabby and the baby." She bore her friend no ill will for his part in handing her over to Goss. With his wife and child's life at stake, Josiah had had little choice but to protect them. She was convinced no other inducement could have enticed him to betray her. "I know you said Kane found them and saw them to her parents' home, but Josiah must be anxious."

"I imagine so. He's got to be frettin' the British plan to hang him, too."

Elise raised her hand to her throat. "I must say I've been concerned about that same fate myself."

"Oh, bosh." Prin rubbed her lower back, her stomach protruding now that she was further along in her pregnancy. "That husband of yours might have a temper a bull would envy, but he isn't gonna let anything happen to you."

"I'm not so sure." Elise tipped her head against the pillows. She closed her eyes for a moment, her head throbbing with tension. "I'm a traitor in my husband's eyes. What if he decides he can't abide that fact?"

"He'll forgive you." Prin sat beside her on the bed and brushed the hair from Elise's brow. "I never saw a man care for his wife so much."

"You don't know him like I do. Both his first wife and former fiancée betrayed him, but he gifted *me* with his trust anyway." Tears sprang to her eyes. "Now that he knows the truth, I'm sure it's killed all his love for me."

Later that afternoon, Elise was supposed to be napping, but she couldn't sleep. Instead, she left her bed, pulled on a robe and went in search of Drake. Itching with nerves, but weak from weeks of little activity, she made slow progress down the stairs. She was gasping for breath against the smooth, wooden banister when the door of Drake's study swung open. He entered the central hall.

"Elise!" He ran to her. "What are you doing out of bed?"

"I need to speak with you." She clutched at the soft material of his shirt, basking in his strength. She'd missed him desperately. It felt so good to have him hold her.

"Why didn't you wait until I came to you?" He cradled her in his arms and started back up the stairs.

"Now that you know about my past as a spy, I thought you might never come again."

Hearing the hurt in her voice, Drake winced. He watched over her every night while she slept, but she had no way of knowing about his nocturnal visits. "I see Prin has told you of our conversation."

"Yes," she whispered. Her soft hair brushed his throat and her lavender scent tugged at his senses.

"Then perhaps you can understand why I have no wish to speak with you at present."

"I know you're angry," she said in a small voice. "You must feel betrayed. But have my worst fears come true? Have I lost your love forever?"

He said nothing as he stalked across the second-story landing and into the bedchamber. The tight grip he'd maintained on his temper began to unravel.

"What do you expect of me?" he demanded, placing her gently on the bed. "You played me for a fool." He turned his back on her. "You deceived me without conscience, but all of that fails to compare with—"

"What?" she cried. "Tell me, Drake. Tell me all the crimes you think I've committed. If you ever loved me, give me a chance to explain. Allow me to set right the wrongs between us."

If he'd ever loved her? Was she insane? Loving her was

a malady, and he had no cure. He berated himself for his weakness. His need for her was part of the war raging within him. Anger twisted him in knots. He shouldn't love her, but he did with an intensity that bordered on madness.

He turned to find her sitting on the edge of the bed. Her lovely hair wreathed her face and fell in thick tendrils over her narrow shoulders and down her back. He should loathe the sight of her. His pride should prevent him from having the smallest thing to do with her. As it was, her beauty stung. Her faded bruises shone like badges of her deception. She was a traitor to England and all he held dear. But that wasn't the worst of her sins. "Do you remember the Hawk?"

She blinked in confusion, then paled. "Hawk? What do you know of him?"

"I know it all, Fox. Including something you do not. His real name was Lord Anthony Amberly. He was my brother."

"Your brother…?" The blood drained from her face by slow degrees. She shook her head in silent, shocked denial. Her hand slipped over her mouth as though she might be sick. Tears welled in her bright green eyes and spilled down her cheeks. "No. It can't be!"

Thinking she might faint and topple off the mattress, he lunged forward in an involuntary bid to catch her. She scrambled to her feet and dodged his reach. He saw her grimace and judged her injuries protested the speed of her escape.

Icy cold swept through him. His hands clenched into fists. "You're the killer I've been hunting these many months."

"I didn't kill him! I promise I didn't." Her face was wild, filled with the fear of a trapped animal. "You *must* believe me. He tried to hand me over to the enemy. I had no choice but to fight for my life. We struggled for his weapon. *He* fired the pistol, not I. It was an accident. I never meant for him to end up dead."

Her confession touched him at his core. He could see the truth reflected in her face, but his pride fought the yearning of his heart. "So you say. Next you'll try to convince me you had no knowledge of my station when we wed. Tell me the truth if you're able. Did you marry me to work your wiles and spy on me?"

"I did know you were a duke, but I married you because I love you."

He wanted to believe her, but he'd be a fool if he did. "And Prin's fate had nothing to do with it, I suppose?"

Trembling, she grasped the bedpost for support. "By marrying you, it's true, I assured her freedom sooner, but nothing could have forced me to pledge my life to you if not for love."

"Surely you don't expect me to believe—" Her pallor concerned him. "Sit down, Elise."

"No." She shook her head. Perspiration beaded her upper lip. "I want you to hear me out."

"I can listen while you're sitting down." He moved with such speed he had her cornered before she could flee. He pressed her onto the feather mattress and covered her with a quilt. "I admire your determination, but you've the babe to consider. He's the only good left in this charade of a marriage."

She flinched as if he'd smacked her. The saner part of him regretted the cut, but under the circumstances it would have rung hollow to apologize.

Elise squared her shoulders and schooled her delicate features. Her chin quivered. "If you truly believe our union is a sham, then all is lost. How can I make you see the truth when your mind is already set against me?"

What *could* she say to ease the battle that raged within him? He should set her aside, end their marriage in whatever way possible. To choose her would be an insult to his brother's memory, yet an unthinkable, unforgivable part of him burned toward Anthony for putting her in harm's way all those months ago. He cleared his tight throat. "Indeed, what is left to say? Perhaps farewell is our only option."

Shattered, Elise watched him storm from the chamber. Without considering the consequences, she ignored her protesting muscles and followed after him. He'd traversed most of the stairs by the time she crossed the landing and grasped the mahogany rail. "Drake, wait! You can't be serious. We have much to say, and none of it includes goodbye."

Spine rigid, he continued his exodus without a backward glance. Desperate, she ran down the steps, nearly tripping on the hem of her dressing gown. "Drake, please come back. I *love* you."

To her relief, he halted before entering his study. He faced her. In her eyes, he'd never looked more like a duke. Cold and intimidating, his frigid manner belied the heat burning in his eyes.

"Don't say those words to me again," he said through clenched teeth.

"Why? You say you want the truth." She refused to let him push her away. "Drake, please. Hear me out."

Remembering the guards at Josiah's door upstairs, she pursued Drake into his study, where the faint scent of leather provoked her already throbbing head. He slammed the door behind her. "You deceived me about Anthony."

"No! I had no knowledge of Hawk's relationship to you until you told me minutes ago. I didn't kill him," she repeated, eager to reach him now that he might listen. "Even so, I've agonized over his death."

"You expect me to believe you suffered over the death of an enemy?"

"We were friends of a sort," she hurried to explain. "He was a spy much longer than I, the first agent I was ever sent to meet. Everyone trusted him. Over time I felt I could trust him, too."

"Yet you never allowed him to view your face."

His sarcasm stung. "I needed to protect the fact that the Fox was a woman. I don't know why Hawk wore a mask, only that he did. Perhaps he meant to conceal his identity as a lord."

"Perhaps," Drake conceded coldly. "Espionage is a shameful business."

His steely condemnation hit her with dizzying force. Her fingers clenched the back of a green leather chair for support. She cleared her throat, frantic to cross the chasm widening between them. "I learned he had a lively, sometimes hateful sense of humor. More than once he played at turning me over to the redcoats. That night he threatened the same. At first, I thought he must be up to his usual tricks."

Drake looked away. "That sounds like Anthony. Always enjoying a prank only he would find amusing."

"I realized he meant serious business when he placed a pistol to my head."

"What? I don't believe you!" His gaze flashed to her face. "He put a pistol to your head? He could not have known you were a woman."

"He learned within minutes, but cared not a whit."

Drake clawed his fingers through his hair in a gesture that betrayed his anguish. She'd never imagined such a decisive man could look so torn.

Shaking with trepidation, she rounded the chair and took a hesitant step closer. "After I came to lov…after I agreed to wed you, I didn't know how to tell you of my previous life. Truthfully, I didn't want to. I convinced myself there was no need. Prin and Kane were free. I had you—everything I dreamed of. Even leaving America was not too high a price to pay for the life I longed to share with you. I reasoned the war would be over soon one way or the other, and none of what I'd done would matter in the end."

"You planned never to tell me." It wasn't a question. "What other secrets have you concealed?"

"None, I promise. I don't know how to convince you, but consider what you would have done if I *had* told you. I believe you would have sent me to the gallows. In fact, were I not carrying your child, I think you would see me there now."

He stepped closer. A muscle ticked in his jaw. Waves of tension emanated from him, encircling her. His eyes were hard as flint. "It's what you deserve. You've no remorse for your spying. My duty to my family and country require I turn you in."

She blanched, but held her ground. "And our child? What will you tell him? That you had his mother hanged moments after he was born?"

He swung away, but not before Elise saw a glimpse of his inner torment. His pain stretched between them and pierced her own heart.

Outside, shouting erupted, giving them both a start. Elise looked toward the open window. She saw nothing except magnolia trees swaying in the cool breeze. A door slammed at the back of the house, pounding footsteps echoed along the central hall.

Drake whipped open the study's door to find Kane sprinting up the stairs. "Miss Lisie! It's over," he shouted. "It's over."

"What's all the clamoring about, man? What's over?" Drake demanded.

Kane stumbled to a halt.

Elise looked past the foyer's chandelier to see one of Josiah's guards come into view on the upstairs landing. Kane spun on the step to face Drake. "The war, suh! Everyone's hollerin' it's all over. The Patriots has won."

"Blimey! You must be mad!" the soldier exclaimed.

Elise's heart stopped in an instant of joy. She schooled her features to belie her excitement and sent up a prayer of silent gratitude. "How do you know, Kane? Where did you hear the news?"

As Kane's dark gaze darted from Elise to each of the two Englishmen, and back to her again, his enthusiasm waned. "I jus' come from the wharf, ma'am. News arrived by ship this mornin'. The British done surrendered at Yorktown, up Virginia way. General Washin'ton got 'em all tied up by land and the French fleet cut 'em off by sea. They had no where else to go."

"When?" Drake asked in transparent disbelief.

"From what I heard, las' week, suh."

"The entire Southern army?"

Kane gave a quick nod. "That's what everybody's sayin'."

Drake groaned. Elise's gaze flew to the guard upstairs. He'd paled a shade lighter than his pristine white breeches.

"Lieutenant, I'm off to Captain Beaufort's. Reposition your men," Drake ordered. "If pandemonium breaks out in the city, I want my wife well-protected."

The young soldier jumped to do Drake's bidding. Kane had disappeared in the confusion. Elise guessed he'd gone to find Prin.

At the door, Drake gathered his tricorn and cape from the rack. He raised his eyes to meet Elise's in a moment of heartrending silence. What could she say to soothe him? He believed the worst about her. And if Kane's report were true, England, the greatest power in the world, had lost the jewel in its crown to a ragtag force of upstart colonials.

With no words to ease Drake's heart or his pride, she stayed rooted to the spot, pleading silently for him to come to her.

He turned away. With haste, he took his leave, shutting the door between them on a note of haunting finality.

Chapter Twenty

Elise awakened the moment a heavy hand covered her mouth. Her eyes flew wide and a jolt of panic raced up her spine. Eyes straining to see in the moonlit parlor, her startled cry died in a palm that stunk of sour ale. Fear crippled her as she imagined Goss or one of his henchmen had escaped the prison barge and come to finish her off.

Kicking furiously, she met empty air as she clawed at her captor. She rolled her head and gritted her teeth, but her shadowed assailant managed to gag her. He wrapped her in a quilt and stuffed her into a large box. Her mind raced. A trunk? A coffin? With her legs bent at the knee to fit her in the confining space, she couldn't even kick in protest. A scream borne of panic welled in her throat, but she choked it back, determined to keep her wits about her when she had her child to think about.

The strength of her fear crippled her. The quilt made it difficult for her to breathe. Anger and frustration began to override the terror. Muted male voices penetrated her shroud, alerting her to more than one captor. One of them took pity and uncovered her face. She could see nothing in the dark. Cool air bathed her skin, but the reprieve ended when the lid banged shut.

Agitated, Drake popped his head out of the coach window in an attempt to judge the traffic. The cloak of night made it difficult for him to determine accurately, but if the noise and number of coach lanterns were anything to go by, a week would pass before he traveled half a mile.

His meeting with Beaufort had concluded an hour ago, and he would have been home already if not for the congestion. As it was, he pondered his quandary with Elise. Truth to tell, he'd thought of little except her since he'd left the house that afternoon. The need to see her had grown to unmanageable proportions. What information his brain happened to filter from Beaufort's ramblings happened by chance. The captain had droned on, blubbering on more than one occasion as he confessed Britain's ghastly state of affairs in North America.

Mayhem outside drew Drake's attention to the window. Small bonfires blazed along the street, illuminating the hornet's nest of humanity to be found there. So far that evening, he'd seen as many revelers celebrating the British surrender as protesters. Drake hated to admit the unthinkable, but Cornwallis's surrender at Yorktown signaled England's certain withdrawal from the Colonies. The loss was no small thing. It was humiliating and vexed his pride, much like finding out his traitorous wife was entangled with his enemies.

In principle, he could make no excuse for Elise's actions. Had she been a man, he would have seen her hanged at the first opportunity. But she wasn't a man. She was his wife, the other half of his soul, the mother of his unborn child.

He wouldn't give her up. He defied anyone to try to take her from him.

Old bitterness began to swell in his chest and he could feel himself slipping back into the darkness that had plagued him so long after the deaths of his family. Anger rose inside him like a fountain of acid. "I thought she was a gift from You, God. Now I see You only meant to torment me."

The box landed with a thud that rattled Elise's bones. The lid lifted and candlelight glowed above her like a celestial orb.

"Elise?" Christian said, incredulous. "Are you all right?"

She squinted as her eyes adjusted to the blinding glow. Seeing a friendly face, she sagged in relief. With her trepidation gone, her temper flared. Her entire body screamed with the agony of her cramped position. She struggled to sit up, but the quilt hobbled her.

"What have those idiots done to you?" He reached in and untied the gag.

"Help me up," she sputtered, gasping for a deep breath of air. "Why…why have you brought me here?"

He set the candelabra he held to a side table and helped her from the box. "I sent Adam and Hargus to rescue you and Josiah."

"How did you know we needed help?"

"Several days ago, Father received a letter from Tabby explaining the whole story of Goss's duplicity. She's been worried sick. She and the baby have joined her parents at their plantation up river."

"They're both safe then?

"Yes."

"Has Josiah been taken to join them?" she asked, unable to conceal her worry.

"No. The lads sent a missive with Captain Travis when he brought you upriver from Charles Towne. According to the letter, Josiah's being kept on the second floor of Amberly's house. They weren't able to reach him."

"Yes, he is upstairs. It's been impossible to speak with him. What's to be done? We can't abandoned him."

"We won't." Christian stooped to unwind the quilt from around her legs and helped her to the parlor's settee. "Tabby feared Amberly had learned of your past as a spy. Is it true? Does he know you're the Fox?"

She nodded, unable to say more as sensation clawed up her legs like a thousand stabbing needles. She held her breath to keep from crying out.

"Are you all right?" Christian asked worriedly.

Rubbing the cramps from her calves, she frowned.

He backed away. "I know that look."

"An eternity passed in that box. I thought I would suffocate."

"There were holes in the top," he said quickly. "You weren't in danger."

"Why didn't they tell me you'd sent them?"

"I don't know. Perhaps time didn't allow or they feared any noise might alert someone to their presence." His gaze settled on her rounded stomach. His jaw tightened. "But considering the similarities in your girth, I think we should be grateful the lads didn't confuse you with Josiah and send you to Tabby."

She sent a pillow flying straight for his head. "I'm with child, you lummox. And I'm nowhere near the size of Josiah."

Christian ducked just before the pillow hit the wall behind him. Chuckling, he sauntered to the cabinet and poured them both a glass of water.

"Thank you," she said when he handed her one. "That gag made my mouth as dry as a bale of cotton."

She sipped the refreshment, revived by the cool liquid on her parched tongue. Once she'd had her fill, she asked, "How did they sneak me past the soldiers?"

"By getting rid of them first, of course."

"They didn't kill them, I hope."

"I didn't order them to finish anyone, but I won't know if it came to that until I've talked to Adam and Hargus. After putting you on the ferry they stayed in town in case they were followed."

A nippy breeze blew through the room, carrying with it a faint, familiar song from the direction of the slave cabins. Elise shivered in the chill and handed her glass back to Christian. "Where have you been? It's been weeks since I saw you last."

"I returned from Virginia this morning," he said, his face suddenly animated. "Thanks to the information you gave father, I made it to the Marquess de la Fayette in time for him to send word to Generals Washington and Rochambeau. Rochambeau notified the French fleet under Admiral de Grasse in the West Indies. de Grasse did not disappoint. He sailed up the Chesapeake, cutting off Cornwallis's escape by sea. I stayed throughout the siege, then took part in the battle."

"I'm glad you weren't hurt."

"As am I, though I had a close call. A redcoat tried to skewer me with his bayonet, but my pistol took off his face before he succeeded."

She grimaced at the grisly picture he described, but he continued with verve, "As everyone's talking about it, I believe you know Cornwallis surrendered. It's too soon to be certain, mind you, but word is that England will petition for peace."

"'Tis excellent news," she said, remembering she'd given Zechariah the information concerning the British encampment as a means to secure Kane's freedom. She sighed. There was another reason for Drake to despise her.

Christian's brow furrowed. "I expected you to be pleased. The war will soon be done."

"I'm overjoyed, I promise you." She stood and moved to warm her hands at the fireplace. The scent of warm cloves rose from a bowl of pomanders on the mantel. "As a patriot, I'm overcome with pride. If I seem melancholy, it has nothing to do with the political situation."

"It's Amberly, isn't it? Kane mentioned—"

"Kane mentioned?" She faced her friend. "When did you see Kane?"

"A short time after I docked. He was at the wharf."

"Ah, yes, he told us he'd been there when he reported Cornwallis's surrender. I take it you were the one to apprise him of events?"

He nodded. "In return, he told me little is well under

your roof. Faint though they are, I see the bruises on your face. If Amberly's abused you, I'll take pleasure in avenging your honor and beating him to a pulp."

As she watched Christian grind a fist into his open palm, she wondered why he seemed so eager for an excuse to throttle her husband. "He hasn't beaten me yet. However, he may before too much longer."

"That's a rather cryptic reply, dearest."

She picked up the pillow she'd thrown and ran her palm over the expensive blue silk. "Not only does he know I'm the Fox, but Hawk was his brother. Drake believes I killed him."

Silence reigned. For the first time since she'd known him, Christian grappled for words. "It's worse than I imagined. After I spoke with Kane, I sought out Beaufort. He told me one of his spies claimed you were the Fox, but that no one believed it. If Amberly knows the truth, why is Goss rotting on a prison barge instead of being hailed as a hero?"

She repeated the story as Prin had told her. "After Goss beat me senseless, Drake arrived to collect the Fox. When he found me, he believed in my innocence. I've yet to determine if Beaufort wished to curry favor with Drake or if he found it impossible to believe the Fox was a female. Whatever the case, he sent Goss to the barge for assaulting me. Drake saw me recovered, though Prin made the mistake of telling him I'm the Fox a few weeks ago. He confronted me this morning."

"And?" Christian jumped to his feet. "Tell me you did the intelligent thing and lied through your teeth."

She tossed the pillow to a nearby chair and rubbed her

pounding temples. The headache from earlier in the day had grown worse. She'd spent the whole afternoon wishing Drake would return while deep down she feared he would never come back. "Of course not, you idiot. I told him the truth."

"Did he inform you of his plans? Has he deduced the identity of your spymaster? What of Brixton Hall?" he said, displaying an anxious side she'd rarely seen.

Returning to the settee, she mulled over what Drake had said. "I believe he must have worked out Zechariah's role in my escapades because he's aware that I spied in part to win Prin. However, both your reputation as Tories and friendship with Beaufort speak well for you. He must not have solid proof of your activities or redcoats would be breaking down the door by now."

"God be praised." Christian picked up the poker and stoked the fire. "Where is the duke now?"

"When he left me, he said he intended to seek out Beaufort. Perhaps my abduction was a blessing. For all I know, they may have returned to the house with a noose to see me hanged."

"That bad, is it?" The taut line of his mouth softened with compassion. "He must have been angry enough to say the vilest things if you believe he would consider such treatment when you're expecting his child. Did you try to explain?"

"Of course." She swallowed hard and bit her lower lip to stop its quivering. "He refused to believe me. I don't blame him. I'm not certain I'd believe me either if our positions were reversed." She stood and began to pace the

Oriental rug. "I've contemplated the situation from every possible angle, but I've come up with no acceptable solution. How can I convince Drake of my innocence when he believes I'm the worst sort of trickster? As quickly as he decided to marry me, it seems he's determined to leave."

Christian rammed the poker in the fire, causing the flames to flare and pop. "Then let the fool go and stay here with me. I'll care for you and the child as if he were my own."

She quit her pacing, not sure she'd heard him right. "But Christian, I'm a married woman. You and I are naught but friends. I couldn't ask you to—"

"Friends we may be, but I love you, too." His intense blue eyes lifted to hers. "I have for quite some time."

The fire crackled in the silence. She couldn't mistake his sincerity. Stricken with shock, she sank to the edge of the settee behind her. "Some spy I am. I never guessed."

"I'm as good at concealing information as you are at uncovering it," he reminded her. "I should have declared myself long ago, but you viewed me as you would a brother or…or some sort of harmless pet." Sitting beside her, he leaned his head against the back of the settee and closed his eyes. "I've been in agony watching you fall in love with that arrogant *Englishman*."

She'd been an insensitive clod. "Oh, Christian, I'm so sorry. You know I'd never purposely hurt you. Please forgive me."

He grasped her hand in his and gave it a light squeeze. "Don't fret, Elise. I know you wouldn't hurt a fly. I also know you want Amberly back. I can see it in your eyes. If you wish, I'll send word to him that you're here. Just know

I'll protect you and your loved ones if his high and mighty is too stiff-necked to come to his senses."

She clutched his hand. "Thank you, my dear friend. Your kindness won't be forgotten."

Compelled by his craving to see Elise, Drake abandoned the stalled coach to the capable hands of his driver and walked the remaining miles home. Midnight had come and flown by the time he reached the front steps. Much to his surprise, no guard stood watch as he'd ordered. Candle-light poured from the front windows when he expected everyone to be abed. The stillness of the place warned of something dire.

Tearing up the front steps, he crossed the threshold, calling for Elise.

Prin appeared in the parlor door to his left, her face pinched and reproachful. "She's not here."

Momentary alarm stole his breath. "Where…?"

"I don't know. Last I checked on her, she'd finally fallen asleep after spendin' the whole day frettin' over you." Her voice sizzled with accusation. "Me and Kane went to enjoy the cool air in the courtyard. When I came back an hour later, I found Lisie gone."

Cold fingers of dread took hold of Drake. Goss's promise of revenge came to mind at speed. What if the ferret had somehow escaped the prison barge and sought out Elise to finish her? Thoughts racing, he refused to think on that possibility. He was determined to find Elise and bring her home, he would never forgive himself if she came to harm. Once he found her, he swore he would never let her out of his sight again.

Please, Lord. Protect her.

"What's been done to secure her return?"

"Very little, if you ask me."

Drake flinched under her condemning glare.

"Whoever was here trussed up the guard at the front door and the one outside under Josiah's window. Kane cut 'em loose. They run off as soon as he did. The kidnappers left the guard outside Josiah's door alone. He didn't hear nothin', and neither did we. We thought maybe the other two was goin' for help. When nobody came, Kane went lookin' for Lisie himself. He's been gone over an hour. If he don't find her soon, he'll probably aim for Brixton. The Sayers won't mind helpin' to find one of their own."

Drake felt off-kilter enough to disregard her accusatory tone. "You believe I wouldn't aid in the search?"

Her chin trembled. "Forgive me for speakin' my mind, but I do wonder. Lisie told me what happened between the two of you earlier. Don't seem like you cared enough to listen to her side of things. If you ask me, it don't seem like you love her very much at all."

Her censure hit a raw nerve. "Cease your prattle, madam, you go too far. My feelings for my wife are none of your concern. Regardless, I can't condone her treachery."

"What treachery?" she said, tears slipping down her dark cheeks. "All she did was for the love of her country and to save me from slavery. I told you that weeks ago, but you're holding it over her head like an ax about to fall. What would you have done in her place?"

Drake made for his study without answering. Undeterred, Prin followed him. "Maybe the treachery you can't forgive has to do with your brother? She said you think she killed him."

In the brightly lit study, Drake yanked open the top desk drawer and removed his leather pistol box. Opening the lid, he lifted one of the matched set from the case's blue velvet lining. He loaded the ornately carved weapon before shoving it into the depths of his coat pocket. If Goss had dared to take his wife, the rat-faced vermin was dead.

"Maybe you think she shouldn't have defended herself when your brother tried to kill her?" Prin said from behind him. "Would you be happier if she was the one to die?"

"No!" Drake growled. "How can you even suggest such a thing?" Racked with grief, he collapsed into the seat behind him. Rampant frustration and bitter regret rattled him to his core. His gaze flicked to Prin, where she stood crying beside the desk, her slender fingers clenching and unclenching with tension. "Get out of my sight," he ordered.

Flinching, Prin collected herself with dignity and wiped the tears from her face. "You're too proud, Your Grace. That pride's gonna cost you more than you're willin' to pay, if you're not careful."

"I said get *out*." Drake stared at the cold fireplace until he heard the soft click of the door closing. Images of Elise bombarded him. Her startling green eyes and luscious hair, her soft smile, the sound of her laughter, and the memory of her touch all conspired to torture him. He couldn't lose her. As he'd known months ago, to lose her would mean going back to the cold, joyless existence he'd known in England.

"Dear God, please help me!" he cried out from the depth

of his soul. He remembered the promise he'd made to Elise not turn his back on the Lord again. Remembering how easily he'd allowed renewed bitterness to creep into his soul, he realized he'd broken his word like a spoiled child throwing a tantrum when he didn't get his way.

Another wave of anguish swelled over him. It had been Elise who'd reminded him of God's grace, that no matter what he did or where he went, nothing could separate him from Christ's love.

He bowed his head in his hands, desperate for the Lord's guidance. "Lord, *please* forgive me and my stiff-necked pride. Prin was right. My arrogance kept me from giving Elise a proper hearing when I should have remembered she is a blessing from You. *Please* help me find her, to listen to her, to understand Your will for us."

More at peace than he'd been since learning Elise was the Fox, he stood and crossed to the open window. The streets had calmed, though an occasional coach continued to rattle past. As he gazed at the starlit sky, he silently acknowledged he hadn't wanted to learn the truth about Anthony when he'd known it all along. Ever since Kirby arrived at Hawk Haven with the news of Anthony's death, Drake had sought to remember naught but the good in his brother. Elise's version of events challenged those memories and forced him to see Anthony for the man he really was: a man loyal to no one but himself, a spy willing to kill a woman for a reward and a fleeting taste of glory.

He fingered the scar along his jaw. On more than one occasion, he'd been the target of his brother's wrath. It wasn't difficult to imagine Anthony exploding into violence when Elise resisted capture. How could he blame her for fighting back when anyone would have done the same? In truth, he could only admire her courage.

He could no longer make excuses for his brother's unbridled behavior. He'd love him, but he wasn't to blame for Anthony's decisions. Since the death of his parents, Drake had done his best to protect his family. Elise was his family now, and she was out there somewhere, believing he despised her. He had to find her if only to tell her how much he cherished her.

He weighed the loaded pistol in his pocket once more. Intent on finding Beaufort, he left the house and collected a horse from the stable. The captain would know if Goss had somehow escaped. With no other clues concerning his wife's disappearance, it was the only place to begin.

Drake returned from Beaufort's quarters just as the clock struck six. Exhausted but unwilling to relent in his search when Elise remained in peril, he'd returned to the house for a fresh horse and any available news.

Prin met him at the front door. By her haggard appearance, he could see she'd slept little, if at all. Lines of stress ringed her full mouth and her eyes were bloodshot. The aroma of breakfast sausage drifted through the house from the kitchen. His stomach growled, reminding him of his hunger.

"Did you find her?" Prin asked, her anxiety unconcealed.

He shook his head. "Has Kane returned?"

"Aye, he's sleepin'. I drilled him for you, but with all the goings-on last night, he had nothin' to follow 'cept a cold trail."

Drake ground his teeth in frustration. "What of the guards who deserted last night?"

Prin straightened her apron. "They came back 'bout an hour ago. Said they was gone so long 'cause of the ruckus in the streets."

"I can believe it."

"They wouldn't tell me nothin', but they might have some information they'll spill to you."

"Get them for me," he said as he sprinted up the stairs. "I'll see what they know, if anything."

Drake entered the bedroom he shared with Elise. The emptiness of it tore at his heart. The scent of lavender she always wore teased his senses until he thought he might go mad. Regret twisted in his chest when he thought of how they'd parted.

Please Lord, please let me find her.

After changing his clothes, he went to his study, where the two soldiers awaited him. Both denied hearing an intruder, and neither could tell him anything to aid his hunt for Elise. Drake dismissed them to their duties, though he doubted their competence. Dashing off a note to his cousin, he requested fresh guards to replace them.

Prin delivered a plate of sausage and eggs. "You gotta eat somethin' or you'll be no good to anybody."

He accepted the plate and handed her the note with instructions for Kane to deliver it the moment he woke. Eating quickly, Drake made plans to go to Brixton Hall. The very idea of procuring help from rebel spies offended his sense of honor, but Elise's safety hung in the balance, and she was more important than his pride or his principals.

* * *

A rooster's crow awakened Elise. Red streaks of the rising sun painted the Eastern sky. The muted chatter of servants in the hall beyond her chamber door spurred her to dress with haste. A quick look at the clock told her the ferry was due. She needed to be on it when it returned to Charles Towne.

Locating one of her old dresses in the wardrobe, she changed from her nightgown and tied her hair in a ponytail. Downstairs, she traced Christian to his father's study, where she heard the two men arguing. With a loud rap on the partially opened door, she announced her arrival.

"Come in," Zechariah bellowed from where he stood by the window.

She took a seat in front of her spymaster's desk. "My goodness, the atmosphere is ripe this morn. May I inquire as to why?"

"We're deciding what to do with you," Christian said matter-of-factly. "Father says we should use you as a lure to capture Amber—"

"You wouldn't dare!" Elise hopped to her feet in protest.

"I assure you I would, girl." Zechariah sent her a side-long glance. "Alone, Amberly is worth a fortune in ransom. Think of the sum I could command by holding both of you."

"Think of what you'd lose, you cold-hearted old goat. The war may be winding down, but the British still hold Charles Towne. My husband would have all the evidence he needs to see Brixton Hall seized and you dangling from the gallows."

"The voice of reason," Christian quipped beside her.

"I'm glad you agree with me," she said. "The idea is plain foolishness."

Christian leaned forward in his seat. "Exactly. A better plan is to exchange you for Josiah, *then* kidnap Amberly."

Elise's eyes nearly popped from their sockets. "You must be jesting. How dare you even suggest it?"

"We won't hurt him."

"No, you won't, Christian, because he won't be touched."

"You're being too hasty, dearest. The war is almost over. By ransoming your duke, we'll gain additional funds to aid wounded Patriots and their families. Josiah will be freed, and you will be reunited with your Englishman. Everyone benefits."

Livid, Elise began to prowl the study, aware that Zechariah remained riveted by the view outside the window. "*I'll* see Josiah freed somehow, but you must leave my husband out of this nonsense."

He's been wounded enough already.

A low, sinister laugh emanated from Zechariah, sending a shiver down Elise's spine.

"What is it?" Christian stood and went to the window. He groaned. "It seems our discussion is at an end. His high and mighty has arrived."

"What?" Elise pushed her way through the two men blocking her view. When she located Drake striding up the path from the ferry landing, a shot of joy brought a smile to her lips, but it was quickly replaced by a deep concern for his safety. "When did you send him word of my arrival here?"

"I didn't," Christian grumbled.

"Then how?"

He shrugged. "You'll be able to ask him yourself in a moment."

Elise spun on her heel to leave, but Zechariah clamped a staying hand on her elbow. "Don't betray me, girl. Amberly is worth a fortune to me dead or alive. His family will ransom him either way. You can help deliver him to me and keep him alive or today you will see him dead. A British aristocrat in a cold grave will warm my heart. The choice belongs to you."

With a sidelong glance to Christian, Elise fled the study and arrived at the front door before the footman. She opened it wide and crossed onto the portico just as Drake mounted the steps.

A burst of cool morning air surrounded her, tugging the tendrils of her hair and whipping it around her face. Brushing it back, she searched Drake's face. She held her breath, unsure of his reaction to finding her there. Blatant surprise scored his features and a relieved smile spread across his lips. For one sweet moment it was though no impediments stood between them.

Elise descended a step.

He climbed two, his golden gaze roaming over her in an anxious inspection that conveyed his deep concern for her.

Zechariah cleared his throat behind her, splintering the moment of ease between them. "Good day, Amberly. I see you received my message. So good of you to respond with such haste."

"I received no word from you, Sayer." Drake's deep voice blistered with skepticism. "When did you send it?"

"Why, as soon as Elise arrived yesterday, of course. If

you ask me 'tis unseemly for a wife to abandon her husband."

Gasping at the lie, Elise pivoted on her heel to face the spymaster. His narrowed gaze warned her to hold her tongue. "Would you care to come in and discuss the matter?"

"We've decided to take a stroll," Elise interrupted.

"Then you'll need to fetch a shawl," Zechariah replied with the timing of a seasoned thespian. "'Tis a clear enough day, but we wouldn't want you to catch a chill in your condition."

Drake noticed the silencing glance Sayer cast toward Elise. His anger burned toward the old man. According to Prin, Zechariah had bent Elise to his will for years by using her sister as a hostage. Drake was determined to see his wife freed from the old man's clutches once and for all.

Sprinting up the remaining steps, Drake reached into his coat pocket to feel for his pistol just in case he might need to make use of it. "My wife is right, Sayer. The morn is too fine to waste indoors. However, with all this wind it's perfect for a sail. I thank you for keeping her safe for me, but we'll be taking our leave on the ferry."

His right hand clutched the pistol in his pocket. He set his left arm around Elise's waist and started down the steps. The sharp click of a gun being cocked stopped them the moment they reached the gravel path. Zechariah waited for them to face him before he spoke. "I hate to disrupt your plans, Amberly, but we have much to discuss. Either return indoors with me now or die in the dust where you stand."

Elise knew Zechariah would carry out his threat.

Without hesitation, she threw herself in front of Drake, determined to keep him safe.

Just as quickly, Drake thrust her behind him. "What are you doing, woman? Have you lost your mind?"

She grabbed hold of his shirt and refused to let go. "I won't see you hurt. Yesterday when you left me, I faced what life would be like without you. I'm not strong enough to do it again."

He twisted around to face her. Admiration glowed in his eyes as he tucked a wisp of hair behind her ear. "It breaks my heart to think of how we parted, my love. I can only pray you'll forgive me."

"But I'm the one who needs forgiveness," she said, full of regret. "I didn't tell you of my past. What of Anthony?"

He placed a soft, lingering kiss on her brow. "Let's speak of it later. In the end, though, I suggest we forgive each other and start afresh."

"The two of you are about to give me a case of the vapors," Zechariah complained.

Unconcerned, Drake slid off his coat and draped it around Elise. As he faced Zechariah, he tucked the pistol he'd eased from his pocket into the back waistband of his breeches, careful to keep Zechariah ignorant of his actions. With a flight of stairs between them, he couldn't rely on his weapon's accuracy. He would have to move closer in order to insure a clean shot. He raised his hands in a show of surrender and sighed as though Sayer had him over a barrel. "You leave me no choice, old man, I'll come with you. However, I insist Elise be allowed to return to Charles Towne without further hesitation."

Elise clutched the back of his shirt. "No," she whispered fiercely. "I'll not leave without you."

Zechariah aimed his pistol at the center of Drake's chest. "I'm afraid you're not in a position to negotiate, Amberly. As I told Elise before you arrived, the two of you are more valuable as a pair."

"What is it you want to secure our freedom, Sayer?"

"I believe ten thousand pounds, the freedom of Josiah Smith and your silence concerning my and Christian's identities will do."

"You've thought of everything," Drake said, undaunted. "If I agree, Elise and I must be free to go at once. I'll have to arrange for the funds to be delivered to you. You'll have to accept my word your demands will be met."

The blustery morning rang with Zechariah's laughter. "I think not. You and Elise will wait in my study. I'll have you write and sign orders for Josiah's release. Once I'm assured of his freedom and the ten thousand pounds is delivered safely, I'll set you both free. Not a moment before."

Drake opened his mouth to reply, but the words died on his lips when Elise slid the pistol free of his waistband. She shoved the barrel into his back. The click as she cocked the hammer sent the hair rising at the back of his neck.

"I'm sorry, Drake, but I'm doing this for both our sakes," she said, her voice as hard as flint.

The old man guffawed with delight. "You thought to shoot me, eh, Amberly?" To Elise he said, "I knew you'd see reason, my girl. Bring him inside and let's have this business done."

Palms sweating, Elise prodded Drake with the weapon.

He started a slow ascent of the steps. Without taking her eyes off Zechariah or the gun he directed at her husband, she waited until the precise moment, then, using surprise to her advantage, thrust Drake out of harm's way and pulled the trigger. The explosion echoed on the wind. A cloud of smoke enveloped her.

Through the acrid haze she watched Zechariah fumble his weapon and fall. He squealed in pain before clutching his hand. Christian burst from the house. Shouting for a servant, he bent down beside his father, aiding him as best he could.

Drake extracted the smoking pistol from Elise's blood-less grasp, then pulled her into his embrace, where she trembled against him.

Christian helped his moaning father to his feet. Blood dripped from Zechariah's hand, but she saw he maintained all of his fingers.

"I'm sorry Zechariah, but you left me no choice," she said. "My loyalty is to my husband."

"Come, sweet, we're leaving," Drake said. "The ferry is prepared to sail."

"Elise, wait!" Christian called as they turned go. "Things were never intended to come to this. Remember Josiah. Most of all, never forget what I told you last night. It will always hold true."

Elise choked back the sob that swelled in her throat. Christian wouldn't keep them from leaving because of his feelings for her. Combined with the events of the morning, it was too much to say a final goodbye to one of the dearest friends she'd ever known.

Before she could respond, he turned his back on her and led Zechariah's groaning form inside the mansion.

Drake tugged on her hand. "Swiftly, love, it's time to go."

On board the ferry a few minutes later, Captain Travis inquired about the shot he'd heard. Elise assured him all was well, and asked after his mother to distract him.

Cap in his hands, Travis studied her with concern. "She's right as rain, Miss Elise, but I hope you don't mind me sayin', you don't look so good. Maybe you should sit a spell in my cabin."

"My thoughts precisely, Captain." Drake led her away. "Your kindness is appreciated."

The cabin was a dusty cell, but Elise welcomed the privacy it offered. Sitting on the narrow bed, she watched Drake close the door. White-lipped and face taut, he reminded her of a storm cloud. "Don't be angry with me, Drake."

"Angry?" He sank to his knees before her. "'Tis more like I'm in the throes of shock. Please don't ever endanger yourself like that again."

"I had no choice." She brushed her fingers through his silky hair and cupped his cheek, grateful they'd escaped unhurt. "I knew we had to move closer if I hoped to have a clear shot."

"You are the most brilliant, bravest woman—"

"No, but when he aimed at you, I wanted to kill him, Drake. God forgive me, I would have if he'd caused you harm."

His eyes caressed her face. "I'm the most fortunate of men to have a loyal wife such as you, my love. From the depths of my heart, I thank you for your care. It shames me to think of what I said to you yesterday."

"It broke my heart, but I understood." She ran a fingertip along his full bottom lip. "I want no distrust between us. Will you allow me to explain?"

"There's no need," he assured her. "I didn't want to face it, but I've known the truth since Prin set me to rights weeks ago."

She searched his face for the truth. "You believe me about Hawk?"

He nodded without hesitation. "I loved Anthony and I always will, but with the Lord's help, I was able to remember him as he really was, not the idealized version I'd clung to these many months. Once I realized what I'd done, I had no trouble believing your version of events, especially when you've proven by word and by deed what a woman of honor you are.

"As for your spying, I admit I wish it were otherwise. For your sake, I wish you'd been spared the painful choices that led you down that path. As it is, I can only thank the Lord for bringing us together and I stand amazed at your courage, for I've never met the like."

He stood and slowly, as if he feared she might reject him, drew her into his embrace. "I love you, Elise. I love our child. There's nothing I want more than to spend the rest of my life loving you."

With a prayer of thankfulness, she snuggled close, breathing in his comforting scent. Drake knew her secrets and loved her anyway. Love for him filled her heart to the brim and spilled over. At long last, she knew the meaning of peace.

Epilogue

Elise clipped her long hair at the nape of her neck and checked her appearance in the mirror one last time. Drake would be coming to find her soon. The thrill of anticipation seized her. She was looking forward to a lazy afternoon with him and the picnic the servants had set up near the estate's large fish pond.

God had been faithful, just as His word promised. The Lord truly had seen them through their darkest hours. Now their lives overflowed with goodness. In the eight months since she'd arrived at Hawk Haven, the sprawling estate had become the home of her heart. Though she occasionally missed the warmer climate of South Carolina, England possessed its own lush beauty. Prin, Kane and their new son, Robert, thrived in their own spacious cottage down the lane. Elise had made friends, including

Drake's impish sister, Eva, whom she'd come to love as her own.

She smelled one of the vases of sweet red roses displayed in artful arrangements on the side tables and atop the mantel. When the clock struck noon, she grew impatient and went in search of her husband.

She found him in the nursery across the hall. Through the open window, light streamed into the luxurious space decorated in soft shades of yellow and cream. His black hair loose around his shoulders, Drake rocked their sleeping daughter in the crook of his arm, despite the capable nanny who read a book in the corner.

At three months old, Olivia was the darling of the household and the axis of her parents' world. A wave of tenderness engulfed Elise as Drake slipped his large fingertip into the baby's tiny grasp. She memorized the loving expression on his face and wished somehow she could capture the unguarded moment on canvas.

Not wanting to interrupt him, she turned to go, but the floor creaked, giving her away. He looked up and smiled with obvious pleasure. "At long last." He placed the sleeping baby in a crib frothed in cream lace and yellow silk before gently covering her with a soft blanket.

Meeting Elise in the doorway, he pulled her close and bent to nibble her ear. "Are you ready to leave? I'm starving."

"I've been waiting for *you*," she whispered with a smile, careful not to wake Olivia.

"You were reading a letter when I came to find you earlier."

"That was ages ago."

"How odd." He grinned. "I thought it less than half an hour. Who wrote to you?"

"Tabby," she said. He held her hand as they walked down the hall. "She says all is well in Charles Towne. Moira's nearly a year old and as fat as a sausage. Josiah is well. The Rolling Tide is flourishing. Zechariah has use of his hand again and Christian has left to come here for a visit."

Drake's brow arched. "Come again?"

Elise tried not to laugh at his aghast expression. "Drake, please don't make a fuss. Christian has been my friend for a long time."

His brow drew together. "I don't like it. I still say he's in love with you—"

"Don't you trust me?"

The scowl returned. "Don't be a simpleton. You know I trust you. I love you more than words can say."

"Then don't worry about Christian." They started down the grand, winding staircase lined with the portraits of Drake's noble ancestors. He seemed to relax and Elise continued her account of Tabby's letter. "Tabby asked me to thank you again for releasing Josiah last fall. She'll be your loyal friend forever."

"It made you happy. That's all that mattered to me."

Elise's merry laughter filled the foyer as he swept her off her feet and out the door the butler held open. Bright sunshine surrounded her the same as her love for Drake filled her heart. She flung her arms around his neck, savoring the knowledge that he was hers.

He glanced down at her, a smile warming his face. "Love me, sweet?"

Her arms tightened. "You know I do, my darling. Today and every day for the rest of my life."

* * * * *

Dear Reader,

Happy New Year!

I hope your 2009 Christmas season was wonderful and you're enjoying great success with your New Year's resolutions.

Speaking of resolutions, one of mine for 2002 was to write my first historical romance. Like a lot of resolutions, it almost fell by the wayside. I never dreamed the road to publication for *The Duke's Redemption* would take eight years, but I'm grateful for the friends I made along the way and the lessons in endurance the journey taught me.

I hope if you get discouraged with your goals sometime during this year, you'll stick with it and be like Elise, who knew the Lord would never give her more than she was able to endure.

Thank you for kicking off 2010 with *The Duke's Redemption*. I pray the coming months bring you love, joy and loads of reading enjoyment!

I love to hear from my readers. Please visit my Web site, www.carlacapshaw.com, join my newsletter to learn about upcoming releases and contests and/or write to me at carla@carlacapshaw.com.

Be Inspired,

Carla Capshaw

QUESTIONS FOR DISCUSSION

1. Elise became a spy for many reasons, the main one being she hopes to win Prin's freedom. Have you ever had to do something dangerous to protect your loved ones? Is there a limit to what you would do to keep a loved one safe? What is it?

2. Even though Hawk meant to harm Elise, she felt great remorse over his death. Have you ever had someone try to hurt you, only to have the situation backfire on that person? If so, how did you feel? Were you glad or sad the person was hurt? How do you think God would want you to react?

3. When Elise accepted Zechariah's offer to become a spy, she believed God had answered her prayers to escape her stepfather and help Prin. After Hawk's death, Elise questions whether or not she's really following God's will. Have you ever thought you received an answer to a prayer only to wonder later if you'd believed incorrectly?

4. Drake is estranged from God because family tragedies and personal disappointments have made him believe God has forgotten him. Have you ever suffered through painful events that made you think God no longer cared for you? What made you realize He still loved you and wanted to be a part of your life?

5. Drake's reaction to his brother's death is an immediate need for revenge. Have you ever had something happen to make you long for revenge? The bible says we should leave vengeance to God. Were you able to give the situation to God? How did the situation work out in the end?

6. Though Elise's problems seem to escalate throughout the story, she truly believes the Lord will never leave her or give her more than she can handle. Have you ever been at your wit's end? Were you able to trust the Lord and give Him your burdens? If so, what did you do to give Him control in your life?

7. Elise's home life was less than ideal. Do you agree with the way that she chose to save Prin? Was spying a good means to an end? What else could she have tried?

8. Zechariah is a true believer in his ideals and thinks the end justifies the means. Do you think his treatment of Elise was ever unfair? Do you think if he'd acted differently toward her she would have been more helpful to him in the end? Or do you think because of her loyalty to Drake she would have had to react the same way no matter how Zechariah had treated her?

9. Until a true crisis forced him to choose to live by faith once and for all, Drake's relationship with God ebbed and flowed along with the joys and disappointments

of his life. Do you know anyone who lives by fair-weather faith? Were you ever this kind of person? What made you finally decide to trust God no matter what the circumstances?

10. Do you think Elise should have told Drake the truth about her past once she married him? Was it dishonest of her to keep the information to herself and just hope it would go away once she moved to England? What would you have done in a similar circumstance?

11. Do you think Elise was wrong to give Zechariah information after she married Drake? Was it disloyal of her, or did she have to help Prin and her family? What would you have done in the same situation?

12. Once Drake learned the truth about Elise's identity, do you think he reacted fairly? Do you think he took too long or not long enough to accept the reasons for her actions? Do you think she actually did anything he needed to forgive?

13. If you married someone whose secret past was brought to light, how would you react? Would you be able to forgive and forget or would you continue to feel betrayed? What do you think the Lord would have you do?

14. Is there anything we can learn about God's forgiveness from the story of Drake and Elise?

15. Zechariah tells Elise that he's risking his life and more because of his ideals and hopes for the birth of their new country. Have you ever thought about the sacrifices our American forefathers made? Many of them risked/lost their wealth, families and lives. Would you be willing to make those sacrifices in a similar situation?

*Scandal surrounds Rebecca Gunderson after
she shares a storm cellar during a deadly
tornado with Pete Benjamin.
No one believes the time she spent with
him was totally innocent.
Can Pete protect her reputation?*

Read on for a sneak peek of
HEARTLAND WEDDING by Renee Ryan,
Book 2 in the AFTER THE STORM:
THE FOUNDING YEARS *series*
available February 2010
from Love Inspired Historical.

"Marry me," Pete demanded, realizing his mistake as the words left his mouth. He hadn't asked her. He'd told her.

He tried to rectify his insensitive act but Rebecca was already speaking over him. "Why are you willing to spend the rest of your life married to a woman you hardly know?"

"Because it's the right thing to do," he said.

Angling her head, she caught her bottom lip between her teeth and then did something utterly remarkable. She smoothed her fingertips across his forehead. "As sweet as I think your gesture is, you don't have to save me."

A pleasant warmth settled over him at her touch, leaving him oddly disoriented. "Yes, I do."

She dropped her hand to her side. "I don't mind what others say about me. You and I, *we,* know the truth."

Pete caught her hand in his, and turned it over in his palm. "I told Matilda Johnson we were getting married."

She snatched her hand free. "You…you…*what?"*

He spoke more slowly this time. "I told her we were getting married."

She did *not* like his answer. That much was made clear by her scowl. "You shouldn't have done that."

"She was blaming you for luring me into my own storm cellar."

The color leached out of Rebecca's cheeks as she sank into a nearby chair. "I…I simply don't know what to say."

"Say yes. Mrs. Johnson is a bully. Our marriage will silence her. I'll speak with the pastor today and—"

"No."

"—schedule the ceremony at once." His words came to a halt. "What did you say?"

"I said, no." She rose cautiously, her palms flat on her thighs as though to brace herself. "I won't marry you."

"You're turning me down? After everything that's happened today?"

"No. I mean, *yes*. I'm turning you down."

"Your reputation—"

"Is my concern, not yours."

She sniffed, rather loudly, but she didn't give in to her emotions. Oh, she blinked. And blinked. And *blinked*. But no tears spilled from her eyes.

Pete pulled in a hard breath. He'd never been more baffled by a woman. "We were both in my storm cellar," he reminded her through a painfully tight jaw. "That means we share the burden of the consequences equally."

Blink, blink, blink. "My decision is final."

"So is mine. We'll be married by the end of the day."

Her breathing quickened to short, hard pants. And then…*at last*…it happened. One lone tear slipped from her eye.

"Rebecca, please," he whispered, knowing his soft manner came too late.

"No." She wrapped her dignity around her like a coat of iron-clad armor. "We have nothing more to say to each other."

Just as another tear plopped onto the toe of her shoe, she turned and rushed out of the kitchen.

Stunned, Pete stared at the empty space she'd occupied. "That," he said to himself, "could have gone better."

* * * * *

*Will Pete be able to change Rebecca's mind
and salvage her reputation?
Find out in HEARTLAND WEDDING
available in February 2010
only from Love Inspired Historical.*

REQUEST YOUR FREE BOOKS!

2 FREE INSPIRATIONAL NOVELS
PLUS 2
FREE
MYSTERY GIFTS

Love Inspired
HISTORICAL
INSPIRATIONAL HISTORICAL ROMANCE

YES! Please send me 2 FREE Love Inspired® Historical novels and my 2 FREE mystery gifts (gifts are worth about $10). After receiving them, if I don't wish to receive any more books, I can return the shipping statement marked "cancel". If I don't cancel, I will receive 4 brand-new novels every other month and be billed just $4.24 per book in the U.S. or $4.74 per book in Canada. That's a saving of over 20% off the cover price. It's quite a bargain! Shipping and handling is just 50¢ per book in the U.S. and 75¢ per book in Canada.* I understand that accepting the 2 free books and gifts places me under no obligation to buy anything. I can always return a shipment and cancel at any time. Even if I never buy another book, the two free books and gifts are mine to keep forever.

102 IDN E4LC 302 IDN E4LN

Name	(PLEASE PRINT)	
Address		Apt. #
City	State/Prov.	Zip/Postal Code

Signature (if under 18, a parent or guardian must sign)

Mail to Steeple Hill Reader Service:
IN U.S.A.: P.O. Box 1867, Buffalo, NY 14240-1867
IN CANADA: P.O. Box 609, Fort Erie, Ontario L2A 5X3

Not valid for current subscribers to Love Inspired Historical books.

Want to try two free books from another series?
Call 1-800-873-8635 or visit www.morefreebooks.com.

* Terms and prices subject to change without notice. Prices do not include applicable taxes. Sales tax applicable in N.Y. Canadian residents will be charged applicable provincial taxes and GST. Offer not valid in Quebec. This offer is limited to one order per household. All orders subject to approval. Credit or debit balances in a customer's account(s) may be offset by any other outstanding balance owed by or to the customer. Please allow 4 to 6 weeks for delivery. Offer available while quantities last.

Your Privacy: Steeple Hill Books is committed to protecting your privacy. Our Privacy Policy is available online at www.SteepleHill.com or upon request from the Reader Service. From time to time we make our lists of customers available to reputable third parties who have a product or service of interest to you. If you would prefer we not share your name and address, please check here. ☐

Help us get it right—We strive for accurate, respectful and relevant communications. To clarify or modify your communication preferences, visit us at www.ReaderService.com/consumerschoice.

Newspaper reporter Amanda Bodine's boss keeps assigning her fluff pieces about dog shows and boat parades. She longs to prove herself to Ross Lockhart with a serious front-page story. Until her own family becomes newsworthy…

Look for

Heart of the Matter

by

Marta Perry

Love Inspired SUSPENSE

RIVETING INSPIRATIONAL ROMANCE

Two women in the witness protection program have been murdered. Before there's a third victim, reporter Violet Kramer writes an article to put all witnesses on red alert. Big-city cop Clay West comes to watch over her—putting her at a different kind of risk.

PROTECTING *the* WITNESSES

Look for

KILLER HEADLINE

by DEBBY GIUSTI

Steeple
Hill®

LIS44381